REBIRTH

THE JACK RANDALL THRILLERS
BOOK 10

RANDALL WOOD

TENSION BOOKWORKS

For information contact:

Tension Bookworks

248 Nokomis Ave. Venice, FL 34285

www.tensionbookworks.com

Tension Bookworks and the portrayal of the screw are registered trademarks of Tension Bookworks.

Jacket and Cover design by Derek Murphy

Book design by Matty Dalrymple

Cataloging-in-Publication Data is on file at the Library of Congress

Wood, Randall, 1968-

Rebirth / Randall Wood – 1st ed.

ISBN-13: 978-1-938825-58-3 (Ebook)

ISBN-13: 978-1-938825-63-7 (Paperback)

ISBN-13: 978-1-938825-59-0 (Large Print)

ISBN-13: 978-1-938825-60-6 (Hardcover)

ISBN-13: 978-1-938825-61-3 (Audio)

2024122701

WARNING!

The story of The Twelve Shepherds was originally released as a serial novel and was published in several separate episodes. Due to the readers' requests, it has now been re-published in novel form. The resulting manuscript was too large to fit into one novel and as a result the Shepherds saga will now encompass six novels.

This book, *REBIRTH*, is part six of The Twelve Shepherds saga, and also book ten of the Jack Randall series.

The author and the publisher apologize for any confusion.

re•birth
a period of new life or growth

1

"True patriotism hates injustice in its own land more than anywhere else."

—*Clarence Darrow*

NORTHERN VIRGINIA

D ayton drove, and Anna did her best to keep track of where they were. She was unfamiliar with the city and had only a short time to get herself familiar. The flight to Dulles International Airport had been uneventful, and they had been dropped off at the private terminal with their presence unacknowledged. An SUV was parked in the hangar, and Dayton punched in the code to open the doors, before retrieving the keys from under the seat. The items they had brought with them were quickly transferred over.

Now they were doing over eighty-miles-per-hour with the afternoon traffic on 267 as they moved east. Anna spent the time memorizing the map she had brought with her. They would be in suburbia for some time before they reached the city.

Or so she thought. Dayton surprised her by pulling off at the next exit. She read the signs before they turned north and then glanced behind them for any threats before asking.

"What's in Reston?"

"Monkeys."

"What?"

"Sorry. Local joke. I have a few things here that we'll need. What's that map telling you?"

"The place is a suburban maze, but at least it's

wooded. I'm a little worried about the jogging trails. I mean, they're both a blessing and a curse. We can use them to get close without drawing too much attention, but someone can just come jogging right into our plans, too. All we need is some suburban mom or some elderly dog walker seeing us, and the cops will be on their way."

"I thought of that, too. But we don't have much of a choice. We may have to do this in stages. Just keep working on the area with that map I gave you."

Anna exchanged the map in her hand for the one Dayton had given her. It was a military map, complete with gridlines and red terrain markers. Obviously, Dayton was sticking with what he knew best, even though it was an urban environment. Several locations were marked in his own personal code. Most of them were decoys in the event the map fell into the wrong hands, but she knew his codes enough to pick out what he had marked as important.

Their target was in South Kensington, next door to Chevy Chase. An upper-class neighborhood populated by the movers and shakers of Washington DC. The homes ran into the millions and were spread out on large well-wooded lots.

Narrow two-lane roads twisted their way through
the trees, and Anna found that also an issue. It
would provide them cover from passing cars, but
they would have to rely on their ears to warn them
of their approach.

A notation on the map made her pause. Was
this coincidence? She planted a finger on the location and measured the distance. About a mile; a
little more with the curving roads. Less, if one
went straight through the woods. She held up the
map, so he could see it.

"Is this what I think it is?"

He glanced at it and nodded before returning
his gaze to the traffic.

"Jack Randall's residence. Hell of a coincidence, huh? I keep forgetting the man is worth
millions himself. He's not what you picture when
you think FBI agent."

"I'll say."

She returned the map to her lap. Washington
DC was laid out like the spokes of a wheel, with
the National mall in the center. She looked for the
nearest spoke and saw that Connecticut provided
a straight shot into town from where they would
be. About five miles, give or take. It could be covered in minutes, with the right vehicle.

But they wouldn't be going that way.

"You have our exit planed?"

Dayton's face changed, as if the question were both amusing and troubling at the same time.

"For years," was his answer.

Anna decided not to pursue it and returned to her map. It was a discussion for another time.

A few miles later, they pulled into the driveway of a small home. Dayton guided the SUV around the back and up to a small detached garage, before checking the mirrors to make sure they were out of sight from the road. Anna examined the home through the glass and then followed Dayton when he got out.

The house had once been nice. A craftsman style bungalow with a wide front porch. She could see a few places where the owner had put in the time and effort to make it a home. There was a picket fence needing paint. Extensive landscaping needed attending. A downspout that had pulled away from the brick. But other than that, it looked like the average middle-class home you would find on the East Coast. Now, the leaves had mixed with the patches of snow and combined into drifts that clogged the door and path to the home's back door. It was obviously not a home that was occupied by its owner much. Dayton gave it all a cursory look, before moving to the detached garage.

"What's this?"

"This is ... This was my parents' house."

Her eyes widened at the information. His tone and the condition of the house told her they were no longer among the living, but the fact that he had brought her here was something on top of that. With the address, she could find out who had lived there. That information would lead to the real name of Dayton Knox, and he knew it. She turned and glanced at the street, and then at the map in her hand, before stuffing it away in her back pocket. It had all just come together.

"How far to the CIA from here?"

"About four minutes. Little more with traffic," was the quick reply.

It was a confession. Or an admission, take your pick. But now wasn't the time. They had things to do.

She followed him inside the garage to find a red muscle car inside. A lite coat of dust marred its paint only slightly. Dayton gestured to it as he walked past.

"A 1972 Oldsmobile Cutlass Supreme 442. Everything is original. My dad and I restored it when we were both home. Took us years. I forgot to put the cover on it. He'd be pissed."

"It's gorgeous."

"It is." He kept walking to a heavy door in the back of the garage. He bent down and reached under a workbench. She heard the beeps of a keypad sounding as he worked it without looking. The door clicked twice, and he pulled it open.

"Shut the door and come in."

Anna slid the inside lock home on the exterior door before following him inside. She found a storage room like any other you would find in the area. This one had a steel bench with a vice and few tools hanging on the wall. A set of cabinets stood side by side, and Dayton was working the lock of one. She had a sudden flashback of their day in the mountains in the stable.

He flung the doors open, and the contents revealed themselves.

Her mouth dropped open.

MONTANA

CARTER IGNORED the pain in his chest and forced himself to maintain the brutal pace he'd set. The snowshoes now impacted the soft ground as fast as he could keep his legs pumping, and he traded possible detection for speed as he made his way down the mountain. The trees were thick, and his face now bore the marks of tree branches he'd been unable to avoid, but he ignored the sting and let the cold numb them as he plodded on.

He'd watched the men advance through the scope, until the last of them disappeared into the wood line before launching himself into action.

The men had puzzled him at first. Were they the General's men? Out in the mountains for some winter combat training? He wasn't sure, but their number and their actions made him think the opposite. They were coming from the wrong direction, and they were making movements as if the operation were real.

The mansion was under attack.

Jolted by the revelation, Carter made a decision. And once it was made it required action. He'd counted forty men, all heavily armed. They were too many for him to handle with a hunting rifle and a knife. He had to balance the power. He had to warn the General.

But how?

The GPS had offered his only alternative. But could he get there first?

He now leaped from drift to drift with both feet as he worked his way down the steep slope, his lungs burning in the thin air. He was traveling slightly away from the route to the mansion that the attacking party was taking, so he felt it was safe to move fast without worrying about the trail he was leaving behind. Speed was his only savior. Until he had to loop back.

His legs were aching from the exertion, but he ignored them and moved on. The hours he'd spent in the gym were now paying off, and Carter called on his reserves of strength to keep him moving. The long underwear he had pilfered from the garage was now stuck to him by a layer of sweat, and the cold air would occasionally find its way into his coat to chill him. He ignored it all and rapidly sucked in the thin air to feed his muscles, slowing only when he got too dizzy to stay upright.

Eventually, he came to the valley floor and grabbed a tree to stop his forward progress. His breath clouded his view, and his head swam as he took in the view.

There. A mile away down the valley. The barn, and across the stream, the cabin. He fumbled with the binoculars to get a better view and was disappointed to see no signs of life. The chimney had no heat escaping, and the snow around the perimeter was undisturbed. Of course, there could still be someone there, as the snow had been coming down for hours. But he felt sure there would be lights on inside and some signs of the fireplace being in use, if there was someone. He'd find out soon enough.

He pushed himself off the tree and made his way to the edge of the tree line. Keeping just inside it, he passed the barn and went directly for the bridge and then the house. He'd hoped to find a vehicle of some kind on the other side, but nothing presented, making him think there really was nobody present. He shed the snowshoes before mounting the stairs to the deck. A quick look through the windows told him his suspicions were right: There was nobody there. He tried the door and then put a shoulder to it, before cursing its solid oak construction. But there was always another way. He leaned the rifle against the wall and moved around the side of the cabin to the woodpile. Under the tarp, he found the axe right where he remembered it being stowed and hefted its weight as he returned to the door.

The impacts were loud, but less than that of a gunshot. He put his weight and considerable strength behind them and got the job done quickly.

The warmth of the cabin welcomed him as he entered, and he checked the alarm pad only long enough to see that it was active. He searched every room and then checked the shelves and cabinets for any form of communication.

Nothing. No phone. Not even a charger. He needed to warn the mansion! But how?

He gazed up at the cameras. He'd noticed them the second day of his training, and like Dayton, had accepted them as something that he would be subject to while he was here. At the time, he had dismissed them; but now, maybe he could make them work for him? He ran for the stairs.

* * *

THE WHITE HOUSE

THE PRESIDENT HELD STILL and watched his wife as she retied his tie for him. Her face had adopted the pursed-lip and furrowed brow she unconsciously painted on it when she was concentrating. It was a quirk he found beautiful, and he smiled as she tugged and pulled, before finally slipping the knot up in place and folding his collar down around it. Only then did she notice his gaze.

"What? Is this the right tie?"

"I love you. You know that?"

"I do." She kissed his cheek and then held him at arm's length.

"Are you ready for this?"

He patted the inside pocket of his jacket. Inside was an envelope and a small device. It, and his own determination, were all that he needed once he left the room. She would arrive before he did and be seated on the balcony next to a few carefully selected guests. She would leave when he got started, and the Secret Service agents would safeguard her return back to the White House. After that, he was unsure what would happen.

"Henry has the copies?" he said.

"One for each network. He'll hand them out when the time is right. You called the kids?"

"Yes, they'll all be home by the time you get started. I didn't like lying to them, but I simply said we wanted them home tonight. Nick protested, but Mary read between the lines, I think. They'll be there."

"I can move armies with a simple command, but when it comes to my own children..."

"Yes, well ... they'll understand soon enough."

"Indeed."

He walked to the mirror and checked himself. He looked tired, he admitted, but then he had reason to be.

"It's time to go."

"I know." He made no move to leave, though. She joined him at the mirror and held his arm.

"Good looking couple," he remarked.

"Yeah, they cleanup okay," she went along.

Would they be able to look in the mirror after tonight? The question was on both of their minds. The other was if they would be able to face their children. They would have the answers to both questions soon enough.

A knock on the door cut through their moment of reflection.

"Yes?"

Henry stuck his head in.

"Sir, they need you downstairs."

"Very well."

The boy pulled his head back and shut the door, and they turned to face one another. She picked imaginary lint from his suit.

"I believe this is the most important thing you've ever done," she remarked.

"I think so, too."

"Try not to screw it up."

"Yes, dear."

Hand in hand, they departed the room. Outside, they were met by the Secret Service agents and a few staff members.

"Lead on, gentleman," the president spoke. "History awaits!"

The men smiled at the man's brevity. In an hour, he'd be speaking, live, in front of the entire world. The man was allowed a joke if he pleased.

They moved down the hall and descended the stairs, neither of them looking back.

2

"The patriot volunteer, fighting for country and his rights, makes the most reliable soldier on earth."

—*Stonewall Jackson*

THE J. EDGAR HOOVER BUILDING

Jack chose the stairs and took his time. He was still working out why he was here. It was a busy night in DC. One that he had always avoided in the past. Between the president's speech and the numerous parties thrown by the lobbying groups, the town would be packed with people. Add to that the growing number of protestors, and he'd had a hard time getting through the traffic.

The protestors had puzzled him. They now numbered more than he had ever seen at once. He'd read a report about an unprecedented turnout for several causes. Permits had been issued for most, but it was impossible to predict the number who would show up for each. The State of the Union address always drew several protests, this, augmented by the nationwide outrage induced by the actions and revelations of the Twelve Shepherds, had been pointed at by the press to explain the large numbers.

So far, there had been little fallout. Despite their numbers, the protestors were behaving themselves. The capitol police had reported only a few minor scuffles. Jack had almost called Danny to get his take on what was happening, but that would have resulted in a quid pro quo, and he wasn't ready to give up what little information he had on the Shepherds just yet.

Jack arrived at the top floor and pushed his way through the fire door. The hallway was occupied by a few agents, but nothing like its usual level of staffing. Deacon was in. Jack had seen the lights on in his office from the street. He'd check in and see how his boss was doing.

Margaret was at the desk with the TV on in the corner. On it, Jack could see the House chamber. Grey haired men and woman milled about on the floor as they waited for the President's arrival. Jack's skin crawled slightly as he took the sight in. A den of snakes. He couldn't imagine what it was that drew some into their ranks.

"Jack? Were you bored, too?"

"Hey, Margaret. Curious, I guess. Is there anything happening?"

"Not so far. I think they'll be back up in a minute."

"Who?"

"Sydney and Mark. You didn't know she was here?"

"No. She didn't tell me she was coming in," Jack confessed. Evidently Sydney had also found it hard to stay home.

"How's he handling the promotion?"

"Okay. Bit of a shock. He expected it to go to Nick in New York."

"Nick doesn't have the Shepherds case," Jack said.

"True."

Before they could say more, the door opened behind him. Deacon held it for Sydney as she carried in a plate of fries and a Mountain Dew. Deacon followed with a cup of coffee.

"Jack! Glad you could join us. We just went on a coffee run to stretch our legs."

"Evening, sir. You've been here a while?"

"Since this morning," he replied.

"You?" he asked Sydney.

"Since about noon, after I dropped Lenny at the airport." She shrugged, and Jack realized she didn't have an excuse to be here either. She went around him and set the plate of French fries down in front of Margaret, who immediately grabbed one and stabbed it in the ketchup.

"Oh, these are so good. Thanks, Sydney."

"No problem." They shared a smile before following Deacon into the office. Sydney took Larry's desk chair and Jack used the one in the corner. Deacon grabbed the remote and turned on the TV. It was more of what Jack had seen out in Margaret's office.

"Larry's on his way in from Reagan," she said.

"He find anything?"

"I guess not, or he'd still be out there."

Jack nodded and pointed at the TV.

"Anything new this time around, sir?"

"I haven't seen a copy, but from what I hear, no. Just more of the same."

Jack sat back and sighed.

"Any threats?"

"Outside of the usual? No. We're following a possible lone wolf up in Boston. Nothing really to go on, other than he started hanging with the wrong crowd online, wearing more traditional clothing, and missing a lot of work. His old girl-friend tipped us off. So far, he's just running his mouth. We haven't seen him shopping for weapons or bomb-making materials yet, but if he does, we'll pick him up."

Jack nodded at the news and said nothing simply because he had nothing to add. His focus had turned to the domestic side.

"Well, let's hope it's a quiet night."

KENSINGTON, MARYLAND

THE SUV WAS A CADILLAC. One with all the options, including tinted glass. As such, it blended into the neighborhood with ease, and they cruised its streets without drawing so much as a glance from those out and about. On the oft chance that they were stopped by a curious patrolman, they had kept the gear inside large gym bags and hidden under the cargo cover in the back. On the seat between them were a few printouts from a local real estate website. Any officer who stopped them would receive a barrage of questions about the neighborhood and a request for directions. From experience, Dayton knew that most would quickly lose their curiosity and then disengage as soon as possible.

Dayton slowed the SUV at the site of the jogging trail. It had paralleled the road for the last half mile, dipping in and out of the trees on their left. Now it crossed the road near the target and then the small stream on the other side. Dayton pulled off the road and then spread the map out on the steering wheel for the benefit of anyone passing by. He spoke to Anna without turning his head from it.

"See that little bridge over there? How much space you think is under it?"

She examined the bridge. It was only a foot or

so off the water and more decorative than needed. A few small shrubs had been planted on both sides to prevent erosion, and they created a shadow that only served to hide the space underneath.

"I think that would work. Big enough to hold what we brought, and there's some cover in those trees on the right."

He traced a line on the map. "The trail and the water lead to Rock Creek and then go under 495 toward DC. Plenty of places to stash the car and then jog back here. Plus, we've got this small curve here."

"I like it."

"Okay. Get ready while I do a lap."

She unbuckled and began crawling over the seats to the back, while he put the SUV back on the road. A half mile later, she was ready, and he did a U-turn.

"I'm at Old Spring. I'll give you a countdown."

"Okay." She was now in the backseat with both heavy bags on her lap. The items gave off metallic sounds when she moved as the objects inside knocked against each other.

"Road's clear, behind," she called out.

"Clear in front," he answered. "Five seconds."

Anna opened the door a crack, before she

grasped both bags firmly. The SUV braked hard and stopped in the road right next to the trail.

"Go."

A second later, Anna was out the door and running for the bridge. The door slammed itself shut as Dayton sped away. In twelve steps, she was at the bridge. She threw herself down on its cold wooden surface and stuffed the bags underneath. They were quickly swallowed up by the darkness. She rolled to the other side to see if they could be seen before throwing herself to her feet and jogging in the direction Dayton had gone. The process had taken her less than ten seconds.

She stayed on the trail and maintained a moderate pace. Just another suburban mom trying to stay in shape. A half mile later, she saw him approaching, and she checked behind her.

Nothing. The rush hour crowd had not left the city yet. She angled to the road just as he pulled up and was back in the passenger's seat a moment later.

"We're good. Heavy bastards. Plenty of room for them, though."

"Okay. What's next?"

"Escape routes. Let's shop for houses some more."

"Okay."

Dayton slowed at the next intersection and signaled a dog walker to cross with a polite wave. When they moved on, she noticed his smile.

"What?'

"I was just thinking about our effect on future home prices."

It was dark humor, but she understood its purpose. On top of that it was just plain funny, and they allowed themselves a short laugh before getting back on mission.

"How far to the next exit?"

"It's ... right here. Turn left."

THE NATIONAL MALL

THE CROWDS of protestors stopped their rotation and slowly gathered at a few key buildings. All of them had cell phones, and they were checking them more often than usual. A few were watching the TV coverage of the Address, while others were conferring with other members of the group.

"Look at the cops on the end there."

Her husband turned his head slightly to do so. He saw a group of three officers, all listening to the radio one of them held in his hand. They seemed a bit agitated.

"Hold on," he told her, as he reached in his pocket and changed the frequency of the small radio. He had the police band pre-programed and now listened in to their dispatcher. His wife waited and hopped from foot to foot in an effort to keep warm. The wool mask on her face keeping the cold at bay, only allowing her eyes and mouth to be seen.

"What is it?" she prodded him.

"The cops are seeing the crowds moving in from the streets. Not sure if it's just a few nervous rookies, or if they are sounding the alarm. No incidences reported; just a big crowd moving in."

"Well, we've been getting them used to that sight for a few weeks now. Let's hope they don't get scared and do something stupid."

He nodded and then held up a finger to listen.

"They're getting ready to move the president to the Capitol building."

They both looked up and noticed a change in the crowd. No doubt they had gotten the same news.

"Time to take our positions."

Ronald Reagan Washington National Airport

Larry stretched in the aisle of the aircraft, while he waited. The flight from Montana had been a long one, and the hours spent in the narrow chair had only added to the several he had spent in a car over the last few days. His frame was just not made for it, and it had taken its toll. Now, he ached all over. He vowed to ask—no, beg—Jack for his plane if this ever happened again.

And he had nothing to show for it. He and a crew of field agents had covered every train and rail yard between Denver and Canada with no luck. A few tramps had been held for questioning, but most had no idea what was even going on in the country. They didn't know who the Twelve Shepherds were or what they were doing. Their worlds consisted of the trains and the next meal or bottle they could acquire, and not much else. After a few days Larry had given up. The trail was cold again. Their guy could be in Canada drinking whiskey, or in Mexico doing shots of tequila. Until another lead came to them, they were back to square one. He'd put himself on plane for home.

The plane was on time for a change and Larry was surprised. In his experience the later the flight, the more likely the delay was to happen. But the weather had cooperated, and he had been lucky enough to sit next to a skinny bookworm this time. The woman had kept her nose glued to a Rosalind James novel the whole trip. He had glanced at the cover long enough to see what the story was about. Romance in New Zealand. He doubted there were any professional assassins in the plot.

Now he stood with the other "spring-butts," as he called them. The people who jumped to their feet the second the seat-belt sign went off. He never understood the action. They just had to wait until the door opened anyway, and then again until all the people in front of them left and made way. He'd rather sit while he waited, but the book-worm had asked him for her bag, so he had stood to retrieve it for her. His cramped legs had wel-comed the activity, so he chose to stay upright.

He searched his memory while he waited. Had he driven here or taken a cab? There had been so many lately he had to think hard. Cab. Good, at least he didn't have to walk through the snow. Was there snow? He bent over to see out the window and orient himself. In the process, he noticed the look of fear on his seat mate's face.

"Ma'am? You all right?"

Her eyes traveled from him to the Colt Python

.357 revolver hanging in his shoulder rig. It had become exposed when he'd bent over.

"FBI. Over thirty years," he quietly told her.

"Oh ... I'm sorry. What you must think."

"It's okay. Happens all the time."

The woman offered another overly displayed smile by way of apology, and Larry waved her off, letting her stand and walk out ahead of him. This airport was close to several law enforcement, intelligence, and military facilities. There were probably a dozen guns on board every plane flying in or out, but he didn't think it was the time to tell her that.

He made his way off the plane and into the terminal and was surprised to see it low on foot traffic. Whatever the reason he took advantage of it and increased his pace. He found a line of cabs waiting outside and let himself be ushered into the first. Thankfully the man had the heat cranked up.

"Where to tonight?" the man asked.

"Hoover Building."

"You got it, G-man."

The young man dropped the cab in gear, and they were soon out of the airport and angling toward the highway. The lights of the capitol shining bright. But something else soon caught his attention.

People. Hundreds of them. All of them bundled up against the cold weather and crowding the sidewalks on both sides of the road.

The crowds got thicker the second he crossed the bridge into the district. He'd seen some footage while waiting for his flight in Montana, but it didn't match the reality. The crowds looked several times what he had seen, and they seemed to be lining the streets on all sides. He watched them after tapping out a message to Sydney at a red light. They were standing in place and looking past him at the bridge.

"What are you looking for?"

3

"A patriot must always be ready to defend his country against his government."

—*Edward Abbey*

THE MANSION

"Who are you?"

William had been deep into a

file from Haney's mystery soldier, when the computer had alerted him of an intrusion at the cabin. The bears in the area would occasionally try the door, in hopes of gaining entry, and once a bison had walked up the stairs to explore the deck. But the bears were all in hibernation now, and the bison herd was in the lower valley this time of year. He tapped keys and soon had a view inside the structure.

A large man. Decked out in civilian hunting gear. A thief? He didn't seem to be. William watched as he passed up the gun rack and the electronics, roaming the house. If he was a thief, he was an industrious one; it was no easy task venturing that far into the mountains just to rob a remote cabin. The man reappeared in the kitchen, with what looked like a bedsheet. He spread it out on the kitchen floor and then crawled across it, his right arm moving in all directions.

"What is he...?"

Suddenly the man stood and flung the sheet into the air. It landed draped across the long couch, directly under the camera. He pulled and tugged until the sheet was spread evenly, before stepping back and pulling off his hat and scarf. William leaned in close to the monitor and examined the intruder's face.

"Number Six?"

William's jaw dropped as he watched the man gesture to the sheet. He taped a key and froze the image, before blowing it up and reading it.

Attack coming. 40 men. Get ready!

"What the hell?"

Number Six stopped waving his arms and moved to the door. William saw him put his hat and scarf back on, before plunging out into the snow. He left the door open, and the snow blew in behind him.

William broke out of his shock and grabbed for the phone.

"Charlie! I need you here, now!"

"What's going on?"

"Just get here quickly!"

THE WHITE HOUSE

THE OFFICIAL SPEECH was in a leather binder, and he had two copies: one, he would hand to the vice president after taking the dais; and the other he would keep to refer to in the event that the teleprompter failed.

He now walked the hallways and office pits of

the West Wing, thanking each person he came across. Many of them were young, called to the West Wing by their inner drive to serve, forgoing pursuits which would benefit them much more than their time at the White House. The president kept a smile on his face as he shook hands, slapped backs, and posed for photos. They were all so driven, so dedicated to a job that paid them so little, yet it rewarded them in ways they could never count.

It was almost a shame to crush that, but he had no choice.

He completed the tour with a stop outside the office of his speechwriter. The few glowing words to praise the man and the document he had produced came off well, and the crowd cheered when the president was finished. The speechwriter got a genuine hug from the president. The speech was a work of art, but it was far from the speech the President had asked for several months ago. The final product had been twisted and tweaked into something that pleased everyone while actually saying very little. He'd found himself wondering if it contained any of his original thoughts.

At a signal from Henry, the president broke away and headed for the door. The young man fell into step next to him, and the President leaned in for one last order.

"Not until I start speaking."

"I understand, sir."

"I won't forget this."

The man's face broke for only a moment before he recovered.

"Yes, Mr. President. Is there anything else I can do for you?"

"I need you to go back to law school and graduate as soon as possible. They'll need you."

"Yes, sir. I will."

The President put his arm around the man and gave his shoulder a squeeze, before breaking away and leaving the building. A few steps later he was in the Beast, and the motorcade was pulling away.

"The first lady?" he asked his escort.

"Secure in the Senator's office, Mr. President."

"Very well. Let's get this show on the road."

"Yes, sir."

MONTANA

AFTER HE CLEARED the snow away, the barn door slid open with little effort, and he pulled it shut behind him. His tracks were being covered by the falling snow, but not fast enough. Either way, the screech it gave off would warn him if anyone else entered.

Ignoring the ATVs and Gator, he searched for a snowmobile. After finding nothing, he made his way to the armory. Knowing the walls were made of steel with a concrete core, he didn't bother trying to break them down, as it would take more time than he had. He'd have to finesse his way in. The keyboard was under a protective plastic cover, and when he raised it, the welcoming red light mocked him.

Unless Dayton had changed it, the first two numbers were eight-five. He'd managed to see them once and had made a mental note of them. Why, he didn't know. He'd never thought he would return here, but it was how his brain worked. There were two more and then the pound key. He just had to figure them out—and fast.

He moved to the stall with the heavy bag hanging inside and scooped up a handful of dust from the floor. He held it up to the keyboard and lightly blew it across, coating the number pad with a fine layer. The eight and five keys clouded quickly, along with the two and the six. He wondered how many chances the pad would give him.

Standard was three before he'd be locked out. He shook his cold hand and flexed his fingers before carefully punching in a code.

8-5-2-6

The red light blinked three times and then returned to normal.

"C'mon."

8-5-6-2

Again, the red light blinked three times before denying him.

"C'mon baby, work with me here."

What could it be? Had Dayton changed the code but used the same numbers? Or was it something else. What if he—"

"Dumbass."

8-5-2-6-#

The light blinked three times and then turned green. Carter wasted no time yanking the door open. The seal parted with a pop, and he was inside.

He dumped the backpack on the floor and moved to the racks. What to take? Long gun? Shotgun? Both? He needed something for both outdoors at long range and indoors and close. He settled on what he knew best: a M2010 Enhanced Sniper Rifle with a scope. He adjusted the sling before setting it on the table. Next, he selected an

Benelli M4 Super 90. Ammo for reach was located under the table, and he soon had both weapons loaded with plenty of extra. A combat vest was found, and he loaded it with as many magazines as it would carry. A full bandolier of 12-gauge shells in double-ought went on the M-4, and several more filled his pockets. Another rack offered a variety of handguns, and he chose a pair of Glocks in 9mm. Both went into belt holsters, and he slid them around so they were just above his belt in the small of his back. Extra magazines went on the belt next to them.

What else?

Grenades. He found a box of frags in a locker and filled the vest with them. A pair of CS canisters were attached to the backpack, and a couple of Willy Pete joined them.

"What else? Think Carter!" he scolded himself.

Another locker revealed a variety of mines. Bouncing Bettys, Anti-tank mines. Cubes of C-4. Detonating cord.

He found what he wanted in the second locker. He loaded two of the concave devices into the backpack with the necessary hardware. It was getting heavy.

He looked at the two Barrett M82s on the top shelf but quickly dismissed them. As much as he could use their range and power, they would be like hauling boat anchors in the snow. He needed to stay as mobile as possible.

"That's it. Get out of here."

He loaded the pickup and was about to leave, when a thought struck him. Were the attackers coming here, first? It only took a second for the idea to form. He returned to the last locker and removed one more item, before closing the door behind him.

"You boys want to play? Let's play."

THE MANSION

THE FLASHING LIGHTS of the district police motorcycles could not be missed. They moved away from the gate, and the first of the Secret Service's SUVs pulled out behind them. It was not an unusual sight in the nation's capital but tonight was different. Tonight, the President of the United States was addressing the country and the entire world. So, on this occasion there were dozens of cameras in attendance. The movement of the most powerful man in the world could not be missed.

And certainly not by the watchful eyes of

William Ockham. As soon as the president had appeared in the doorway and waved to the reporters gathered outside, William had picked up the phone and called the General.

"Sir, he's moving."

"Very well. Send it."

"Yes, sir."

Despite the millions of dollars of hardware at his disposal, William reached for a phone on his desk. The two messages had been in the draft folder of the tiny device for over an hour now; all he had to do was push the button.

"Rubicon," he muttered. He wasn't sure whether it was curse or a prayer.

He pushed the button, and the first group-text went out to twelve people. A few buttons later, another message was sent. This one to thousands.

4

"True patriotism is better than the wrong kind of piety."

—*Abraham Lincoln*

NORTHERN VIRGINIA

Anna paced the house. They were as ready as they could get. The car was fueled and then sterilized. The plates switched out. The radios checked. The maps memorized. Only then had they eaten and then turned on the TV. The usual selection of talking heads were on every channel, and they had quickly tired of the partisan spin and speculation on what the president might and might not say. Dayton had finally lowered the volume and stretched out on the couch. His eyes were closed, but Anna knew he was awake and listening. Their cell phones were quiet. But they expected that to change soon.

How he could be so calm amazed her. She had tried to relax but had quickly given up and began wandering the house. It was like a museum with its décor stuck in the late 90s. The absence of any occupants was there, if one were looking. Empty flowerpots sat on windowsills, and evidence of bugs occupied the nooks and crannies of the floors. The toilets were pink with anti-freeze. The refrigerator empty.

There was another difference, one that she almost expected.

The walls were bare. Even in the small back bedroom, one that had obviously been used as a home office by his parents, the walls held nothing but empty nails and a few oil paintings. Any photographic evidence of its former occupiers had been removed.

She wandered back to the living room to find Dayton sitting up and watching the TV. On it, she could see the flashing lights of a motorcade. Before she could ask, their phones vibrated.

Dayton silenced his and turned to her.

"Time for us to go."

THE J. EDGAR HOOVER BUILDING

JACK STEPPED out of his office with the file he had come to retrieve and bumped into a fellow agent in the process.

"Jack? How you been?"

Jack tuned to see the smiling face of Bradford Williams. He had not seen him since they had taken down a terrorist leader in Africa a few years back. He was now the FBI liaison with the Bureau of Alcohol, Tobacco, and Firearms.

"Brad! How the hell are you?" The men shook hands and paused to talk.

"Good. The new job keeps me busy."

"What they have you doing?"

"Fertilizer at the moment, believe it or not. I

have a team that travels around the country making sure none of it goes missing. It's about as glamorous as it sounds. How about you?"

Jack wasn't surprised by the answer. A former SEAL and EOD technician, explosives were Brad's area of expertise.

"Still chasing the Shepherds. They've gone quiet, so we're chasing the leftovers."

Bradford nodded knowingly. "Working late?"

"Actually, just bored and Larry is on his way in, so I thought I'd come in and watch the speech until her got here. What you doing here so late?"

"One of my guys is retiring and we took him out for a steak and beer. I just came back here to wait out the traffic."

"Come wait with us, we're doing the same."

Bradford shrugged. He had nothing else to do. "Okay."

Jack led the way, and they talked of office gossip until they reached the top floor and Deacon's office.

"You're watching the speech with the Director?"

"It's casual Friday, so-to-speak. C'mon."

Bradford frowned but reluctantly did so.

KENSINGTON, MARYLAND

A FEW MILES AWAY, Haney was watching the same speech coverage. The president was briefly visible as he walked from the door of the West Wing to the armored limousine. The long view of the TV camera panned back enough to include the signs of the protestors ringing the building in its shot. It was what a producer would label "good television." Long on symbolism and short on substance, it was what the viewers had come to expect.

Haney drummed his fingers on the arm of the chair and then reached for the tumbler. He'd made his calls. He'd put the pieces in place. He'd pushed the first domino. Now there was nothing to do but sit back and watch them fall. Harper was out there, and if successful, his actions would serve to fuel their interests for years to come. It brought a smile to his face as he drained the glass.

Shaking the remaining ice, he held the glass out for refilling. When there was no answer, he grunted. It was his own fault. He had ordered them all out so that he could watch the coming speech alone. The staff had been sent away, and he had retained only a few of his security men. Most of them now occupied the kitchen or wandered the grounds outside. He had retired to his study alone, and now he had to make his own drink.

The footage was now of the flashing lights making their way to the capitol building. He had time. He turned up the volume before rising and walking to the sideboard. A fresh glass and three new cubes of ice were assembled before he chose a bottle he hadn't tried before. It seemed like a good night to try new things. Taking the glass to the window, he examined the garden below.

The home had been in his family for generations. It had even prompted the influx of several politicians. Most of them doing so for personal gain. They used their kids. Telling the little boys and girls who to make friends with at school so that they might meet their influential parents and develop a rapport. A shrewd but effective tactic. One that Haney had admired for its boldness. People willing to use their kids to get ahead were willing to do other things, and Haney was not one to let such observations pass unnoticed. They were the kind of people Haney could make use of. He almost wished his grandkids lived in the area.

But it didn't really matter any longer. Not after tonight. After tonight the president would be cowed and have no choice but do as he was told or lose his office. If that happened now or in the next election, it did not matter. What mattered was who held the real power, and to see who that was, he only had to look at the reflection of the window in front of him.

Tomorrow morning, he would be the most powerful man in the world.

He raised the glass to his own reflection.

BRIGHTON BEACH, NEW YORK

"OLEG!"

The man allowed the restaurant owner in close, and they exchanged the traditional greeting. It was more for the sake of those watching than anything else. Oleg owned the man, as he did the beachfront restaurant he had just arrived at, along with three more just like it here in Brighton Beach. While the other members of The Trust preferred their Manhattan penthouses, he preferred to stay here, among those he owned, and an even greater number that feared him.

"Is good to see you! Come, I have table waiting."

Oleg waved his security people back and followed the man to the rear of the restaurant. A private room was around the corner from the kitchen, and as he passed, the smell of dishes he could only get here greeted his nose. It was as close as he could get to home, and it came without the brutal winters. And it was safe; not even the FBI dared to come here. The only threat came from the motherland, and he had taken steps to assure the man he was not a threat. He paid his tributes regularly, and they were both large and well-laundered. The man had little to complain about. Oleg walked a deadly line between The Trust and the Russian president, but it was one he had gotten very good at. Tonight was a good example: He had a copy of the American President's speech in his pocket and had gotten the carefully picked snippets to the Russian President, well ahead of time. They would both profit well from the information. It was an occasion to celebrate.

A few men waited for him inside, and they rose with a roar at his arrival. He endured the loud greetings and several backslaps, before taking his seat. A tall bottle of clear liquid sat in the middle of the table in a bucket of ice, and he filled his own glass before sitting back and downing the vodka with one flick of the wrist.

"*Phaaa!*" he exclaimed, and the others laughed. It was the traditional Russian response to good vodka. His glass was immediately refilled, and this time they all joined him when he reached for it.

"*Za vstrechu.* "It's good we all met here. The men echoed his toast and downed their shots.

"Business is good, Oleg?"

"Business is good, but let a man eat first."

A waiter appeared in the doorway, and Oleg waved him forward. A rapid string of Russian poured forth, and the young man struggled to keep up. Only minutes passed, before plates of caviar, smoked trout with creamy horseradish dressing, and bowls of okroshka hit the table. Georgian champagne arrived and was uncorked with flare, before large plates of *pelmeni* and *kotlety* arrived hot from the kitchen. The waiters came and went at a rapid pace, and the food was consumed between loud conversation and even more vodka.

Eventually, Oleg relaxed and pushed his plate away. Sipping his last vodka and watching the men before him all converse at once. He'd been one of them, once. A man of the streets, like his father before him. A *mafioso*, as they were referred to here. A member of the brotherhood. But when the republic had fallen apart, he had left Yeltsin's shadow and forged his own path, cultivating relationships with those filling the gaps of power and gaining control of several previously state-owned industries. Now he owned one of the largest mining companies in the world. From there, he had branched out into oil, banking, insurance, and agriculture. He owned airports and skyscrapers in many of the world's richest countries. He dined with presidents, prime ministers, and princes in public and dictators and sheiks in private. He was now one of the world's richest men and answered to only a few who were richer. Those men and their combined efforts were making him richer tonight, and he had felt the need to return to his roots and celebrate with them.

Vasily watched him through the door of the room. Close enough to give them the illusion of privacy, yet near enough to be summoned with a gesture. He shared the space with the man's security people and kept his smile hidden. The phone had vibrated in his pocket a few minutes ago, and he had ignored it. He knew what the message was and whom it was from, and he was already engaged. He just needed one more thing.

Opportunity.

As Dayton had taught him, sometimes one had to make their own, and sometimes it was provided by the target itself.

The man he was watching soon did so.

Oleg waved the young waiter forward and ordered a medovukha to go with his vanilla syrniki. A favorite desert from his childhood, it was something he never failed to get when here. Vasily was back with the desert in less than a minute.

"You don't wish to see the American President give his speech, tonight, Oleg?"

Oleg shrugged and reached for the desert drink as it was placed in front of him. "I already know what he will say. The man is ... predictable, in so many ways." This produced a round of laughter and many insults aimed at the Americans they were surrounded by.

"He would not last a day outside his white house!" another boasted.

Oleg laughed with them and reached for his spoon.

WASHINGTON, D.C.

THEY NUMBERED TEN: eight young men and two young women. All of them lean and agile enough for what the mission called for. They approached the armory on sidewalks from all directions, each of them armed with a backpack of supplies and a few tools. The leader held a pair of CS grenades in the pockets of his jacket, but he hoped they would not have to use them. They weren't here to confront people, especially people they considered neighbors.

They had studied the layout and several pictures of the facility for a few days and planned their attack carefully. The first ones in would be the two women. They each had a skill set which made the decision an easy one. They had practiced its execution at a suburban baseball field until it was ingrained. But rehearsals were over; the phone in his hand had just showed him that the president was leaving the White House. It was time to put on the show.

The two tallest men walked to the fence and scanned the motor pool on the other side. It held a variety of military vehicles, the majority of them painted the drab beige of desert camouflage. There were a dozen five-ton trucks with hard covers. Several HUMVs. A pair of fuel trucks, and the usual pickups and sedans. The motor pool was primarily for the movement of troops and supplies. Inside the building was a weapons' cache, one filled with infantry small arms. Ones that could quickly be deployed throughout the city if the need be.

The group was there to prevent that.

The two men saw nothing but cold vehicles and even colder concrete behind the fence. Only one light was on inside. It was the same as it had been for the past three weeks. The facility had only one guard at night, and he rarely, if ever, strayed outside.

"Looks clear."

"Agree. Let's go."

They both turned and put their backs to the fence. Lacing their fingers together, they both adopted a half-squat, their hands out in front of them.

Out of the shadows the women appeared, both of them at a dead run. The squeak of their shoes on the pavement was the only sound they made as they both planted a foot into the outstretched hands. The men straightened and heaved, launching the two women up and over the barbed wire with room to spare. They spun in time to see them both land and tumble forward, each spreading out the force of the impact. A second later, they were on their feet and moving.

The motion detection light came on and flooded the area, and the first woman ran to it and dispatched it with a swing of the baton in her hand, while the other slammed the wedge in the crack of the door and hammered it home. The men all ignored the noise and pulled heavy wire cutters from their packs Attacking the fence with the help of others who joined them. As soon as the opening was big enough, they held it open so the others could squeeze through. The group fanned out across the lot, and the sound of rapid decompressions began to arrive one after another.

"Two minutes!" the leader yelled.

"Watch the door!"

The leader turned and saw a shadow moving across the windows. The wedge they had installed would only hold for so long. If someone applied enough force, it would pop out and allow the door to open. He had to discourage that. To do so, he reached into his jacket and brought out a shotgun. It was full of bird shot, and he hoped it was all that was needed. As soon as he saw the light come on in the window next to it, he aimed the barrel at the steel door and triggered a round.

The bird shot impacted the steel with a boom, which echoed off the football stadium across the street, and whoever was on the other side wisely chose to remain there. The explosions of air continued to sound in rapid succession.

"Almost there."

The leader glanced sideways long enough to

see his people moving down the last row of trucks. They each had six wheels, and the men and women attacked them without mercy. Heavy cable cutters were in their hands, and they made short work of the valve stems, releasing the compressed air inside with hollow booms and rapid hisses. The trucks and HMMVs sank to the cold pavement, one after the other, like dominos. Others used the cable cutters on brake and fuel lines, further rendering the vehicles immobile.

"Time!"

The group finished the last truck and ran for the opening, now large enough for them to slip through rapidly. The leader pumped another round into the door to discourage anyone thinking of following, before he, too, fled. Once they were all outside and back in the shadows, he took a count. All ten were accounted for.

"Ditch the tools and go."

A few chose the weeded lot next door to toss their tools, while others used the nearby sewer grate, but they were all free of them within seconds and moving away in twos and threes. The leader stayed behind and watched the door for a full minute before following. He gave the motor pool one last look before he left.

Every vehicle was disabled. It would take

hours to change the tires out on enough of them to deploy a significant force. By then, all would be over.

He allowed himself a brief smile before turning and running into the dark streets. He and nine others had just nullified the D.C. National Guard.

Now he had other things to do.

5

"When a nation is filled with strife, then do patriots flourish."

—*Lao Tzu*

HOUSTON, TEXAS

He filled the time by checking the stock reports. As a member of The Trust he had access to inside information that hedge fund managers could only dream of. The hardest part was acting on it in a way that didn't draw attention. When he'd seen the final copy of the president's State of the Union address—a speech he had contributed to himself—it had prompted a few changes in his personal portfolio. When the markets opened in the morning, he would stand to make a nice profit. One that his people would move offshore within days.

The elevator arrived on the parking level, and he pocketed the phone before stepping out. His limo waited with the door open, but he stopped on seeing the driver.

"Who are you?"

"My name is John, Mr. Austen. I'm afraid your man David has fallen ill. I was asked to take his place."

Austen paused while he considered the statement. His driver had come to him by way of Mr. Harper—Haney's own right hand. But this man, this man he had never seen before.

As if reading his mind, the man spoke again.

"Mr. Haney sends his regards." The man offered a smile, along with a tip of his hat.

"Very well," Austen grunted.

He took his place in the back seat, and the man

shut the door behind him. He couldn't help but notice the handgun tucked into a shoulder holster before the man straightened his uniform and walked around the car to take the wheel. The limo pulled out of the garage and onto the streets of Houston with ease. Austen watched until he was sure they were headed in the right direction, before settling back into his seat.

He considered turning the TV on to see the speech, but he already knew its contents and didn't need to see the man they employed delivering them. He was more concerned with The Trust's next moves. The war in Syria would drag out, as planned. Russia would be held in check, which produced more opportunities for his company. Fossil Fuels were dying. He knew it, and so did the brothers.

Their efforts were now on two fronts. The access to more cheap oil. Low hanging fruit that they could reach at minimal costs. That meant opening public lands to drilling and setting up operations off the eastern seaboard. It was the only way to keep profits up. The second effort was the constant battle to deny the damage they were doing. It was getting harder. They were up against the world's top scientists and countering their research was getting harder to do. It had become a media war, a battle of advertising budgets. And theirs would always be bigger.

He pulled out his phone and checked the messages from his top propaganda man. The figures looked good, and he crunched them as the car traveled out of the city. The horizon was dotted with cracking towers and their discharge. It was like a dystopian skyline, a city of no return.

WASHINGTON, D.C.

THE CHAIN and lock were just propped in place, as promised, so the group entered with the briefest of pauses. With a few muttered goodbyes and a couple of thumbs-up, they paired off and found the vehicles which matched the keys in their hands. One of each pair carried a full backpack, the other nothing but a map.

The busses were big. Not the normal yellow school buses, nor graffiti-covered transit units. Instead, these were long-distance vehicles. Ones that were complete with TVs, and elevated seats, and large storage compartments underneath. They were usually used to haul tourist around the city or up the coast to the casinos. Today, however, they would serve a much different purpose.

The drivers moved to their seats and fired up the diesel engines, letting them warm up while they adjusted seats and mirrors. Their partners checked every seat, and even the bathroom, to make sure no one was aboard before pulling the backpacks off their shoulders and unpacking their contents. They chose a seat halfway down the narrow aisle, and concentrated on their device, ignoring the outside view, as the busses left the parking lot and headed into the city. Then each split up and headed to their assigned intersections. The ride was a slow one and the driver checked his watch at every stop. The lighted dome of the capitol building got closer with every red light.

"We early?" the passenger asked.

"Only about a minute. You ready?"

"I will be. Just give me a countdown."

"Remember to take out at least two of them."

"I will."

The light turned green, and they traveled on. The passenger, now squatted on the floor, duct-taped the device to the leg of a seat. He'd practiced with the same size container at home, and had counted how long it took it to empty: thirty-seconds. The timer on his watch was set for forty-seconds. The driver claimed that would be enough for him to do his part, so that's what they were going for.

"Six blocks," the man shouted.

"Six blocks," he echoed back.

He double-checked the connections and then powered up the phone. After making sure they were both ready, he slipped the phone in his pocket and glanced outside. The bus was moving at a moderate pace through the DC streets, and he was happy to see that they, and the sidewalks, were mostly clear. The spot had been chosen carefully. They were on a major approach into the city, but it was in the old section of town and the streets were narrow, built in the day when gas powered vehicles were not yet conceived. While they were on their own here, other busses would be working in pairs, and in some cases even greater numbers. But he couldn't worry about them right now; he had his own mission to complete.

"One block. Find a spot!" the driver yelled before tugging on his seatbelt.

He didn't bother answering this time. Instead, he planted himself in a seat next to him and hugged the one in front. He felt the bus swerve, and the tires squealed on the cold wet pavement as it angled across the intersection.

"Brace!"

A bump from a car that was parked too close, and then another as they jumped the curb. The impact was not as strong as he had expected, but it still served to rock him in his seat. There was shattering glass and the scream of steel changing shape, and then all was still.

He opened his eyes and jumped to his feet. The driver was still strapped in but was now holding his head. He ran forward and grabbed the man.

"You okay?"

"Yeah ... yeah, help me up."

He unbuckled the man and yanked him to his feet. The man wobbled once and then stood straight. A bruise began to swell on his forehead.

"We're here. Everybody out." He smiled at his own joke and yanked on the door handle. It opened just enough for them to squeeze out. They stepped out and turned to see the results of their actions.

The bus had crossed both lanes under the driver's guidance and planted its nose into the corner of a building. The rear end had swung around, impacting the parked cars across the street, effectively wedging itself in and blocking travel in both directions.

It was perfect.

He shoved the man toward the rear of the bus.

"Get the back tires. I'll get the front."

The man moved off, and he glanced up at the faces peering out of the buildings above them before dismissing them and pulling his knife. It made quick work of the front tire, and the bus settled to the ground. A second later, the rear joined it. He pulled out the phone and hit the speed-dial button.

Inside the bus, the valve on the plastic gas can opened, and its contents began to pour out onto the grooved rubber surface of the center aisle. The bus's new angle caused the gas to move aft at a rapid pace. It had forty seconds to reach the bus's rear.

The men were over half a block away when the gas ignited. The whoosh was enough to move a few onlookers back, and the smoke soon filled the bus's closed interior. Several people used their cellphones to call nine-one-one, but most got a recording telling them that all the lines were busy. Traffic began to pile up behind the now closed intersection.

One by one, the fires sprang to life all over the

city, creating a ring and separating it from the world outside. Over a dozen buses and several smaller cars now blocked the bridges over the Potomac, and the highway overpasses were clogged by both the fires and the snarl of traffic that immediately accumulated behind them.

The drivers and their passengers faded away into the crowds.

MONTANA

CARTER WATCHED them through the scope.

They were good. Only one man moved at a time, but they did so rapidly, the others providing cover as the man moving dashed to his new tree. No doubt there were others on the ridge acting as overwatch. Some of them might even be scanning the area he was currently hiding in. He hoped none of them had an infrared scope. If so, he would never hear the shot.

Eventually, they reached the trees nearest to the stable, and three men stacked up to move to the door. One of them pointed to Carter's tracks in the snow. When he saw that they only lead into the building, they slowed their approach. Carter had left out the back and kept himself among the trees until he reached this setoff boulders looking down on the barn. He'd covered himself with snow and waited, but not for long. He'd barely started to get cold when the men had arrived.

Once he determined that the three men were the only ones aiming to enter the barn, he swung the rifle away and looked for other targets. There were many, and he scanned them looking for a man with an antenna. But there was nothing; modern communications were so good that bulky antennas were no longer needed. He spotted two men close together. That usually meant leader-ship, or a crew-served weapon. It was the latter. The barrel of a machine gun stuck out of a white sheet cover. He centered his scope on the man's chest and waited.

THE MAN NODDED, and his companion yanked hard on the barn door. As soon as the gap was wide enough, the other two stepped in and broke left and right.

"Clear."

"Clear."

"Safe that door!"

The first man spotted the open door at the other end, which his partner had indicated just as the third man came in. Unlike the first two, the third man stopped and looked for targets. What he found instead was a present left by the previous occupant.

The wire had been hidden in the snow and was now wrapped around his foot. He froze in place and rapidly traced it with his eye. It led off toward one side of the barn, to a pair of ATVs. Both sat next to a fifty-five-gallon drum of fuel.

"Get out! It's a—"

His shout was cut off by the explosion. The charge blew from the top down, and the exploding gas spread across the floor, filling the space with burning fuel in a fraction of a second. The door they had entered through was now launched across the snow-covered valley, and flames shot through each stall window. The contents of the barn were immediately incinerated.

PALM BEACH, FLORIDA

THE PRIVATE CLUB cost over two-hundred thousand dollars a year to join, and the membership was quite filtered. It was an echo chamber of political thought, and only chosen members of the power elite were allowed in. He'd identified many of them, and his access to their conversations had allowed him to grow several files in William's archives. Many had even made the list of potential targets. He'd spotted several names on tonight's guest list, and he spent the first hour matching names to faces. Now it was time to put that knowledge to work.

The man he was here to see was sitting at table sixteen. It was one of the preferred tables near the terrace, which looked out over the Atlantic as well as holding a nice view of the stage. Tonight, a band had played soft dinner music while waiters delivered plate after plate of food and drink to the men and woman in suits and dresses that rivaled their yearly incomes. Marcus watched it all from the side of the room, his eyes expressionless as he gazed about with crossed hands and an earpiece showing in his ear. A security man, he watched the party goers with a detailed eye, while they ignored him in return.

That was fine. It was what he wanted.

The man he was here to see had flown in two nights ago on his Boing 737 from Michigan, where he headed the company started three decades ago by his father. Since taking over, he had leveraged his billions into every political race he could in order to buy politicians who would do his bidding. He not only had tripled his wealth and acquired a membership to The Trust, he had financed their operations both in and outside the country. His main role was now money laundering. The world-wide business he'd inherited was perfect for washing bribes and hidden profits for those who could afford his rates. It had only cemented his place in the organization further. The trips to the club were disguised as vacations, but they were actually a way to contact as many of his clients as he could in one place. The irony was that he still wrote the trips off as a business expense.

The target had chosen the lamb tonight, and by Marcus's eye, he had downed at least three martinis with it. A fourth had been ordered as they prepared to watch the president's speech, and the man sipped it now with a smile on his face. He reached for the drink again and then set it back down without drinking. The man was a fidgeter, one with a small bladder and a phone addiction. Marcus was sure he was looking for a way out of the room so he could take a piss and check his phone. It was only a matter of time.

Five minutes later, the man pushed his chair

back and made his excuses, before heading toward the door Marcus manned. The man made it as far as the doorway on wobbly feet, before being stopped by someone's trophy wife and forced to make small talk. He finally pulled away and examined the hallway in both directions. His phone vibrated again and this time the man's eyes bulged when he read the message.

Marcus moved to intercept him.

6

"The highest patriotism is not a blind acceptance of official policy, but a love of one's country deep enough to call her to a higher plain."

—*George McGovern*

WASHINGTON, D.C.

He was seventy-four-years-old, but he wasn't letting that slow him any. While he couldn't keep up physically with the group tonight, he could contribute in other ways. He checked the time, and with a last look at the TV, he killed its sound and walked to the dining room of his small home. It was covered in a variety of equipment, and it was time for him to use it.

He'd been a gadget man his whole life. The kind of kid who took apart his mother's appliances and built elaborate Rube Goldberg devices in his father's garage. Electronics had soon dominated, and he'd spent his life keeping up with the ever-changing technology. Many of the teenagers he taught were surprised when the old man demonstrated the inner workings and capabilities of their own cell phones. It was a skill that had not gone unnoticed.

Tonight, he would work from home. While the other members of the group braved the sidewalks and cold, he would do his best to help them from his dining room table. They were still with him, in a way. Their voices, anyway. He had spent a day writing short scripts and recording each of them reading one. Now, it was time to put all that work to use.

He picked up the first phone in one hand and held it next to the speaker. With the other he worked the mouse and selected an audio file on the screen of the laptop. With a finger on each button, he was ready. He clicked the phone first.

"Nine-one-one, what is your emergency?"

He clicked the file, and the voice of a young man spoke from the speaker.

"There's a bunch of people starting fires on Rhode Island at U street! Got to be at least two houses burning! There's like twenty of them burning stuff. Better hurry!"

"Wait. Who is this, please?"

He ended the recording and the call. The phone went into a bucket of water on the floor next to him, and he picked up the next. This time, he selected the file for a young woman.

"Nine-one-one, what is your emergency?"

"There's a bad wreak on Maryland and Eighth. A bus and two cars! One of um's on fire! The drivers are fighting. We need the police and the fire department."

"Maryland and Eighth? Who is calling please?"

He ended the call as fast as he had the first, deposited the phone in the bucket, and picked up the next one. He had twenty-four more lined up next to it.

"Nine-one-one, what is your emergency?"

ATLANTA, GEORGIA

CONVENTION CENTER WORK SUCKS, Ben thought, for the hundredth time. But it got him the access he needed. Being a Shepherd gave him a lot of free time, so finding the right temporary agency and getting the minimum wage job of working the floor of the center, and of the adjoining hotel did not take up too much of his time. He was basically on-call for whatever event they were having. So far, he had worked a car show, a few trade industry conventions, and a few political rallies.

Like he was tonight. The death of a senator had sparked a special election, and his target was now a candidate on the road. Something Ben had watched closely. Once the agency figured out that Ben was both reliable and available day or night, he got called in for everything. Tonight, he was an escort. Leading parties of two and three people from their rooms upstairs, around the convention center floor, and back again. His access key allowed him to use the freight elevators and the service corridors in order to keep the VIPs separate from the attendees.

It also got him an earful of what went on behind the scenes. The amount of acting these people had to do was tremendous. Cater to this group. Pander to that group. They discussed manipulation strategies and talking points as if he were not even standing there and it made his real mission that much more easily vindicated. Politics were nothing but a game of numbers to these people; there was nothing off the table when it came to getting the necessary number of votes. He'd heard them promise something to one group, only to promise the opposite to another thirty minutes later. Not once had he heard the candidate express his own thoughts. It was all about power to him.

And money. Having access to the rooms these people were staying in allowed him to plant listening devices after their people had swept them. Once, he even did so while the security people were still in the room. He had picked up many conversations with the man himself meeting donors and throwing numbers around. In the last few hours alone the man had excepted several checks. He hoped they were still in his pocket.

He now watched from the edge of the stage as

he gave a rousing speech to the crowd before him. These were the voters, the ones who thought they elected the people into office. Most had been chosen by the process for the candidate and didn't even realize they had been marginalized. Like extras on a movie set, they were little more than nameless faceless filler for the cameras. He watched them cheer and chant meaningless slogans for twenty minutes, before stepping back and checking his watch.

The candidate was an anomaly. A man with his own money. In his former life, he'd made billions off the health care industry, and despite getting caught in the largest case of Medicaid fraud in history, he had managed to survive intact and successfully run for governor. The heavily gerrymandered state, combined with a billion-dollar ad-buy had assured his victory, and from day one he had set about making the money back. A series of inside deals and back-channel negotiations had padded his pockets back to their original sum and then only added to it. His term as a governor had been even more profitable than his years as a head of business.

His reign cut off by term limits, he now sought to repeat the process, this time as a Senator. The campaign had started early, and with the various watchdog groups examining every contribution, he was forced to be extra careful while gathering funds for his election. That meant more hours on the road pandering to the people, even on the night of the State of the Union address. The rally had been scheduled months in advance.

The governor's schedule was tight, enforced by both him and his campaign manager. A man who insisted they all refer to the candidate as Governor still, obviously a strategy to remind the voters they had voted for him before. The campaign manager was a weasel in Ben's opinion, and a foreign one at that. He wisely kept himself off the cameras, as his Russian accent would not go over well on television. Ben ignored him and focused on the target.

The man preferred several short naps throughout the day in leu of a full eight hours of sleep. Tonight, would be an early one by campaign standards. This speech, followed by a few private meetings upstairs with some donors, then a nap, before he and his staff watched the president give his State of the Union address. Then back to bed for an hour, followed by a ride to the airport.

The man was scheduled to visit LA tomorrow to meet with some defense industry donors. That meant a plane ride instead of the bus. William had already forwarded him the flight plan that the pilots had filed a few hours ago. The campaign manager had told everyone that the man was to be in bed no later than midnight. That was fine for Ben; he was scheduled until even later. Copies of the schedule had been passed out to several people, and Ben had managed to snag a copy. It made planning so much easier when the target cooperated.

The crowd got louder as the man ramped up the rhetoric for his big finish, and Ben used the opportunity to fade back into the group gathered backstage. He found his way through the adjoining kitchen area and then to the service elevator. Traffic around it prompted him to loiter, and he untied and re-tied a shoe in order to stall until he had the car to himself. After getting off on the floor below his target's suite, he found his way to the stairwell.

There, he paused to send and receive a quick message from William. Between each floor, there was a small door in the wall containing a fire extinguisher. He opened it and retrieved the item he had secured there a few weeks prior and tucked it in his belt. Assured by William that the cameras were off, he then climbed the stairs and made his way down the hall to the candidate's room. Letting himself in, he cleared the space before leaving and finding his way across the hall to the maid's storage closet. Inside, he found a comfortable spot between the towels and toilet paper to wait.

It would not be too long.

CAPITOL HILL

THE CROWD WAS LOUD. Their shouted slogans and chants were enough to pierce the armored hull of the president's limo, and this time he did not avert his gaze. The angry faces swept past at a rapid rate, growing in number the closer they got to the building. He marveled at their grit. He could see the fog of their breath rising above them as they waved gloved hands holding signs in his direction. It was well below freezing outside, and yet these people had turned out in the thousands for the last few weeks. He'd been doing his best to ignore them, to push their shouts aside, each time telling himself that they just didn't understand.

He was wrong. They did understand. Much better than he had allowed himself to see. He realized now that if he were not the man in the limo, he would be one of them on the sidewalk. Well, there was a time and place for that.

"Mr. President?"

He turned from the view outside to see his Secret Service agent addressing him.

"Yes."

"There's been some questionable activity in the city being reported."

"Such as?"

"A few busses have been set on fire, and there's a large accident blocking the Roosevelt bridge."

"Terrorism?"

"No, sir. We're really not sure yet."

"Handle it. I have a speech to make."

"I ... Yes, sir."

The agent went back to listening to his earpiece, and the president returned to gazing out the window. A few moments later they were through the police perimeter and the crowds stopped at their line. Regardless, their voices could still be heard. His view was blocked by the backs of agents in long black coats, and the shadow of the canopy appeared. It was erected for his arrival every time. He'd asked once, and the one-word explanation had been "snipers." A comforting thought.

"Are you ready, sir?"

"Let's go, John."

The door opened, and the shouts of the protestors rose by several decibels. The president had no time to even wave to them, before he was swept along in the middle of his detail, and he barely felt the cold before they were inside. They paused long enough for him to shed his coat before he was led upstairs, the old speech held firmly in one hand, his other griping the small device in his pocket.

He waited until he reached the main floor to paint a smile on his face.

BOSTON, MASSACHUSETTS

TERRANCE CARVER LEFT his office as the streetlights were coming on. His wife would be upset at his late arrival, but he had several men on a conference call that would simply not end. All of them demanding projections on the quarterly profits and the changes that would come from the president's words tonight. It had taken over two hours to convince them that their efforts and political investments would pay off. Now exhausted as he was, he had to get home and play host to several more of his company's senior staff. It had become an annual event at their winter home on the Florida coast. A State of the Union party. You had to be rich as hell to even say that with a straight face. A profit party was more like it. They would all make several figures tonight while they drank and congratulated themselves for the chess game of donations and outright bribes they had placed on the congressional chessboard. It was going to add to his fatigue, but it was well worth it.

He dropped the car into gear and pulled it out of his private spot, before goosing the engine enough to squeal the tires. A former fighter pilot, he was now chained to a desk, and the car was the only thrill he had left. He had vetoed the suggestion of a chauffeur years ago. Once on the street, he let the Jaguar lose, and it weaved in and out of the West Boston traffic with ease. He had ten minutes to enjoy himself before he arrived at his gated communities set among the high rises of the downtown area. The weather had cooperated for once and the streets were free of snow to the point he had pulled the Jaguar out of storage. Now the lights of the harbor passed rapidly as he made his way along the tree-lined boulevard.

Rounding a corner, he was forced to grab for the papers on the seat next to him to keep them from ending up on the floor. It was a copy of the president's speech. One he had quoted for the board members and several key stockholders. The speech promised more war, and for them, that translated into more missiles, more bombs, and more planes. The cheapest of them well over a million dollars apiece. They were looking at healthy profits for the next several years. Everyone had been happy.

Returning the papers to the seat, he steered his way up to the gate. The reader on the pole scanned his car for the barcode sticker and promptly opened the gate. It was an improvement over the maned gatehouse as he didn't even need to roll down his window and lose the warm air inside.

It also kept the noise out, and the person following him knew it.

The Mansion

"Is that Number Six?"

"Yes. I verified it while you were on the way."

"How did he get here? And what's this attack he's talking about?"

"Did the drones fly today?"

"No, the weather was too bad."

"Get one up. Soon as possible."

Charlie thought about what William was saying. The mansion had four drones that would normally be launched every morning to track the movements of the bison, as well as patrolling the perimeter of the property, but the snow and wind had been so bad the last few days they had all been grounded. They had lost one last year because of the weather and still not found it. It was now under several feet of snow.

Charlie grabbed the phone.

"Hawkins? It's Charlie. Get a drone in the air right now ... I don't care—just do it. Check out the cabin to the east and the stable first, and then head..." He tapped William on the arm.

"East. The pass between here and town."

"You hear that? Good. Let me know as soon as you see anything." He hung up before the man could reply.

"Should I send a snowmobile up there for him?" he asked William.

"I ... I would wait until the drone footage was in. Mr. Carter is capable of taking care of himself. Until we know more, I would wait.'

"Yeah, okay. I've got to go alert security. Call me

if you see anything more!" He turned and ran for the lock.

"Charlie!"

"Yeah?"

"That plan I told you to make?"

"I did. It's ready."

"Okay."

7

"Patriotism was a living fire of unquestioned belief and purpose."

—*Frank Knox*

NEW JERSEY

The beach house was modest but still considered top-end due to its location.

The man had carefully selected it for its landscaping and gated entrance—it allowed him to come and go without being seen. The three-story structure was on stilts and had survived the wrath of Hurricane Sandy because of it. One of his neighbors' homes was still being rebuilt, and on his last visit they had suffered through the pounding of nails and the scream of saws. He'd almost called and complained, but that would have required giving his name. That was not an option.

The location served another purpose: it was directly on the route to and from his drive to work. He could stop there for an hour or so every few days without his wife suspecting anything. His many cars were already checked regularly for tracking devices, and he only used the security people when traveling. Otherwise, he preferred to remain as independent as possible. The drive to and from his massive home to the south and the headquarters of his company was often his only alone time, and he preferred to spend it enjoying the ride at the speed he wished, with the music he wished, at the volume he wished. And if he wanted any further diversion, there was the beach house.

The current occupant's name was Sasha, a girl

he'd been introduced to while in New York six months ago. She had already outlasted her predecessors by several months. Her age was at least thirty years younger than his and he had never actually inquired as to the real number. He was sure the answer would be a false one and he really didn't care if it was. What he did care about, she was very good at.

Her dark beauty and Slavic features were tantalizing to him in a way the American girls he'd harbored in the house before her had never been. Added to that was her skill and enthusiasm. The combination was something he couldn't get enough of. The first time he had arrived after moving her in, she had been floating in the pool, covered only in a fine sheen of oil and a pair of sunglasses. She had attacked him on a chaise lounge, and the memory of that day was still fresh in his head. He'd found it difficult to concentrate at the many meetings he'd attended today. How was he supposed to calculate profit margins on drugs sold in Africa when he knew she was waiting for him after work? He'd been entertaining thoughts of an extended business trip with her, but The Trust had too much going on. A pity.

There was wife number three to worry about as well. He suspected that she knew, but so far, he had not detected any action taken on her part. She seemed content to travel, and shop, and spend his money seemingly as fast as he could make it. And as the CEO of the world's largest drug company, he made a lot of it. He'd married her eight years ago, when the surgery was still fresh, and everything was in place. Now age was winning the battle, and the surgeons could no longer keep up. He'd purchased the beach house four years ago, and ever since had installed a revolving door of young flesh to keep himself happy.

Tonight, he'd have a few hours to indulge. He used the excuse of the State of the Union address to make it a late evening, telling her he would be watching it with a few business friends. His wife had no interest in politics and made her own excuses for letting him go, sparing herself the drudgery of having to watch it with him. He'd chosen the Audi R8 that morning to celebrate and now floored it on a straight stretch of road to separate himself from the traffic behind him. He didn't wish to be seen pulling into the gate when he arrived.

The seashell driveway crackled under the tires as he pulled inside and closed the gate behind him. The trees swallowed him up, and he parked the car out of sight behind a low concrete wall.

The sea breeze mussed his thinning hair as he pulled himself out of the car, and he smoothed it back down before climbing the stairs and letting himself inside.

The dress was made of some space-age fabric he didn't know the name of, but its inventor deserved the highest award in the industry as far as he was concerned. It hugged her form in way that could only be described as predatory, and she made it more so the way she walked forward to great him. His hands found her shape and he caressed it as her tongue found its way into his mouth. After a minute, he hoisted her small form up and carried her to the bedroom.

SIMON WATCHED it happen on the tiny screen from only a dozen feet away. He had accessed the property from the waterline after a long walk from the south, the waves erasing his tracks as fast as he made them, defeated the alarm system, and let himself into the house before the sun had come up. The cameras he had placed weeks ago were still in place, and he had watched the girl sleep until noon before getting up and completing a workout in the home gym. She had followed that with a meal and a lazy afternoon of watching TV. It was not an unpleasant view. His target had good taste, even if the woman was bought and paid for. After the TV, she had left for a few hours of shopping, and he had followed her travels on the GPS locator he'd affixed to her little convertible while she hit a few high-end stores in the area, before she returned with several bags. He'd then been treated to her modeling the outfits in the mirror while she spoke to a friend on the speaker phone in Russian. Evidently, the woman on the other end was in the same line of work, and he smiled as they compared their keepers lack of skill in bed. Twice, he'd had to stifle his own laughter at their comments. The friend was thinking about making an upgrade—a richer colleague of her current owner had made an interesting offer. The conversation then shifted to the pros and cons of the new arrangement. Simon put money on the upgrade, the girl sounded like she had a head for business.

Eventually, the target called to confirm his arrival. Something William had already messaged him, and Simon shifted quietly in the closet while he waited. The girl made a dress decision and then proceeded to paint her face for his arrival. All while watching some inane reality TV show that was obviously scripted. Simon suffered through it as best he could.

The arrival of the man himself was announced by the roar of a V-10 engine outside and Simon switched cameras on the tiny tablet in time to see him exit the car and head up the stairs. Simon got to his feet before she killed the TV and then went to the door. Killing the device in his own hand, he waited. If it was like most visits, they would not be in the entryway long.

He was right. Within minutes of his arrival he had drug the girl off to the bedroom. He waited until she was making the appropriate sounds and then used them as cover to leave the closet behind.

He fingered the items in his hand. They were called auto-injectors. Something Dayton had added to their training in the mountains. They were simple devices: basically, a spring-loaded syringe that, when stabbed into a muscle, automatically delivered a metered dose of whatever drug it had been loaded with. He and Stephen had both had brief training on them in the army—they were to be used on yourself if you were under chemical attack. But beyond basic training, they had not been a priority. He had never thought of them as an offensive weapon until Dayton had showed him their flexibility.

He now held one in his hands. They'd been originally intended for the injection of epinephrine, a common drug used by people who had a severe allergic reaction to bee stings. Two of them were now loaded with something called Telazol, the other two were loaded with Versed. Ironically, the drugs were manufactured by the target's company. Something Simon took a bit of pleasure in knowing. They were marked one and two, and he had instructions for both. He'd practiced with another set a few times and even made a makeshift holster out of a shotgun shell holder, so he could assure quick access when the time came to use them.

That time was now.

He crept to the woman's bedroom door and found it open a crack. Inside, the girl was riding atop the man at a frantic pace, her cries getting louder as she flung her hair about. It was an Oscar winning performance. A part of him hoped that she wouldn't give the old man a heart attack and deny Simon his mission.

A few minutes later her cries suddenly ceased. She had completed her mission, and like a good actress, saw the portrayal to the end, collapsing on him in feigned exhaustion. Simon almost rolled his eyes, but he stayed on mission, trying to interpret the new sounds into their actions. The man regained his breathing and rolled the girl off him. She collapsed and splayed herself across the bed for him to ogle.

"Stay there," he ordered.

She whispered something in Russian, and he smiled before rolling out of bed and heading for the bathroom. Simon listened for the click of the door shutting. As soon as it reached his ears, he moved.

He was through the door, across the room, and on her before she could open her eyes. His hand clamped down over her mouth, and his bulk pinned her to the bed as he plunged the needle into her shapely thigh. Her eyes went wide in horror as she gazed fully into his eyes from inches away, and she bucked twice in a futile effort to throw him off her. Her slight 110 pounds was no match for his 220 pounds of muscle, and she struggled in vain. A few seconds later, she weakened and then went limp, the drug taking hold fast due to her recent physical exercise and rapidly beating heart. A quick check of her pulse confirmed her unconsciousness, and he pulled the envelope from his back and placed it in her hands. He left her naked form in place and turned her head away from the bathroom door, before planting himself behind it.

He waited.

THE MANSION

CHARLIE WATCHED the screen over man's shoulder as he raced the drone up the valley. Bison and trees occupied its view until the cabin came into sight.

"Some tracks from out of the wood line." He pointed.

The drone banked and did a slow lap around the building. The pilot zoomed the camera in on the deck.

"The doors open. Looks busted down. More tracks."

"They're headed toward the barn. Go that way."

The drone had barely spun and faced the structure when it was obliterated in a cloud of orange flame. The shock wave hit the drone a second later, and it rocked a few times before leveling back out. The two men stared at the remains of the building as debris rained down all around it. The rumble of the explosion rattled the windows a second later.

"What the hell?"

The drone pivoted, and they caught sight of a few shapes in the wood line before one of them flashed three times and the screen turned to static.

"I lost it," the man spoke, before reaching out and hitting the reset button.

"Don't bother; they shot it down. Get to your station."

"What? I—"

"Get to your station! We're under attack!"

HUDSON BAY, NEW YORK

HUGH LISTENED as the men got louder. Whoever had called, their words had come as a shock, and the two men had immediately punched new numbers into their cell phones. After getting no answers after multiple tries, his boss had ordered the boat back to the dock. Hugh had advanced the throttle to appease the man, and rounded the island faster than normal, but when the chop hit the bow head-on, he used it as an excuse to throttle back. The man was obsessed with whatever news he had just received and didn't notice. Both men in the salon now barked into their phones, trying to piece together what was happening to their colleagues.

The waypoint got closer, and Hugh set the autohelm to follow the track he had plotted, before reaching under the console and removing the envelope. He placed it on the helm and wedged it in place. He didn't want it to fall and be missed. With a last look at the two men in the salon, he activated the box and silently left the bridge.

He made his way aft, stripping off his clothes as he went. By the time he reached the stern he wore only a black dry suit. Reaching into a locker, he found his fins and a spare air tank. It would give him about ten minutes of air, enough to get close to the island without being seen. He donned the fins and fixed the goggles on his face before sitting on the boat's rail. He caressed it once by way of apology—the boat had been a good one, and it was not its fault; he almost hated to leave it. But that was no longer an option, so he wasted no further time lowering himself into the cold water of the Hudson.

Bobbing to the surface, he saw the boat already yards away, its shape a silhouette against the lights of Manhattan. It sailed on through the light chop, held on course by the autohelm and oblivious to the fact that its pilot had left it. Hugh dismissed it and struck out for the island, cutting through the cold water with powerful strokes. The current was about three knots, and he adjusted his course into it, letting it speed him to the rocky shore. The bright paint he had used on the rock now shone in the darkness, and he angled for it, slipping only once as he pulled himself out of the water. He sat and rested for moment, looking for the boat now a half mile away.

Soon.

"Hugh! How long until we're back?"

"Look at this crowd around the capitol building!" His college pointed at the screen. "It's huge!"

"I can see that. You get through to Charles?"

"He's not answering either."

"God damn it. Where the hell is everybody? Hugh!"

"We still on course?"

"I think so. Hugh!? Where is he?"

"Maybe you should check, Jamie?"

His partner's phone rang, and he began

yelling at whoever had called. Jamie gave up on his fellow Trust member and went in search of his captain.

"Hugh?"

Getting no answer, he headed for the bridge. The liquor was taking hold, and he grabbed the railing to keep his feet as he ascended the small flight of stairs. The cold wind bit into his light clothing, and he shivered a bit as he looked around.

His captain was nowhere in sight.

"Hugh! We need to get back! Where are you?"

Getting only the wind for an answer, he set down his drink and pulled himself to the cockpit. A glance at the screen showed them to be on course, but where was the man who kept it there? Had he gone over the side? He glanced at the stern but saw only the trail of the boat disappearing into the chop, and the lights of Liberty Island behind them.

"Where the hell ...?"

His eyes found the GPS screen again, but this time he noticed the envelope. The letters on the side were illuminated by the red numbers of a timer sitting next to it. What the hell?

TTS.

His eyes went wide, and the blood in his veins

chilled. Struck sober, he reached for the timer as it counted down its last few seconds.

WASHINGTON, D.C.

THE DEVICES WERE SMALL. Handcrafted by himself with items bought at various locations around the state. He had been purchasing them for months, always paying cash or utilizing a stolen card. The disassembly process had been accomplished in a weekend, and the new items had been crafted on a homemade assembly line.

Now he had a box of them taped to the creeper as he pulled himself along behind the row of cars. The device allowed him to stay inches off the ground and silently mobile at the same time. The fence had been breached a few nights prior with the aid of some wire cutters, and the floodlight had been taken out with the aid of a pellet gun. They had yet to replace the broken bulb, and as a result the lot was in darkness.

The creeper allowed him to silently roll from car to car as he placed his creations under each back wheel. He'd painted them all with a coat of flat black paint, and they disappeared once they were tucked under the black rubber tires. His only fear was of running out before he got to the end of the row.

The last vehicle was an evidence recovery unit. A truck like he was used to seeing delivering packages in his suburban neighborhood. Only this one was black and had the symbol of the Washington DC police department on the side. He hesitated. Was it a worthy target? Did it double as a SWAT vehicle? It wasn't worth the risk. He stuck the last two devices under the wheels and spun the creeper around to go back the way he had come.

It was done. From here he would leave and return to his own block and keep watch over his home and that of his neighbors. There were some in the city that would see tonight's events as an opportunity. And with the police immobilized or busy elsewhere, it would be up to the people to police their own.

He was through the fence and back on the street a minute later. Leaving the creeper behind, he walked four blocks to his car and started it up. The seat warmer drove the chill from his bones, and he held his hands to the heater for a moment before dropping it in gear and moving west.

The spike strips he had purchased had produced sixty spikes. He'd disassembled them and made those spikes into sixty one-spike units. They were designed to let the air out slow, so as not to cause a sudden loss of control if used on a vehicle traveling at a high speed. If any of the cars in the police lot moved tonight—and they certainly would—they would find themselves with two flat tires before they had gone a few blocks.

They could not defeat the police, but they could make them immobile. And that would be enough.

He turned on the radio to hear the man's speech.

8

"Patriotism is often the cry extolled when morally questionable acts are advocated by those in power. When these cries of patriotism drown out any logically based dissension, it is usually the American soldier that is given the order to carry out some ill-conceived mission."

—*Chelsea Manning*

C arl sat in the dark and watched the tiny screen. His feet dangled over the dark chasm, and the machinery moved the elevator car past him again only a few feet away. Despite the drop of several stories, he was perfectly calm. High places were his element. He cycled through the twenty-odd camera views, looking for any indication that they were aware of his presence, but it looked like it was business as usual. He looped the lanyard tighter before reaching up and using the overhead beam to reposition his ass on the cold steel he had been sitting on for the past several hours. It was an uncomfortable hide, especially when compared to the rooms just outside the elevator shaft he was currently hiding in, but it was the safest spot to be in a building full of cameras.

Cameras. He had gone over the building plans and the security system for months. There were over a thousand cameras in the hotel, casino, and parking structures. While most were concentrated on the casino floor, the rest of the building was not lacking. Working with William, he had planned a route inside which required them to spoof, or temporarily disrupt, over thirty of them. Even then it had required a fake security pass, a uniform, and a false employee file to be entered in the casinos computer system. All of which had been removed as soon as he had arrived at his perch.

The security box he had wheeled into the service doors and right past the guards had contained the usual empty money bags and lockboxes they were used to seeing, and he was sure they would no doubt be full of cash by days end and on their way back the bank. He didn't care. What mattered to him was the false bottom that contained his gear. With it he had entered an elevator, where, with William's help, he had ascended to the top floor without security seeing him. There, the seemingly empty car had paused long enough for him to bypass the alarm and exit through the escape hatch. There, he had left the car behind and climbed his way past the final two penthouse floors, to settle onto the beam supporting the giant motor serving the car. At that point, he had conducted a wardrobe change and a camera check, before settling down in the most comfortable spot he could find to wait. William had helped by patching a TV signal through to him, so he could watch and time his mission appropriately. And while it passed the time, it did not make the cold steel any more comfortable.

A new screen appeared in the corner of the tablet, and Carl clicked it. Another camera feed, this one courtesy of William as well. This one was not from the casino's system though, and Carl stifled a laugh when he realized it was from the target's own laptop. He was looking across the penthouse apartment, just one floor below and maybe twenty yards away, at the man he was here to see. Carl watched him as he sat down on a leather couch and adjusted the seventy-inch TV mounted on the wall.

The view of the floor-to-ceiling windows drew Carl's attention, and he counted the panes of glass peeking out from under the curtains, to confirm the man's location. The setting sun made the curtains necessary; otherwise, the man in the chair would have been blinded. But then, in a way, he already was.

Where was his wife? Or worse, one of the mistresses? If one of them showed up, it could be a problem. Carl tapped the screen for the audio from the feed and heard nothing but the sound of the man's TV and the rattle of ice in his glass as he worked on a tumbler of amber liquid. Carl had no doubt that there were security men in the penthouse somewhere, but unless they were in the room with him, it would likely not matter.

He checked his watch. He could go at any time, but he decided to wait a few more minutes and be sure the man was alone first. He began mentally rehearsing his moves once he left the shaft, while he checked the coil of rope around his body.

THE MANSION

THE FLASH OF THE EXPLOSION, and the ball of orange-black flame rocketing skyward, pulled the General's attention away from the TV screen and to the window. The shock wave rattled the glass and shook loose the accumulated snow. The General reflexively moved back a few feet and checked the tree line for any moving shapes, before examining the cloud again.

"Hello, Angler," he muttered.

A few seconds later, Charlie burst through the door. The General made note of the armor and holstered weapon, before gesturing to the window.

"We have some uninvited guests, I take it?"

"Yes, sir. But there's more. Number Six is here."

"It was him?"

"No sir, but he's here as well. The alarm went off at the cabin. We saw Six there. He gave us a warning and then left. We launched a drone, and it got there just as the stable blew. I think that was

Six's doing. There's about forty of them, sir. That's all I could see before they shot the drone down."

"Mr. Haney, I presume."

"How did he know—"

"That's irrelevant now, son. Take me to William."

"Sir, I have to get you away from here."

"This changes our plans, and William will need guidance. You've alerted security?"

"Yes, sir."

"Then take me to William, and we'll figure it out from there."

Yes, sir."

The General reached into his desk's top drawer and pulled out a battered 9mm, like the one Charlie wore on his thigh. Like most soldiers, they returned to trusted friends when the situation called for it. The pistol was tucked under his leg where he could reach it quickly before he gestured to Charlie.

"Let's move, son."

NEW YORK CITY

Two thousand miles away, Stephen sat in a similar elevator shaft. Unlike Carl, he still wore his security uniform and badge, as he would need them on his way out. He also sat atop the elevator car itself as it cycled its way between the floors. It was the executive elevator, one used by the man he had come to see and few others. So far, he had ridden it up and down twice without it containing his target. But Stephen was a patient man.

His trip to New York had been uneventful, and the storage unit in New Jersey he and Tommy had visited on the way into the city was found undisturbed. They had quickly extracted the items they needed and set off into the city in a van they had abandoned only a few blocks away. Neither of them had offered a goodbye—if all went as planned, they would see each other again very soon—but Stephen couldn't help but watch Tommy disappear into the city. When he was no longer in sight, Stephen had pushed all thought of him aside to concentrate on the mission.

Now safely at his staging point, he reviewed his steps. He'd left the keys in the van and the door unlocked, so he sincerely doubted he would find it there if he returned, which he had no intention of doing. Arriving at the building itself cancelled his fear of being recognized by someone on the street, and the new fear of the false ID not holding up replaced it. But William had delivered, as always, and his name was in the contracted security company's system. His new-guy act was quickly bought by the guards behind the desk, and he'd been given the crap assignment of patrolling the top floors, before they dismissed him. They turned back to their televisions before he had even reached the elevators.

Home of the largest bank in the country, this was a building that was never without a steady stream of workers. He was soon a part of the crowd, walking through various departments and universally ignored by the traders staring at their multiple screens. He'd ignored them right back and followed the map in his head until he found the storage room with the door in the back leading to the elevator shaft. It had required a climb of five stories before he was at the top, and another thirty minutes of waiting before he was able to step off the steel ladder and onto the roof of the car. Once there, he settled in to wait. With William's help and a cell phone, he kept tabs on the happenings in Washington, and when the president arrived at the capitol building, he removed his own coil of rope from around his waist.

It was much shorter than Carl's.

THE MANSION

THE EXPLOSION WAS AN EXPECTED SURPRISE, and unlike his target, Carter didn't flinch. He instead completed his squeeze of the trigger, sending a round on its way across the valley. The man's head had turned slightly to take in the sight of the exploding barn, and Carter saw his eyes narrow just as the round completed its flight and punched through his chest. He toppled over backward and sprawled in the snow.

His companion let out a shout, which Carter saw through the scope but couldn't hear. A second later, rounds began zipping past him, impacting the trees and snow. He rolled left and took shelter behind the boulder until there was a lull in the incoming fire and then slid down the rock and into the trees.

It was time to move. He set out down a trail offering shelter from the incoming fire, pushing his body hard to propel himself through the snow.

"CEASE FIRE!"

The men quit shooting but continued to scan the ridge.

"Son of a ... gimme that radio," King ordered.

The man next to him pulled the device from his sleeve pocket and tossed it over. He keyed the mic and spoke quickly.

"Wolfpack to Moose. Expedite the silence. Repeat, expedite the silence. Do it now!"

RURAL MONTANA

"ROGER, WOLFPACK. GOING QUIET."

He turned the radio off and gestured to his companion.

"Knock it down."

The man smiled and turned around until he could see the distant tower. Without any fanfare, he pulled a phone from his pocket and hit the speed-dial button.

The tower held both power and communication wires and was one of several that dotted the mountainside until they disappeared over the far ridge. He had spent the last few hours climbing it and selecting a few key structural points. By the time he returned to the ground, the small back-pack he had taken with him was empty.

The charges blew in rapid succession, and the tower buckled in slow motion. The wires arced and showered the snow-covered field with sparks, before grounding out with a loud tone and snapping. With the wires no longer adding to the tower's rigidity, it accelerated its trip to the ground, crashing hard and throwing up a large cloud of powdered snow.

"Wow," was the man's only comment.

"Dams are better. Bridges more fun."

"True, but it all pays the same. Let's get out of here."

The two men loaded themselves back into the old pickup truck they had bought two days before and headed out down the mountain. Their job was done. Rig the tower. Blow it on signal. That was the job. Two miles later, they tossed the phone and remaining hardware over a cliff, where it landed in snow so deep it would be well into spring before it all melted.

"Easy money."

"Yup."

THE MANSION

WILLIAM WAS VERY BUSY. Reports were coming in from a variety of sources, and he was struggling to keep up. Shepherds were checking in. The national TV services were reporting on the president's speech, while the local channels were reporting on bus fires. He'd intercepted a report of vandalism at the National Guard armory, and another of a massive pile up on the bridge over the Potomac River. So far, he hadn't heard any mention this was a coordinated attack. Good. The longer they stayed in the dark, the better. Now he had Number Six and an attacking force to worry about.

The sound of the airlock cycling distracted him for a moment, and he glanced behind him long enough to confirm it was Charlie and the General, before going back to his screens.

Another Shepherd checked in, just as the two reached his side, and William sent the acknowledgement reply without thinking.

"William. Where are we?"

"At least four of the Shepherds have completed their assignments, sir. Maybe more, but they haven't checked in yet."

"We advised them not to unless it was safe to do so."

"True. But I'm a little more worried about this group outside our door."

"Understandable. But I need you to stay focused on Rubicon. Charlie and I will handle the battle here."

"Sir, you should leave. I think—"

"Now is not the time to flee, Mr. Ockham. Now is the time to fight. Have you sent the files?"

"He's not started his speech yet."

"Expedite. How long will it take?"

"For the entire library to transmit? A little over an hour. And then I have PRISM to deal with."

"Send them now."

"Yes, sir." William reached for the command button and, with a deep breath, pushed it. The progress bar appeared again and rapidly grew. Through the thick glass, William saw the servers lit up, their blinking lights showing an uptick in their work progress.

"The off-site servers have the download command. The remaining ones, here, will take about an hour to send everything."

"Then we need to buy an hour. Charlie, we need to—"

The darkness descended, in a fraction of a second, cutting off the General's order. They waited in the red glow of the emergency lights, and William's screens came back to life as the emergency power kicked in.

"They cut the external power," Charlie whispered.

William checked the backup connections and the progress bar. The commands had made it out.

"They're too late."

9

"Patriotism demands of us sustained sacrifice."

—*Chiang Kai-shek*

THE CAPITOL BUILDING

"Mr. President."

The president didn't know the man beyond his name, but he

vaguely recalled his face from prior speeches. Whatever his title was, it didn't really matter; all the president knew was that he should follow him. He did so, while waving and exchanging quick handshakes with capitol staffers. This was as close as they would come to the chamber tonight, and many had waited for hours after their normal quitting times to spend five seconds with the president as he traveled the halls. The corridor of well-dressed staffers eventually deposited him in front of the house chamber, and there he stopped to tie his shoe. The crowd shifted nervously while they waited and the elderly man before the president nodded a greeting to the entourage, as they made their way through the crowd to be by his side. His speechwriter broke the silence as soon as the president stood.

"Is there anything—"

"No, Sam. The speech is locked. You did a great job." He patted the young man's arm, reassuring him for the twelfth time tonight.

"Thank you, sir."

He took the time to shake the hand of every one of them before turning and facing the man in front of the chamber door. The crowd fell silent as the president closed his eyes and whispered a quick prayer.

"Mr. Jacobs, would you tell the speaker I'd like to see him, please?"

Mr. Jacobs nodded, before turning and throwing the chamber's double doors open. The murmur of the crowd inside died to the sound of a gavel, and before it was gone completely, the man's voice overpowered the rest.

"Mr. Speaker ... The President of the United States!"

Preston entered the chamber to the deafening applause.

NEW YORK CITY

CHARLES GAZED over the balcony at the crowd below. They'd been there for a few days now, and their numbers were growing. The fact that he'd been forced to wait while his car made its way through them was one thing; the constant insults he'd had to endure while walking from the car to the building were another. And he took his frustration out on the buildings staff.

He'd chewed the security people a new ass for subjecting him to this, but until the parking garage was through with its renovations, it could not be avoided. He quickly dismissed the crowd and rode up to his penthouse apartment with two security men in tow. One of them waited in the foyer, while the other sat just inside the entry door after a quick sweep of the entire floor. Charles had merely grunted at the man when he was informed that it was safe and made his way straight to the bar to mix himself a drink. It was the price one paid for accumulating such wealth as he had. The scotch poured over the three cubes of ice, and he relished the first sip as he walked to the balcony.

From his elevated position, he could just make out their protests and it irritated him to no end. *Little people with little voices*, he thought. Let them scream; it would matter little. With a frown, he walked back inside and slid the door shut, cutting them off completely.

He wandered to the kitchen and rummaged in the cupboards before finding a jar of nuts to munch on. The clock on the microwave informed him that he had only a few minutes left, so he carried the jar and the glass down the hall and to his private study. There, he settled in and turned on the TV.

State of the Union coverage was on every channel, it seemed, and he selected Fox, as usual, to watch it. Not to be informed, but rather to make sure the news was delivered as he wished. A copy of the speech had been in his pocket all day, the majority of it written by people who worked for him and many of the passages would be his own words. He took great satisfaction in that. If the president of the United States was commonly referred to as "the most powerful man on earth," then how powerful was the man who told him what to say?

He smiled at the thought. He and his brother owned the country; the man on the screen merely performed a role for him. *This*, he thought, *this is what true power is.* He was going to enjoy the man saying his words tonight. Too bad his brother wasn't here to enjoy it with him, but he preferred his home in Kansa to that of The Big Apple. He pulled his phone from his pocket and tapped out a quick text. David answered him immediately: yes, they would talk after. Charles traded the phone for the TV remote and thumbed the volume higher to hear the sergeant at arms announcing the president.

His words echoed through the entire floor. Traveling down the halls and through the various rooms, before reaching the kitchen.

OFF THE SPACIOUS kitchen was a pantry. One whose entrance was hidden by a cabinet face which allowed it to blend in with the rest of the kitchen. Stocked with a variety of food and other household necessities, it was only accessed by the chef and the maids. Despite the thick door, the sound from the TV reached the interior with little difficulty.

Tommy stood inside, ready to meet anyone who tried to enter. He'd been there for hours and had waited patiently for the man to arrive. The tablet computer he'd brought with him served to provide him a view of the outside, and the various security cameras allowed him to follow the man's progress of entering the building and making his way up to the penthouse. The hacked feed and running loops had allowed Tommy to roam the entire floor for over an hour prior to Charles arrival. Everything was in place.

He tapped the small screen, and it split into four separate views. One of the foyer, where the security man now lounged in a chair. The second of the entry, where the second man was doing the same. The third was of his target, alone in his study. The fourth was of the House chamber, where the president of the United States was now making his way to the dais to address the nation.

Despite Tommy's preparations, it would be the man on the last screen that would set Tommy in motion. He fingered the items hanging off his belt and waited.

WALL STREET, NEW YORK

IT WAS the largest bank in the United States. It claimed to have 1.5 trillion dollars in holdings. It housed itself in one of the New York City's tallest towers, where it could be seen by every resident every day.

Its walls were made of glass.

The crowds had been gathered outside for days, always moving and always shouting the same thing. The money men arrived in their private cars and security cleared a path so they could enter the parking garage below without having to hear the outcry. Most of them barely looked up from their cellphones and spreadsheets as their cars entered the black hole. From there, they were taken by private elevator to their offices, which were well above the reach of any sound from below. They were like gnats one of them said, something to tolerate, but certainly nothing that would change what they were doing.

But tonight, the gnats were angry, and their numbers were great. The news hitting the airwaves, combined with the expected words of the President, had pushed many to their breaking point. For some, it was the buildup of righteous anger; for others, it was a planned event. They were creating opportunity for one another, and they didn't even know it.

The security men watched the crowds through the lobby's thick glass. The last banker had left hours ago, and the doors had been securely locked ever since. The garage's heavy gate had descended and been secured, as well. They'd settled in for another long night of gnat tolerance.

"Fired up tonight, aren't they?"

"If they beat on the glass again, we'll have to call the police."

"For what? All they do is run them off for a half hour or so. They come right back."

"Getting tired of it."

"You're tired of them interrupting your TV shows."

"That, too," the guard admitted. He smiled at his screens, one of which was tuned to his nightly dramas, the rest showing revolving views of empty hallways and war rooms.

"I'm going for a coffee and a piss. You got this?"

"Yeah, I got this. Piss for me, too, will ya?"

"You got it."

OUTSIDE THE BUILDING, a pair of men watched as the guard walked away. That left the one behind the desk. They'd been watching them for weeks, looking for patterns and gauging their skill level. The men were unimpressed. The guards did little but give the illusion of security. Their jobs consisted mostly of escort duty, keeping protestors in place, and staring at video monitors. They called the police to handle anything that might remotely be physical.

Good.

The two men shared a look. It was time. They each unzipped the backpack of the other. They had been modified with sewn-in loops at the top and holes cut in the bottom. Holes that corresponded with the back of their long coats. From inside them, they each pulled a sledgehammer.

"Well, all right!" one of the protestors shouted on seeing the pair.

Without hesitation, they both cleared an area around them and swung away. The ten-foot-tall glass panels shattered and rained down inside to the marble floors of the lobby. The men repeated the effort twice, and the crowd stormed into the building.

"What the hell!"

The guard had time to hit the alarm before he was mobbed by the crowd. He was dragged away from the desk and shoved in the nearest closet as the crowd surged throughout the building.

Among the protestors was a group there for a select reason. They ignored the vandalism and other acts of protests, and instead ran up the stairs, peeling off from the group in twos and threes to enter certain offices. There, they shut themselves inside.

One immediately began ripping the hard drives from every computer he could find, while the other utilized a crowbar to open any locked file cabinet. They didn't bother reading anything—there would be time for that later; they simply loaded as much of the paper as they could in their packs, before leaving the office behind and fading back into the crowd.

They didn't bother waiting for the others in their group; they made their exits as soon as they were done and disappeared into the surrounding streets. Behind them, the protestors shouted in defiance and victory as they destroyed everything they could.

They split up again as the sirens got closer. It sounded like the cops were sending everything they had.

They were already too late.

Most of the information would be on the web by tomorrow.

THE DIRECTOR, Jack and Sydney were catching up with Bradford when Margaret walked in. Her expression was enough to silence them.

"What is it, Margaret?"

"Sir, there's reports of some possible rioting taking place around the city. Security has warned everyone to stay inside."

Deacon glanced at the TV screen, but everything in the House chamber looked normal. He then turned and pulled the curtains apart. The others joined him at the window.

The glow of the fires could be seen in a few areas. The crowds of people on the streets below had grown in size, and the streets were clogged with traffic.

"What the hell?"

Deacon snatched up the phone and hit a speed dial number.

"What's happening?" He demanded from whoever answered. The others waited in silence while he muttered a few answers to what he was hearing.

"Call me back when you have confirmation." He hung up and faced them.

"We've got a buses and cars burning at three major traffic arteries, including a couple bridges, and the armory was attacked. All of the vehicles were disabled."

"Is it coordinated?"

"They don't know. The 9-1-1 system is getting overrun with calls. The DC police are responding, but they're already short-handed due to the speech. The cell towers are jammed with traffic. There's also a report from New York about a mob breaking into the US Bank building."

"So, what are we doing?"

"A level one alert for now. They'll shut down Reagan and take control of the bridges. All government buildings are being told to shelter in place. The hospital is on alert. I'll know more in a few minutes. Let's move this party to the ops center."

The three of them gathered their things and followed the man out, leaving Margaret alone. Jack paused at her desk and whispered a quick question.

"Can you get ahold of Debra for me, tell her to stay inside?"

It was technically forbidden to use a government line for personal use, but with the cell towers jammed with traffic Jack didn't have a choice. Margaret had access to FBI lines that they didn't.

"I'll try."

WASHINGTON, D.C., AIRSPACE

"DELTA FLIGHT 286, Reagan control. Come left heading 123 and descend to ten thousand. You are instructed to divert to Dulles, contact 348.6. Reagan is closed to further traffic by order of Homeland Security."

"Delta 286. Uh, roger, Reagan control, coming left to 123 and descending to ten thousand." He dialed in the new heading while simultaneously addressing his copilot, "What the hell is this all about?"

"I don't know but take a look outside."

He pointed, and the pilot followed his lead to see the familiar traffic grid of Washington DC below them. Something was off, though. Fires were burning below. A lot of them. They seemed to circle the downtown area.

"What the hell?"

"Check out the bridge!"

He looked and saw a pile of burning cars, and buses piled its entire length. The flames reached a high altitude and reflected back at them off the river below.

"Riots?"

"Who knows? Looks serious, though."

"Let's get this thing on the ground, and then we'll find out. Landing checklist."

The copilot tore his eyes away from the view outside and did what his pilot needed. But the image was burned into his mind. His home was down there, and so were his wife and kids. They lived far from the downtown area, but still.

"You with me here?"

"Yeah, sorry. Flaps to forty."

THE MANSION

CARTER BREATHED SLOWLY. In through his mouth and out through his nose. The escaping breath was blown sideways on the slight breeze, and he hoped it was not enough to give away his position. The sheet he had yanked from the bed and used as a message board was one of two. The second he had slashed a hole in and used as a cover, much like the down blanket he had made a poncho of, only this one had a different purpose: Its white color now worked to help him fade in the snow as he waited for the men to arrive.

He fought off the shiver and willed his body to accept the cold. After the prolonged physical effort of running through the snow, he had then circled back on his own tracks and found a spot to work from. The device had been set up and covered in a matter of seconds, and he now waited between two large pines for them to approach. The sweat he had worked up now chilled him as the snow he had flung over his body melted and found every crack in his clothing.

There. A tree had moved out of sync with the others. He slowed his breathing more and concentrated on the gap in the trees. He had placed himself in the attacker's shoes. They would not come straight up the valley—it was too open—and the bison would announce their presence. They would split up, with one half moving through the trees on this side to attack the mansion from above, while the other would travel across the valley and attack from the lakeside. This way, they could watch over each other in the event of an ambush.

He was taking a chance, hoping that they thought he had fled to the mansion. If they feared him sounding the alarm, they would come fast, hoping to put a bullet in his back and stop him.

Or, they would assume he had a radio and take their time.

He saw them on the second sweep of the trail. A diagonal black stripe moving over the white landscape. It was the sling of a rifle across the chest of the point man, his body wrapped in white. The shotgun he held in his hands was wrapped in white, as well, and he blended in so well that Carter was lucky to see him. He ranged the man at one hundred and fifty meters. An easy shot. But he needed to know where the others were first. The man paused and took a knee while he examined the tracks Carter had left in the snow. The tracks said the man he was following was in a hurry, and Carter was counting on that to make him lower his guard.

There. He counted ten more, about fifty meters

back, and looked beyond them for a trailing element. After a ten-minute scan, he saw nothing and deduced the main party was on the other side of the valley.

Good.

He moved the scope back to the point man. He was good. Alternating his gaze from near to far regularly. Moving in short sprints, with pauses to look ahead. Avoiding the path Carter had taken directly and instead following it off to one side. He examined the trees above as much as he did the ground he was treading on. Carter examined the weapon in his hand. Would he keep it? Or would he switch to the rifle?

He was going to find out very soon. He moved the scope back to the main group and measured their progress. About ten more meters. He glanced at the point man again. Five meters. He counted to ten and then triggered the device.

The M18 Claymore mine is a popular antipersonnel mine. Shaped like a paving stone and possessing a slight curve, its twelve-ounce explosive charge was sandwiched between a steel plate and a layer of ball bearings that, when detonated, produced a cone-shaped kill zone of fifty meters. They could be detonated one at a time or in series, depending on how many feet of wire one had and the person's imagination. Carter had wired two together in series and detonated them remotely.

The result was a cloud of snow and smoke that swallowed up the main party in a horizontal rain of steel. The double blast echoed across the valley like a clap of thunder, and snow fell from the trees as the shockwave passed.

Carter used the cover of the falling snow to mask his roll to the right. He was back behind the scope, scanning for the point man as the snow fell around him. Some landed on the scope itself, and Carter cursed it as he brushed it away.

The boom of the shotgun reached his ears as the pellets whistled overhead to dump more snow on him. He gave up on the scope and rose to his knees, aiming down the barrel as best he could.

The man had him in his sights and was pumping rounds in his direction as he walked sideways toward the nearest thick trees. It was the smart move; he was at the maximum effective range of the shotgun and was doing nothing but keeping Carter's head down until he reached the trees and had time to get the rifle off his shoulder and into play.

Carter sent a round his way that only managed to knock the snow off a branch and send his target to the ground. Cursing the fogged scope again, he rolled twice and then brought the rifle back up. The man was on his feet now and sprinting for the trees. Carter forced himself to clear the lens, before putting his eye back to it.

The snap of rifle rounds passed through the trees to his right, and he flinched before staying put. It was the men across the valley; they were shooting at where they thought he was, and hampered by the cloud of snow his mines had thrown up. Most of which was now drifting down the valley. He ignored it and searched for the point man.

There. He caught some movement around the edge of the tree. A weapon poked around its trunk.

The rifle. The man had dropped the shotgun and deployed the rifle while running.

"Smart bastard," Carter mumbled.

He stayed frozen and continued to watch. The rifle fire got a bit closer, but he knew they were firing at vague shapes. As long as he stayed still, they would most likely not see him.

Most likely.

The barrel was followed by an arm and still Carter waited. The cloud of snow continued to dissipate.

The rifle had a scope as well, and Carter watched as it slowly turned toward him. He selected the spot five inches above it and waited. If the rifle kept coming, the head had to follow.

When it did, he could hardly see it. The white balaclava blended into the snow cloud behind it, and he could barely make it out. Barely.

His finger tightened on the trigger.

The rifle kicked, and he immediately rolled back behind the tree. A second later, it was pelted with rounds from across the valley as the men zeroed in on his muzzle flash. The tree splinted and showered him in bark and snow as the rounds chewed into it. He waited for what seemed like an eternity, but eventually they stopped.

He only listened. To look would invite a bullet. All he got in return was the whistle of the wind through the pines.

Ten meters away was cover. A crack in the side of the mountain that he had first hoped would be a good observation point. Unfortunately, it had not provided the view he needed, but if he could get to it now, he'd be able to pass through and use the saddle on the other side to reach the mansion.

Ten meters. It might as well be a hundred. There was no way he could cross it without them seeing him and punching a hole through his back.

10

"Dissent is the highest form of patriotism."

—*Howard Zinn*

KANSAS CITY, KANSAS

D avid smiled at the brief message from his brother before placing the phone down and picking up the report from Haney. It was like most, short and to the point. A copy of the man's speech was also on the table, and he had read it twice to confirm that it held the words he and his brother had selected. He'd already moved money into the stocks which would be affected by the man's speech; if the predictions by his staff proved to be true, he stood to make a tidy profit in the next few hours.

Outside, the sun had settled, and darkness occupied the land around his hundreds of acres. The glow of city lights drowned out the stars, but he still preferred this view over the city skylines. It was one of the few ways he and his brother differed.

The TV showed the president still making his way through the chamber, on his way to the podium. It would take a few minutes, and he chose to leave the volume off until then. He had sent the staff away tonight, not wanting to be disturbed. The only thing moving outside was a security man by the pool and one of the cats creeping along the fence. Gazing past them, his eyes traveled the tree line, and he tried to remember the last time he had gone hunting. It had been too long; perhaps he could convince his brother to fly out and join him for a few days. After tonight, they would deserve a break for all their hard work.

LEE COULDN'T HELP but smile when the man seemed to look right at him. Hidden in the tree line and wrapped in an insulated ghillie suit, he knew he was invisible to the man a half mile away, but it still felt odd to have him look right at him through the high-powered scope.

He was tempted to pull the trigger, but the glass between him and the man in the chair was at an angle. Though not impact resistant like his Florida mansion, the windows here were still triple-paned and insulated. Tough enough to deflect his round after its five-second journey and result in a miss. He had two other possibilities, both more direct angles and therefore less likely to throw his round off. He hoped to see the man in one of those windows soon. If not, he would have to either take the lower probability shot or abandon the rifle in favor of moving in closer. Either one was well within his skill set, but the rifle offered a higher probability for a successful escape.

In his head, he retraced the route he intended to take out. The two miles of ground he had walked, crawled, and slithered over, all while dragging the rifle with him, had been challenging. He had endured rough terrain and thorny vegetation, as well as the bitter cold, during the entire journey. Three times patrolling men on ATVs had passed. One of them within a few feet of where he laid, but his camouflage had proven itself sufficient to keep him hidden. A full day's effort had been spent to get him to the location he was at now, and he had spent the hours since then lying motionless in the thick trees, waiting for his quarry to arrive. The man had passed right over him in his helicopter to land on the other side of the massive home only a few hours ago. Lee had marked the occasion by taking a piss; he wouldn't have time on his way back to the river.

Swinging the rifle to the left, he located the security man. There was a total of three, plus the pilot, at the home now, and Lee was surprised the man didn't have more. The file from William had been detailed when describing the security measures. They relied too much on electronics and not enough on personnel. Something Lee was taking advantage of at the moment. The file had contained a detailed map, and Lee had carefully navigated his way around and through the grid without triggering any of the sensors. William had also provided an addition to the software, and now Lee, with the simple activation from his cell phone, could shut the whole system down, or trigger a trail of false flags to lead the men off in the opposite direction. He hoped the breach in the system had not been discovered, as he was counting on it to get him the two miles back to the river unopposed.

The security man made a lap around the massive pool before returning to the chair he had placed against the wall of the home. Lee doubted it was for any other reason but to warm himself up and he didn't blame him. The temperature had dropped with the setting sun, and even his insulated ghillie suit was struggling to keep him warm. He had chemical hand warmers ready for when the time came; he couldn't afford to have his hands clumsy on the trigger.

If he missed, it would be his fault. The rifle he had chosen for this shot was the best in the world. A CheyTac M300 chambered for .408, it was accurate out to 2500 meters and carried enough punch to travel through the window and beyond. He had practiced with and adjusted the rifle for weeks until he was confident his cold zero was within the high-probability range. Without a practice shot, there was no way of truly knowing if he would be on target, but a practice shot was not in the cards tonight. He would get one chance, maybe two if he were lucky, and then he would be on the run.

Unfortunately, the rifle would not be coming out with him. Despite its light weight—only twenty-one pounds—he would be switching to the machine pistol in his backpack the second he stood up to increase his speed. Between that and a few other items he had brought along, he was confident in his escape. The only wild card was the helicopter. But he would worry about that when it came.

Pushing the thought aside, he moved the scope back to his target. He was still in the chair and watching the TV. Lee could see its reflection in the man's glasses and even make out the president himself on the screen. The speech was about to start.

It was time for Lee to warm up his hands.

BRIGHTON BEACH, NEW YORK

THE YOUNG WAITER placed the items in front of him and quickly departed. Oleg barely noticed him and dismissed him just as quickly. The men around him were getting louder, and he smiled at their banter.

Oleg's smile turned to a frown after he took a drink. The medovukha was a bit bitter, not its usual sweetness. Perhaps, his palette needed a cleanse? He sipped from his water glass and tried again. *Nyet*. He would order another.

The desert beckoned, and he took a taste only to find that his tongue was fouled. The bitterness would not leave. It filled his mouth and then his nose. He coughed.

"Oleg?" the man across from him asked. "Are you well?"

Oleg's chest began to burn, and he saw the man's face turn to one of horror as he lurched to his feet and clutched it. The tightness spread across his body, and he became unsteady on his feet. His mouth suddenly filled with secretions, and he struggled to breath past them. The men jumped to their feet in shock as they watched him struggle.

"Oleg!"

His mouth now freely frothed, and the spittle ran down his face as his skin turned blue. His eyes bulged as he struggled for air, and his hands grasped for the men watching. They recoiled in horror as he lurched toward them only to collapse onto the crowded table of food, his chair flying across the room behind him to impact the wall. The men's voices screaming at each other were the last thing he heard as the darkness arrived.

One of the men yelled for silence and pointed. The others gazed in the direction indicated and saw it.

The chair. The one Oleg sat in every time he came. It had come to rest on the floor with its bottom facing them. Secured to the wooden surface was an envelope. The lettering on its surface was clear from across the room.

TTS.

WASHINGTON, D.C.

HE CHECKED himself in the mirror again. His face was clean-shaven now, and he sported the quasi-military haircut worn by many of the agents his age. The uniform was black and displayed the logo of the FBI Hostage Rescue Team. He'd washed it several times, and then left it wadded in a ball for a day until it was sufficiently rumpled. The weapon on his belt was real and what the team currently carried. The jacket he wore over the uniform had FBI on the back in one-foot-tall letters.

The ID was current, and he'd tried it already on a gate at Fort Mead. The young gate guard and his scanner had passed him with a polite buzz, and he had driven a circle before letting himself out. He was assuming the stickers he had applied to the windshield would also work. He'd had no time to check them. The plate was from the government and had a Department of Defense sticker in one corner. It should be enough to get him past the gate at the Hoover building. After that, he would just walk away.

In the cockpit with him was a metal lockbox. One designed to hold deposits and other valuable outgoing mail. The idea being that the driver could toss them in and then they could only be retrieved once he had returned to the companies' shipping warehouse, where someone would have the key. The idea was to cut down on losses from robberies. Harper had improved on the idea. Inside this box was another. Stronger and fireproof, it would survive tonight's mission and deliver its contents into the hands of the FBI.

It held a file. One carefully forged to appear as if it were authored by the Twelve Shepherds. Inside, it contained information on every agent working the case, Agent Jack Randall was chief among them. Harper's mission was to turn the tide of public opinion. To make it look as if the Shepherds had attacked innocent lives to protect themselves. One of the nation's most widely recognized and respected lawmen. And he would do it right in the middle of the nation's capital, where all would see it. The Shepherds would become the enemy, one hated by over three-hundred-million Americans.

Still, there were a lot of unknowns. And because of them, he had taken some steps to assure he had alternatives if they should be needed.

He hoped the first mission would be over quickly, and without incident. He wanted nothing to interfere with his second mission of the night.

He pulled out his phone and punched up the picture. Debra Randall, sitting in a chair by the fire with her feet tucked beneath her, reading a book. She looked very much at peace.

That was about to change.

THE WASHINGTON POST, WASHINGTON, D. C.

DANNY WAS SITTING in his cube, watching the overhead screens. Every major network had footage of the president's State of the Union address running. Not that it was "must-see TV" at the moment—the man was still working his way to the podium. Danny did notice a lot less glad-handing on the way in though. The president seemed to be tolerating it as he moved forward, whereas before he treated it as an opportunity to broadcast relationships to the nation. A presidential smile and handshake was worth serious political capital to any up-and-coming politician, especially when done on live, worldwide television.

"That man does not want to be there," Steve said from the next cube over.

Danny frowned. He wasn't the only one noticing it. He was about to open his mouth to ask Steve's opinion when his phone vibrated on his desk. He reached out to silence it, but a second later heard the sound of other cell phones in the room.

What the hell?

He glanced at the message and bolted upright when he saw the name of the sender.

The Twelve Shepherds

"Steve? You getting this, too?"

"Yeah."

"Me too," Danny's other neighbor called out.

"I just got a second one!"

The ringtones continued to sound as every reporter in the room received message after message. Danny spun to his computer and opened his email. They were arriving at a steady pace. He was already up to twelve when he reached out and clicked on the first one.

It was a file. Hundreds of pages thick. He scanned the first page for the subject but found only a man's name. A wealthy industrialist, one of the richest men in the world. He quit scanning and started to speed-read it, scrolling through the pages as fast as his brain could process the information.

"Oh, my God. Steve!"

"I'm reading it, too!"

The room began to buzz as conversations started and only built for the next several minutes.

Ed appeared in the gap between their cubes.

"Ed! What the hell is this?"

"We're not alone. *The Times* is getting it, too. So is *Chicago, Dallas, Denver*, and *LA*."

"What do we—"

"I've called everyone in. Start verifying this

stuff, and I mean *now*. As soon as you have any-thing, we run with it online."

"We don't have to verify it," Steve said.

"What do you mean?"

"They've done that, too. Look at page fifty. Bank records. Money transfers. PAC accounts. Tax returns. They have it all right there. Somebody did some serious homework."

"I don't care. I want it all double-checked. You two take this first file, I'll assign the others. Now get moving."

"We're on it."

They both continued scanning the documents and taking notes. A round of applause sounded from the TV, as the President climbed onto the podium. It served to plant an idea in Danny's head.

"Steve?"

"Yeah?"

"You think he knows this is happening?"

"Who? The president? Not unless he got it be-fore we did, but if he doesn't..."

"What?"

"He sure as hell will soon."

Danny watched the man on the screen give a half-smile to the crowd of clapping suits and ties in front of him. Danny watched his face closely.

"You're right."

"Who's right?" Steve asked, his eyes glued to his computer screen.

"You. He doesn't want to be there. I think we better hear what he has to say."

Steve stopped reading and looked up at the TV screen too. The look on the president's face was made of stone. He watched as the man nodded to the applause again, before turning and handing the vice president one of the folders in his hand. The other he placed on the podium before him, before reaching in his pocket and pulling out an envelope. From inside it he removed three sheets of paper and spread them out before donning his reading glasses.

"He doesn't need those for the teleprompter."

Danny slowly stood up and increased the volume.

"What ... is he doing?"

11

"The heights of popularity and patriotism are still the beaten road to power and tyranny."

—*David Hume*

THE HOUSE CHAMBER

The president eventually reached the dais and climbed its stairs under the gaze of the Vice President and Speaker of the House seated above and behind him. Their smiles were politician's smiles. Practiced and mechanical as that of any seasoned actor. The president returned them with his own, hoping the façade held up. He shook hands with each and then handed over the leather binders containing the speech which had been prepared for him. They both set them down without a glance, and then resumed clapping until the president took his place behind the podium. It was time for more ceremony. The vice president stepped back to allow the speaker access to the microphone.

"Members of Congress, I have the high privilege and the distinct honor of presenting to you the President of the United States."

The room once again came to its feet, and he endured another round of cheers and applause. The cameras panned across their faces, and they all made sure to keep up appearances until they were done and focused back on the man they were here to see. The president acknowledged the crowd with several waves and smiles for the cameras and a special nod to his wife seated in the balcony. Eventually, the noise faded, and the people took their seats. President Preston located the cameras which were dead ahead and took a deep breath.

"Mr. Speaker, Mr. Vice President, Members of Congress, my fellow Americans. Tonight, marks the third year that I've come here to report on the state of our union, and much has changed.

"I stand before you today to address a matter that has been heavily in my thoughts.

"This is a time when our democracy, our values, our principles, and yes, our very survival as a nation of the people, are in question. There have been times in our nation's past when the state of our union was in great danger. I am here to inform you, that now is such a time.

"The state of our union is in jeopardy."

A rumble traveled through the crowd, and several members of congress rapidly consulted their copies of the speech and then their neighbor's. The president watched them as the teleprompter scrolled over the opening remarks again and again, trying to prompt him back on track. It was too late for that now. He looked to his wife and saw her stoic face. She put her hand over her heart, and it brought him courage. Gripping the sides of the podium, he waited for the murmurs to subside.

The White House

THEY ENTERED the press room together and were immediately accosted by them all at once. The reporters gestured to the TVs overhead and shouted one question after another at the Press Secretary without waiting for an answer. She tried to get a word in but eventually gave up. She took the stack of papers from him and slapped them down on the nearest table, before spinning on her heel and leaving the room. She had her own letter to write.

Henry watched as they dove on them like vultures and retreated to their tiny cubicles at the other end of the room. The man was right; it was the story of the century, and he hadn't even gotten to the good part yet.

He'd had a hand it that himself and now wondered what the fallout would entail. He doubted they would come after him. There were only two men who knew of the mic he had planted in the Chief of Staff's office and the other was on TV right this minute.

He watched them now, each of them feverishly reading and highlighting their copy. Pulling quotes for the story they would all publish in minutes.

It was what the press had become: a race. It wasn't about the truth of what they reported or the fallout; it was about who got there first. Who got the story up and out there, where it could be clicked on and shared and liked and placed next to whatever ad was running that day. Stories translated into dollars, and that was all that mattered to them and their corporate overseers.

"Cronkite must be rolling over in his grave."

"What?" said a passing staffer.

"Nothing." He shook his head at the reporters and walked back to the Oval Office. For the first time in a long while, he found himself with nothing to do. He wandered a bit and then entered the President's private study. It had a TV, and he and the man would often watch football there, where the first lady wouldn't bother them. He turned it on, now to see the speech, and was shocked by what he saw instead.

HOUSTON, TEXAS

A BUMP in the road brought his head up. The car had left the main road and was bouncing down a secondary one. The towers were closer.

"Where are you going?" he called. The driver responded by raising the divider, cutting off his view out the front.

"Hey! I asked you where we are going!"

He got no reply. What was going on? He reached for the small bar on the side of the car and pulled open a drawer. The gun he kept inside was gone. In its place, he found a large envelope. He gapped at the writing on its side. The car slowed to a stop as he pulled it free.

TTS

"What the ..."

The car's engine was shut off, and the divider came down. The driver turned and looked at him, his face expressionless.

"Who ... who are you?"

"You ask the wrong question," John replied. "We ... are the future."

A gun appeared in his hand and boomed twice in the tiny space. The rounds were like a baseball bat impacting his chest. The man stared in horror at his killer, before his eyes glazed and his head slumped forward. His many chins holding it in place. The envelope stayed in his hands. John thought it most appropriate.

Despite the gloves, he took a moment to wipe the interior down with a bleach-soaked cloth before leaving the car and moving to the trunk. He popped the lid with the remote and found the man's bodyguard right where he had left him. Still bound and gagged and sleeping from the dose of drugs John had injected him with. The lid stayed open, and John left him and the car behind, walking down the dead end in the direction of the city lights. The road had ended at the fence of one of the man's own properties, and the sign warning anyone not to go further seemed to mock him now. John didn't care. His days as a Shepherd had just ended.

A short walk later, he came to his pick-up truck. He shed the chauffer's uniform and shoulder holster, before climbing in. It was about four-hundred miles back to his home outside Dallas. He estimated it would take him about three and a half hours. May as well get started. He paused to send a short text message before starting the engine.

He dropped the truck in gear and made his way to the highway. On the way, he found a news channel on the radio and listened to the many breaking headlines as they were reported. The events in DC were astonishing.

It was proving to be an eventful evening.

THE MANSION

"WHAT DO YOU SEE?"

"Main column is down. Those had to be Claymores. At least two of 'em. Fucker."

"Patterson?"

"He's down, too. I got the guy pinned behind a tree; soon as he moves, I'm taking him out."

King checked his watch. "You stay here and keep him off us. We have to move. He's one guy, and we've got work to do. Don't take forever."

"I hear you, boss. One minute."

He settled in behind the scope, as the others moved past him. The noise of their departure was soon swallowed up by the snow-covered trees. The man slowed his breathing and kept his eyes on the tree.

"C'mon, now, Little Bunny. Let's see you try and hop away.'

CARTER PACKED the snow down as carefully and as completely as he could without leaving the shelter of the tree. He'd only get one chance at this, and it was a slim one at that. But it was all he had. Once the snow was as ready as he could get it, he planted his feet and aimed the rifle skyward.

The wind was with him. All he had to do was pick the right one. He examined every branch over his head. The pine was tall and sported several branches, all covered in a heavy layer of snow. Carter needed a smoke grenade, something to hide him while he sprinted for the trees. But he'd forgotten to grab one and was now forced to improvise. The shotgun was gone, behind him somewhere buried under a few feet of snow.

The rifle bucked and sent the round skyward. It impacted a two-inch branch and traveled on to hit another. Both dumped their snow on the branch below, and the process repeated itself for several cycles. Carter rapidly slung the rifle over his shoulder and planted a foot against the trunk.

The snow arrived with a hiss, as it fell through the bare branches of the lower trunk. Carter flinched as it hit his open collar but used it as a starting gun. He pushed off into the cloud of snow he had created and bolted for the rocks.

"Son of a—"

The view through the scope had changed to nothing but a white cloud, and he almost shot early. He held the breath he had reflexively taken further and scanned through the scope. A shape appeared and was gone, and he triggered the round at it. Bringing the scope back on target, he saw nothing but falling snow. He panned left and right and searched the snow for tracks, but nothing presented. He opened his other eye and scanned further, but there was nothing except trees and the last bit of falling snow. His target had escaped.

"Nice trick, Little Bunny. I'll have to remember that one. See you soon."

With one last look at the spot he'd last seen his adversary, he began crawling backwards into the trees. Once he was under concealment, he moved off after the others. They would need him to watch their backs now when they made their attack on the mansion.

The man was still out there.

PALM BEACH, FLORIDA

"SOMETHING YOU NEED, SIR?"

The man pulled his pale face from the message on his phone and looked at Marcus as if he had suddenly appeared in front of him by magic.

"I need a room where I can make a call. A private one."

"This way, sir."

Marcus led the man off toward the resort's offices and pulled a key from his pocket. The man followed him to one in the back, away from the traffic in the hall, and Marcus opened it before stepping aside. The man entered and looked it over. Spotting the washroom in the back, he headed toward it, addressing Marcus as he went.

"See that I'm not disturbed."

"Yes, sir."

Marcus stood in the doorway until the man closed the door behind him. He then closed the outer door and locked it before creeping to the door. The shadow under it and the ting of the man's belt hitting the tile floor told him his target's posture. He reached inside his jacket.

The gun was a .22 automatic. One with a specially machined slide lock that allowed him to only fire one subsonic round at a time. The silencer was overly large and also designed for one shot only. The two pieces had been hidden in an air conditioning vent a few months ago, and Marcus had retrieved them within an hour of his arrival that night. He joined the two together with a few deft twists while the man inside barked into the phone.

"What do you mean you can't reach him? Get a hold of his security people if he's not picking up!"

Silence. Marcus waited, curious as to how the man would react.

"Dead! How?"

More silence. Marcus smiled. He could almost feel the man's fear growing as he listened to what his Shepherd brothers had accomplished.

"No, no, I'm leaving now. Tell him I'll call him once I'm in DC, and he better have some damn answers when I get there!"

The conversation ended, and the man's feet shifted around. Marcus determined there was nothing more to gain by waiting. He turned the knob and shouldered the door open.

The man was literally caught with his pants down. His shocked face looked up at Marcus as he entered and shut the door behind him.

"What the hell are you—"

Marcus cut him off by tossing the envelope into his lap. The man grasped it and read the letters on the outside.

TTS

"You ...?"

Marcus shook his head. "No, not 'you'; we. As in 'We the people.'"

The man just looked at him, still not getting it. Marcus realized he was wasting his time. He raised the pistol and stroked the trigger. The round entered the target's forehead, freezing the look of outrage and confusion on his face and decorating the wall behind him with a circular splatter pattern.

"We." Marcus corrected him again before pocketing the pistol. He checked his shoes for blood before opening the door and locking it behind him. He was through the outer door a minute later and walking into the parking lot soon after. The keys to a member's BMW he had copied months ago found their way into his hand, and he was soon rolling out onto the beachside drive. At a red light, he stopped to tap out a text to William. Once rolling again, he divided his time between the police radio and the news coming out of DC on the car's radio for another thirty miles, before exchanging the car for his own in an industrial section of town. Leaving the keys in the ignition practically guaranteed the car would be in a chop shop by sunrise. He didn't give it any thought; the car had served a purpose.

If all went well, he'd be back on his boat in a few hours. He followed the night's events on his radio, as he made his way home. He was planning a sailing trip, the destination depended on the events unfolding in DC.

The House Chamber

"WE MUST NEVER MEEKLY ACCEPT the slow infestation of corruption into our democracy, nor should we adopt laws that encourage it. The personal attacks on the integrity of our representatives should not be supported by the very system that they strive to work in. These are not just threats against principles, freedoms, and institutions for the benefit of those with money, but an attack on our citizens faith in democracy. The greed of the few should never outweigh the well-being of the many.

"But the never-ending greed has taken hold. To

ward off this greed we must stand up to it. We must rail against its flagrant disregard for truth or decency, its reckless actions, most often for the pettiest and most personal gains, gains that have nothing whatsoever to do with the prosperity of the people that we have all been elected to serve.

"These horrendous features of our present system should never be regarded as a new standard. We must never allow ourselves to lapse into thinking that this is just the way things are now. If we become accustomed to this state, thinking that this is just politics as usual, then heaven help us, for we have contracted a terminal disease, one that is self-inflicted.

"Corruption is a cancer, one that eats away at the very core of our democracy. It is the enemy of development. The greatest foe of investment in our future. An adversary of the very morals on which this great nation was built.

"There must be no compromise when corruption is revealed, it must be exposed and dealt with immediately.

Behind the president, the Speaker of the House and the VP exchanged nervous glances. From their vantage point they could see the recording device in front of the president and the fact that it was inches from the twin microphones was not lost on either of them.

But they were trapped. Glued to their seats by the television cameras and the millions of people on the other side.

They had no choice but to see this through to the end.

Atlanta, Georgia

"Congratulations. Should we call you Senator yet?"

"Little early for that yet," the man smiled.

"Well ... if you say so," the CEO said. "There's more where that came from."

He nodded toward the check in the man's hand, and the candidate couldn't help but give it another look. The number of zeros was impressive, even by dark money standards. The name at the top of the check was that of a generic patriotic-sounding PAC—there were so many out there now he had lost count. Not that it mattered. Bribery of this sort had been voted legal years ago, even endorsed by the Supreme Court. The governor had often wondered how big the check had been to pull that off, but he would never ask. To men like the one in front of him, it was a pittance and simply the cost of doing business.

"Oh, I think this will hold me over for a while. You can assure your board that it was money well spent." He slipped the check into his pocket, where it joined a few others of similar amount. The day had been a lucrative one. He rose to walk the man out.

His aide, a young man from the swim team of the state collage, jumped up to attend the door. The two men made the usual empty promises to get together for a round of golf or other such activity, each of them knowing that their calendars would never allow it. The young man closed the door behind the departing CEO before turning back into the room.

"Will you be needing anything more, Governor?"

The governor almost replied to the affirmative but reluctantly ruled it out. It was too dangerous while out on the road—too many press people about, too many insecure places. They'd almost been caught a month ago when someone tripped the fire alarm in the hotel they were at. His aide had barely made it back through the door joining their two rooms before the security people were pounding on the door. It was a lesson he had to remember. All it would take was one slip-up, and he would lose the evangelicals.

The fact that many of their group had been caught in similar situations themselves didn't seem to hamper their ability to point fingers. The hypocrisy was on an unmeasurable level. But the money would dry up, and that was what really mattered these days. That, and his wife was getting tired of covering for him. He was too close to re-election to risk it.

"Not a good time, Jerry," was all he said.

Jerry frowned but left it alone, bussing the man's cheek before letting himself out.

The Governor smiled for his benefit and then locked the door behind him before returning to the bed and sitting down with a sigh. The clock told him the meeting had lasted a half-hour past what his campaign manager had demanded. He knew why the man had been so insistent: the candidate was exhausted, and it was starting to show. His eyes were darker, and his skin had lost its healthy tone. His heart would often flutter from the numerous caffeine hits he would take in throughout the day. It was no wonder politicians aged so fast.

He struggled out of his suit coat and lay down

with the checks in his hands. He shuffled through them and added their accumulated amounts repeatedly, reveling in the sum he came to. He was closer. With a few more of these checks, he'd practically guarantee his election. And then the checks would only get bigger.

With a satisfied smile on his face, he rolled over and turned out the light. He needed thirty minutes. Just enough to recharge for the night ahead. They'd watch the State of the Union address, and then discuss it for a bit, and then head for the airport. He could maybe sleep a bit on the plane. He forced himself to relax and close his eyes and was quickly asleep.

THE WHITE HOUSE

COOK IGNORED the knock on his door. It was the third in as many minutes, and his secretary had finally warned the last person away. The press secretary. The communications director. The speechwriter. His assistant chief of staff. Whoever it was didn't matter. Not anymore.

The words of the president continued, and Cook could not ignore them. In a way he wasn't surprised. They had painted the man into a corner and then expected him to just do what he was told. He had tried to warn them, but they had refused to listen. It just wasn't in the man's character.

The words the man was speaking were true. There was no denying it. He knew better than almost anyone else. He also knew what the words meant for the future.

Haney. Him and the brothers. They had pushed things too far. And he had helped them. And for purely selfish reasons. Like them, he had been consumed by his own greed and lust for power. What had become a few favors had quickly snowballed into outright corruption. All so he could sit in this office.

He gazed about it now. It was modest by most standards. What it lacked in size or view, it made up for in location. The door on the other side of the room led to the Oval Office. A place he had considered occupying at one point, only to be told no.

And he had accepted that ruling, from men who had no title, and had never been elected to office. Why? Because they had money. That was all it took now. The people had no vote anymore. He had become an employee, one with a boss who was merely a figurehead.

His eyes found the wall of frames. Every person in government seemed to have one. His own face was in almost every one of them. Him with the president at a state dinner. Him watching the man being sworn in. Several of him with leaders of the world and many celebrities. Then there were the donors, the brother's chief among them. That was what they still called them, anyway: the donors. In truth, they were the puppet masters, pulling the strings of those they had placed in office. He examined his own face in several of them and realized his smile was different in them. Forced, that was the word he labeled it. As if his subconscious refused to do his brain's bidding.

One picture in particular caught his eye. Him and Haney. Both seated at a dinner of some kind. Both mugging for the camera. Cook had his arm around the man's shoulder. He reached out and took the frame down, carrying it back to his desk. He sank into the leather chair with a sigh, before placing the frame down on top of his copy of the man's speech. A speech which would never be heard now.

More noise outside his door. Parker. Trying to get past his secretary again. He tuned it out.

His gaze found the frames on his desk now. His wife. His kids. The twin grandkids he hardly ever got to see. His daughter-in-law was keeping them at a safe distance from their grandfather, and he understood why now.

The President was still listing his grievances on the TV. Cook watched as the audience glanced at each other nervously. They had reason to.

The phone in his desk vibrated. Haney. He reached for the drawer and pulled out the device. The phone vibrated in his hand, and he clenched it, trying hard to make it stop. Eventually, it did so.

It was time for him to stop, as well.

He stood again. This time with purpose. His old leather briefcase was found, and he emptied its contents onto the floor. The pictures from his desk were stacked neatly inside, and he added a few personal items in the remaining space. From the wall, he took one frame: him and the President at a campaign stop in Iowa. They were standing together in front of a crowd, waving. The sun was on their faces, and the smiles were genuine. It had been a good day. Their first win. He remembered it as a time when he'd felt really good about what he had chosen to do with his life.

A month later, he had met with the brothers in a hotel room. A month after that, the president had meet with The Trust in another.

Cook realized he had not felt good about himself or what he was doing since.

He walked back to the desk and stowed the photo inside before closing the lid. The desk held nothing but the speech and the phone now.

He deposited both in the trash before walking out the door.

12

---

*"The tree of liberty must be refreshed from time to time
with the blood of patriots and tyrants."*

—Thomas Jefferson

BOSTON, MASSACHUSETTS

A hundred meters over Carver's head, and fifty meters behind him, buzzed a drone.

Will sat even higher in one of the nearby condominium towers which dominated the area. The apartment he had rented had not changed at all. What few things he had moved in occupied the kitchen table, which he had moved into the main room, from where he could see out over the city through the open sliding glass door. The wind blew the cold air inside, and despite him moving the heat to its highest setting, he still needed a coat to ward off the chill.

But the open door was necessary; he couldn't afford the possible interruption in signal between him and his drone. He guided the device along its route with practiced skill, his feet up on a chair as he maneuvered the device over the city.

The drone was heavily modified. Scraped clean of any serial numbers, stickers, and brand names, it now sported a layer of flat-black paint that rendered it practically invisible in the night sky. Its pilot was an expert, and he kept the device over the middle of the street and high enough to avoid any wires or trees as it followed its target on its journey home. He paused only briefly, when the man stopped at the gate before feeding in a little forward stick to stay with him as he cruised the rest of the way home. Will's made the drone drop a little lower, as Caver's destination neared.

The window of opportunity was narrow, but he'd been practicing.

———

CARVER ROUNDED the last curve and muttered a curse when he saw the full driveway. His guests had obviously assumed he was already there and parked their cars in the driveway, blocking all access to the garage. He'd have to park on the street and walk.

"Damn it, Lisa. Told you to hire a kid to park the cars," he complained.

He found a spot in a neighbor's driveway. One he knew was out of town, so he pulled the Jaguar in. Sitting behind the wheel, he examined the sky. Was it going to rain? If so, he'd have everyone move their damn cars. He hated rain on any of his collection, and the vintage Jaguar was one of his favorites. He was examining the clouds out the sunroof, when his view was suddenly blocked.

WHACK!

Something landed on the roof, and he jumped. His surprise quickly changed to rage, when he saw what it was. He threw the door open and stepped out to see it.

A drone? Some kid's toy! He reached out and

snatched the device off the roof and examined the car for damage. A scratch in the paint and another in the tint. Damn it! He turned his attention to the drone.

There had to be a way to track this thing to its owner. He turned it over, looking for a number or an address. Instead, he found three letters.

TTS.

What did that mean? Was it the manufacturer? He searched his memory for the company.

———

WILL WAITED. His finger was on the button, and there was no hurry now. He watched the man's face through the camera, waiting for him to put it together. The man's expression went from confused anger to enlightened horror. Will couldn't help but smile as he pressed the trigger.

The flash of light was visible from his seat just inside the balcony doors, and the sound reached him a few seconds later. One cube of C-4, a plastic explosive created by the man's own company, had been more than enough. The drone had been capable of carrying more, but he didn't want to risk bystanders. In leu of more explosive, he had instead added a handful of buckshot. Between the blast and the flying shrapnel, he was sure the job was done. He silently retracted the antenna and stowed the gear in its hide, before closing the sliding glass window and turning his attention to the two televisions. One was tuned to a national channel that was broadcasting the State of the Union address, the other to a local news station. He watched both as he tapped out a message to William and then thumbed up the volume of the local station.

Both would be very busy very soon.

The House Chamber

"This danger comes not from a foreign land or from any extraneous source. It is a danger from within. There are those here that have come to accept the politics of destruction and despair. Elected leaders who encourage the indecency and discourse we hurl across the aisle at one another. Counterfeit representatives who embrace the compromise of our moral authority in favor of sowing division. And they do so not for the people, but for those that would assure them their place. And new words dominate the political spectrum, the first of which is complicity, the second, corruption.

"Corruption that has not only found its way into every aspect of our system but has also been legitimized and made legal by those it has corrupted.

"And we let it happen.

"And with our complicity in this alarming and dangerous state of affairs, we hasten the death of our democracy and move further toward oligarchy.

"To me, that is unacceptable. It is time for our complicity and our accommodation of the unacceptable to end."

The members of the house were now physically shaken. Where was the president going with this? He could see the fear crawling onto many of their faces. But there were others watching him with stoic faces, and some with even a hint of a smile. It was clear for all to see who the man was speaking of and who he wasn't. he paused long enough to survey every face and hoped that the TV cameras were doing the same. The people needed to see this.

Out of the corner of his eye he saw the first lady rise and make her way out of the chamber. Fortunately, the cameras were all locked on him.

With a deep breath, he removed the recording device from his pocket and set it on the lectern in front of him.

"I have a story to tell you. It's about a soldier. A young pilot that was sent into harm's way only to be shot down and captured by a ruthless enemy. What he didn't know, was that his greatest danger was back home."

ATLANTA, GEORGIA

BEN WAS CHECKING the peephole for the tenth time when the light under the door went off. He'd heard the aide leave and was a bit surprised. The two men were a couple; despite their age difference, it was plain to see and universally ignored by his staff, and Ben wondered for how long they could keep it under wraps. Not that it mattered. If the night went as planned, the young man would have his heart broken, but Ben didn't really care about that.

He waited twenty minutes before checking in with William via the cell phone. He was treated to camera views of the hallway in both directions and found them clear. Opening the door, he crossed the hall and slid his master key into the lock. It opened with a soft click, and he cringed as it echoed in the silent space. The lights in the hall went out as he eased the door open, and he silently thanked William as he slid inside.

The man's shoring only slightly relaxed him, and he moved to the curtains to pull them fully shut before throwing the lock on the adjoining room.

Standing over the Governor, he noticed the checks on the nightstand. He picked them up and examined the amounts. Should he save them for William? No, they were past that point. He had another idea.

Pulling the gun from his belt, along with a pair of zip ties, he tapped the man on the head. He snorted and jerked away but remained asleep. Ben tapped harder and then aimed the gun at his nose from inches away as he woke.

"Jerry, no. What the—?"

Ben stuck the barrel in the Senator's mouth to cut off any outburst. The man gagged, but wisely didn't struggle.

"Not a word, Senator. Or I vote with my finger. You understand?"

The man gave the slightest of nods, his eyes

wide with horror. Ben extracted the barrel and planted it against the man's head.

Keeping the gun firmly in place, he flipped the man over and placed the ties around his wrists and ankles before rolling him back upright.

"I have money. I can give you whatever you—"

Ben tapped him hard with the barrel, and it silenced him.

"Another word, and I visit Jerry next. You understand?"

The Senator wisely chose to nod.

Ben picked up the checks and read them in the dim light.

"Impressive total. I have to wonder, does it get easier, swallowing your humanity? Don't answer that; we already know the answer."

"We? I—"

"No more talking, Governor. We've heard enough."

Before the man could say anything further, Ben stuffed the checks deep into his mouth. The man struggled and bucked, but he held him down easily and watched without emotion as the man's face turned red and then blue. His eyes bulged and the veins in his neck stood out as he struggled to breath. Ben kept all his weight firmly planted on the man's chest, and eventually the struggling lessened and finally stopped. Ben retreated to stand over him and waited a full five minutes before checking for a pulse. Finding none, he swapped the gun in his hand for the envelope tucked in his belt. Shaking the sterile one inside it out and onto the man on the bed took only a few seconds, and he left it where it landed.

Eight minutes. He was under his estimated time. The man would have an aide knocking on his door soon, so as not to miss the scheduled watching of the State of the Union address. Ben almost wished he could stay and hear their reaction when they found him. But he was needed downstairs. It was time to go.

A check of the phone assured him safe passage in the hall, and this time he went up the stairs several floors, before taking the elevator down with a group of guests.

Entering the convention floor, he was surprised to see everyone gazing up at the televisions mounted throughout the floor. He joined a group and voiced a question to the man next to him.

"What's going on?"

"I'm not sure, but something's happening in DC."

The Mansion

"Are you sure?" the man asked.

"Yeah, just don't get shot down before you get there."

"All right. Get clear."

Charlie checked the tape one last time before stepping clear. The four rotors of the drone spun up until they could barely be seen, and the device rose rapidly into the air. The man let it climb much higher than normal before setting it on a course for the valley above them. Charlie joined him and checked the monitors. This drone had two cameras: one optical and one infrared. They were used mostly to locate the buffalo herds but also worked when needed to find predators.

Bears and wolves were not the hunters they were looking for tonight, though. There were men out there. Men with guns and ill intent. They had to locate them.

"Don't stay still," Charlie warned the pilot.

The man nodded and began banking the drone left and right, as it moved up the valley. The drone was tactical—painted a flat black and without any external lights, it was invisible in the darkening sky. He kept it at a high altitude, as Charlie had instructed, and used the moonlight off the snow to keep his bearings. Soon, they were looking down on the ruins of the barn. Its remaining frame of timbers still burning in the cold air, lighting up the infrared screen.

"Barns gone, but the cabin is still standing."

"Follow the wood line on the south side."

The drone did as he asked, and Charlie kept his eyes on the infrared screen. A few nocturnal creatures appeared here and there, but nothing like he was looking for. Where had they gone?

"There!"

They were taking cover, but the deep snow was slowing them down. The shapes appeared and disappeared behind the trunks of the trees, but it was evident they had found the attackers.

"Shit. They're close. Get a count but keep the drone moving."

Charlie held his breath as the drone bobbed and weaved in a circle. He estimated at least twenty, but it was hard to be sure.

"Closer?" the pilot said.

"No. Break off before they take a shot at us. Check the other side of the valley."

"Okay."

The drone banked hard and raced across the bare snow before crossing the stream and angling up the other side.

"Got some bodies, here. They look like they're cooling off."

Charlie examined the men lying in the snow. Their arms and legs told him they were not in that position by choice. The temperature readings backed that up.

"They're dead. About twenty of them. An ambush?"

"Those explosions we heard?"

Charlie put it together.

"Mines. That's Carter's doing. We need to find him."

"Who's Carter?"

"One of ours. We need to get him inside. Find him. He's between there and us."

"I'm on it."

The drone circled at a higher altitude and then set off on a course that would bring it back to the mansion. Again, a few woodland creatures presented, but nothing that was the size or shape of a human.

"Slow down."

"You said stay fast and move around?"

"He won't shoot and give away his position. And he doesn't know if we know its him. We'll have to win him over."

"Got it."

They watched closely as the drone moved over the trees.

"C'mon, Carter. I have a present for you," Charlie muttered.

"What's that?" The man pointed at the screen. "Behind that tree?"

"That's him. Nothing else it could be. Here's what I want you to do."

———

CARTER PLANTED his back against the tree and slid around it in an attempt to stay out of the drone's sight. He couldn't see it, but the buzz it gave off was clear in the still air. His mind was weighing options. Was the drone from the mansion, or the men across the valley? He had no way of knowing.

"Shotgun," he whispered.

He needed a shotgun to take it out, but his was lost in the snow, and the only one around belonged to the dead point man, and there was no way he was going back for it. He raised the rifle. Should he take a shot? It would give away his position, but obviously the drone had a camera that could see him in the dark. So what did he have to lose?

He had just planted his feet and was about to

spin around the tree when the sound of breaking branches reached his ears. The high-pitched buzz of the rotors crackled and died, and the white mist of falling snow once again blanketed him in an impenetrable fog. He shut his eyes and braced for the explosion.

Nothing. Nothing but the sound of falling snow. He cracked an eyelid and then brushed the snow from his face.

The drone had crashed. He stuck his head out for less than a second and saw it sticking out of the snow a few meters away. He gave it a four count and, when nothing happened, stuck out his head for a longer look.

It was big. Its black shape was half-buried with two of the four rotors still in the air. Its belly as exposed and looked to hold two cameras and a long cylinder of some kind.

Deeming it no longer a threat, he left the shelter of the tree to examine it further.

The damage was extensive. He poked a rotor with his rifle and the blades crumbled onto the snow. Making sure he was out of the cameras view, he circled it. The tube caught his eye again.

It wasn't a tube. It was a rolled-up piece of paper. With a shock he read what was printed on the side.

"Carter"

He reached out and peeled the tape and note free.

The message was short. And under it was a carefully drawn map.

"Well alright, Charlie," Carter said. "Whoever you are, I'm on my way."

He picked up the drone and turned the camera to face him. He repeated the message a little louder and then offered a thumbs up to the camera, before setting it down and moving out.

"He saw it!" the pilot said.

Charlie let out a sigh. He wished they had another way to communicate, but he had done what he could. The rest was up to Number Six.

"What now?"

"Make sure the door is open and then go back to your post."

"I'm on it." The man left the controls on and grabbed his rifle, before moving out. Charlie lingered long enough to watch the blob of heat which indicated Carter fade into the trees on the screen.

13

"Guard against the impostures of pretended patriotism."

—*George Washington*

NEW JERSEY

I nside the bathroom the man willed himself back into performative shape. The miracle of modern pharmaceuticals helped him along, and he was getting his breath back for round two. Damn, this woman was amazing. The little blue pills were paying off for him in every direction he looked. Including the bedroom. He ran through several mental images of what he wanted to do with her next, knowing she would be receptive to them all. Between the president's speech and the events he had planned following it, he felt he deserved a reward. It was going to be a very good night.

He was ready. With one last grin at himself in the mirror, he turned and opened the door. She was on the bed, her breathing making her ample breasts rise and fall, drawing the eye. Young and firm and real, they were the opposite of his wife's, who was on her third of forth pair, he couldn't remember.

"Sasha? Wake up, pretty girl. I want to play some more."

He padded toward her in his stocking feet and reached out for her shoulder. Her frame rotated easily, and she let out a snore as her head flopped to the side.

"Sasha?"

His eyes fell to her hands. They held an envelope, one with letters on the front. What was this?

He reached out and took the object from her, before holding it up to read in the faint light.

"TTS?"

His mind had just found the explanation for the three letters when an arm encircled his neck from behind. His head was pulled back by another hand, and the pressure on his neck increased. He flailed about, but the attacker was strong, and the man was lifted off his feet. He punched and kicked as the darkness began to intrude, but the arm around his throat was like a steel trap. He clawed at it in vain as his strength left him. His vision tunneled further and then faded altogether.

Simon dropped the man's limp form on the bed next to the girl. She stirred slightly and then returned to snoring. Simon checked them both. If he had calculated the dose correctly, the girl would be out for another thirty minutes. More than enough time.

He pulled the man up the bed and propped him up on the pillow. The remaining auto-injector found its way into his hand, and he checked its number to assure it was the right one.

The needle plunged into the man's fatty thigh with little resistance, and the drug was in his bloodstream less than a second later. It delivered a dose several times that of the girl's.

Simon exchanged the first auto-injector for a second one and used it on the man's opposite thigh. Again, the drug was delivered in less than a second. Simon removed the envelope from where it had been dropped and placed it back in his hands. It seemed only fitting.

Stepping back, he checked his work. The first drug had rendered the man unconscious, just as it had the girl. The second would paralyze his muscles within the next minute. Including his diaphragm. The man would stop breathing and die long before the drug wore off or the girl next to him woke.

The girl. She would wake up to the horror of a dead man in the bed with her, but she had made her own decision, so Simon didn't feel sorry for her fate. The man's sins were not her fault, but she had certainly benefited from them. Something told him she would find another sugar-daddy in a short time. Perhaps the one her friend was leaving behind? Either way, he didn't care.

Simon made one more check of the room before stepping back to the door. The man's breathing was already slowing. He dismissed him and made the rounds through the rooms and outside, removing the pinhole cameras and their transmitter that he had hidden in the attic. By the time he was done and returned to the room, the man was already turning blue.

It was time to go.

He briefly considered taking the man's car. Simon was a fan of fine automobiles, as well, so the Audi was very tempting. But no, that would be foolish. He instead let himself out by way of the pool and snaked his way through the trees to the edge of the property where it met the sand. Keeping himself in the shadows, he made his way south until he came to another beach house.

This one empty and closed up for the winter, its owners somewhere in South Florida. Rounding its base, he found the car right where he had left it. He opened the trunk and pulled a set of warm clothes from inside and quickly changed, the cold breeze off the water urging him along. In the bottom of the compartment was a burner phone, and he tapped out a quick message to William before getting inside. The clothes and the phone went into a bag with a weight in the bottom. It would find its way to the bottom of the nearest body of water he could find. With a hat on and dressed for the cold, he fired the engine up and weaved his way through the thick trees to the road.

He set off south, his next stop somewhere in Florida.

THE MANSION

KING STOPPED and dropped to his belly in the snow, before crawling forward until he could see over the top of the small rise. His men followed his lead, fanning out to the left and right until they were all on line and facing their final target.

He cupped the lenses of the binoculars, so they would not give away his position, and examined the castle. It was vaguely familiar from the few images he had been able to find, and the most recent satellite images confirmed the additional walls and outbuildings that had been constructed since it was first built. It was a castle, one built along English lines but still distinctly American. Its walls were two stories high and the structure behind them poked above it in various places. The rock walls were thick, and the timbers matched. Some of them looked to be more than ten feet around. It was a masterful example of architecture, and a small part of King's mind admired the man's taste.

But his military mind saw the General's real goal. The massive stones and thick timbers served a dual role. The building was a fortress. One that could withstand an attack by anything other than a full assault with heavy firepower.

To meet that requirement, his men had labored hard. And fortunately, they had survived the ambush intact.

"Range?" he asked the man next him.

"Three thousand two hundred meters."

"That'll do. Set it up here."

With hand signals, the men advanced from behind him. They took one look over the edge at the target and then backtracked into the base of the rise. Their heavy packs came off, and they immediately began to stomp the snow down with their snowshoes. Packing it down until their boots no longer sank into it. Only then did they unpack the weapons they had been struggling with for the last day.

The two thirty-pound base plates were put in place first, followed by the bipods, scopes and cannons. In all, the two mortars weighed in at 200 pounds. Their weight now shed from their backs, the men felt as though they could leap several stories into the air.

King ignored the activity behind him and examined the castle from end to end. It looked deserted. Not one person could be seen. The windows were all blacked out, and except for the few floodlights here and there, it was without power. He listened for the sound of a generator, but either it was hidden, or the distance was too great. He would know soon enough.

"They're set," he heard in his ear.

He pushed the throat mic tight against his neck, before replying, "Feed them."

The three-man crew soon had a line of visitors, as every man in the group made their way to their position to drop off the three rounds apiece they had hauled over the mountain. Each of the crew was more than happy to leave the ten-pound rounds behind, knowing they would not have to lug them out when this was over. No doubt they had cursed the heavy ordinance for the past day, but they would be thankful they had brought them very soon.

King was joined by two other men.

"Approach?"

The men didn't reply at first, each of them examining the terrain and the available cover. They factored in the snow and the sporadic moonlight, before one of them answered.

"I say we use that wood line to get to that spur at two o'clock, then get across that open area with the help of the mortars. Snipers there, there, and there, for overwatch. I'll leave the 240s and a pair of 203s in the wood line, until the assault party is across for anything that pops up. I only see one issue."

"What's that?"

"It's pretty obvious that's the only real approach. It's either that or go across the ice. Or maybe down from the top of the mountain behind them, and we don't have time for that. Too steep, and we'd be in the open too long. We have to go through the trees. They may have something waiting for us."

King had already determined all that, but it felt good to hear it said, anyway. They both looked for anything they had missed, while the head of the mortar crew shot a few azimuths and scribbled out a range card.

"What do you want first?"

"The tower. I'd have a man up there directing traffic. Take it out, first. Then the two corners. Once those are down, fire a spread with one barrel, while you take the gate down with the other. After that, it's what you see or what we call for. Save the gas and smoke until I say otherwise."

"Got it."

They all knew what the finality of the last order: if they called for the smoke and gas, it meant they were retreating.

"The Willys?"

"We'll call if we need them. Otherwise, they wait until we're done."

King checked his watch and then the setting sun.

"We move in ten."

The two men said nothing. They stowed their gear and crawled backward down the snowy slope, leaving King behind to examine the castle again. A face appeared in a window and was just as quickly gone. It was an elderly man, his silver hair making him immediately identifiable.

"I'm coming for you, General. Are you ready?"

HUDSON BAY

THE LOW CRUMP of the explosion traveled on the wind and reached Hugh only seconds after the flash of light. The mast buckled and fell first, followed by the fire that quickly consumed the canopy and sails. The boat slowed and then healed around, as the mast hit the water to drag the boat to a stop. A secondary explosion sounded as the fire found the fuel tanks, and the boat began to drift back toward the island, carried along by the current as it started to sink at the stern. Hugh watched long enough to determine that no one got off.

It was time to go.

Putting the goggles back on, he slipped back into the water and felt his way down the rock to the bottom. The sled was right where he had left it. Anchored to the bottom and tied off to the seawall. He snapped a chemical light stick he had tied to its chain and used it to check the gauges.

The battery's charge was nearly what he had left it at, and only a few sea creatures had taken up residence on its surface. He brushed them away and then turned the machine on. Attaching himself to its safety line, he quickly detached the lines holding it. It remained buoyantly neutral, and he took up the piloting position, before activating the power to the prop.

The Sea-Doo Seascooter was a civilian version of the sea sleds he had used in the Navy. This one had a top speed of just over two and a half knots, enough to counter the current of the Hudson and get him to where he needed to be without surfacing. Between it and the two spare-air tanks he had fixed to its tiny hull, he would not have to surface for almost an hour. It was more than enough time.

Using the compass, he guided the craft around

to the west, skirting the edge of the island, until he felt the current pull him south. He surfaced just long enough to check for traffic and pick out a landmark, before aiming the sled at it and diving back under. With the aid of the glowing gauges, he guided the tiny craft through the blackness, counting off the seconds in his head and measuring the current's pull.

After an allotted time, he surfaced again to see himself just off the shore of the Liberty National Golf Club, its landscaped grounds deserted this time of night. He slowed and checked the boardwalk for late night strollers, but as expected the walkway was bare. He motored in slowly, angling for the dark spot where he had taken out two of the walkway lights with a well-aimed BB gun a few days ago.

The seawall here was made of boulders, and he searched for one to stow the scooter under before finding it. He flooded the buoyancy bladder and wedged the device under the rocks. If it were found, there would be no way to trace it, but he didn't want to leave a trail.

A minute later, he was out of the water and into the trees, picking his way through them to the parking lot. He paused at the edge to determine that it still held the van. Plain, white, and possessing a city of Greenville license plate, it had been left alone by whoever checked for such things. He swapped the plate with a New Jersey one hidden underneath its bumper, before slipping the keys from around his neck and opening the back.

The van was just as he had left it. Good.

Inside, he stripped off the wetsuit and changed into comfortable clothes, before drying his hair on a towel and slipping into the front seat. The van was well stocked, so, other than filling the tank, he would have no reason to stop for over a thousand miles.

He pulled a phone from under the seat and tapped out a quick message to William, before dropping the van in gear. The lights of New York City were soon fading in his rearview mirror. The phone went out the window and into the water, as he crossed the bridge headed west.

THE HOUSE CHAMBER

"THIS IS NO SMALL TASK. The disease is malignant and has found its way into every facet of our system. It operates out of the people's sight, and it is self-replicating.

"But we must fight it. It affects us all. The children are watching, and they will someday ask us why we did not. What will we tell them?

"When those of us in the position to combat this affliction remain silent and fail to act, we become an accomplice to this exploitation. When we *know* that silence and inaction is the wrong thing to do—because of political considerations, because we might make enemies, because we might upset the big money donors, because we might provoke a challenge to our position, because ad infinitum, ad nauseam—when we surrender to those thoughts in spite of what should be greater deliberations and imperatives in defense of the institutions of our liberty, then we shame our values and forsake our duties.

"Those principles are far more important than politics, and certainly more important than personal greed.

"So, I stand here today to say ... enough. We must dedicate ourselves to defeating the corruption that threatens us all. We have fooled ourselves for too long into thinking that our system provides the necessary checks to ward off such exploitation. It is now necessary for us all to shine the light on those who would enslave our democracy for their own personal gain."

The crowd in the balcony was now rumbling, and the president held up his hands for silence. The politicians before him were already dumbstruck. He ignored their glares and pushed on.

"A former president named Roosevelt had this to say about the presidency and a citizen's relationship to the office:

"'The president is merely the most important among a large number of public servants. He should be supported or opposed exactly to the degree which is warranted by his good conduct or bad conduct, his efficiency or inefficiency in rendering loyal, able, and disinterested service to the nation as a whole. Therefore, it is absolutely necessary that there should be full liberty to tell the truth about his acts, and this means that it is exactly as necessary to blame him when he does wrong as to praise him when he does right. Any other attitude in an American citizen is both base and servile. To announce that there must be no criticism of the president, or that we are to stand by the president, right or wrong, is not only unpatriotic and servile, but is morally treasonable to the American public.'"

The president paused again to glare at the men

and woman seated before him before turning back to the cameras.

"The only way to fight such an adversary is to expose it. Even if doing so exposes one's own self in the process. James Madison, a wise man and one of our founding fathers once said, "Ambition counteracts ambition." I feel this to be very true. Conscience and principle is the manner in which we express our morality, and as such, loyalty to conscience and principle should surpass loyalty to any man or monetary sum. Too often, we rush not to save our values, but to forgive and excuse our failures, so that we might accommodate them and go right on failing—until the accommodation it-self becomes our principle.

"In that way and over time, we have learned to justify any behavior and sacrifice almost any form of integrity. Until we wake up one day and realize that the system we have studied and aspired to make better has instead become a hollow shell of what it once was. A system that is now corrupted at every level.

"I'm afraid that is where I now find myself."

The president paused and scanned the room. Despite its size and volume of people, it was stone quiet. The rustle of the papers on the podium as he selected the next could be heard without strain.

Across the nation, people leaned into their televisions and thumbed the volume higher. World leaders questioned their interpreters to ensure that what they were hearing was accurate. It was if the world had simply stopped.

The President took a deep breath and then continued.

"I have a story to tell you. It's about a soldier. A young pilot that was sent into harm's way, only to be shot down and captured by a ruthless enemy. What he didn't know was that his greatest danger was back home."

14

"We, the People, recognize that we have responsibilities as well as rights; that our destinies are bound together; that a freedom which only asks what's in it for me, a freedom without a commitment to others, a freedom without love or charity or duty or patriotism, is unworthy of our founding ideals, and those who died in their defense."

—*Barack Obama*

Las Vegas, Nevada

Carl adjusted his ass one last time, before shutting off the video feed and stowing the phone in a pocket. He zippered it up tight and then checked the others, before getting to his feet. He shook his legs to get the blood flow back, before moving to the door and planting an ear against it. The screen had told him it was clear, but you could never be sure. A smoker could use the space to feed his habit, or a pair of horny co-workers might think it a good place for a quickie. You never knew.

But he heard nothing and, after cracking the door open, saw nothing, as well. The roof was deserted. The stuffy interior of the elevator shaft gave way to the fresh air of the desert and a view that stretched for miles in every direction. He allowed himself a quick scan of the surrounding rooftops, all of them below his current position, before moving to the far corner and pacing off the distance.

Here.

He marked the spot with a piece of chalk, before moving to the nearest air conditioner. It was huge. Several feet high and wide and supported by I-beams at least eight inches thick. Anchored by large bolts to the roof, it was not going anywhere. In only a few seconds, he swung his rig around its metal base and secured it.

Playing the rope out, he walked it straight to the chalk mark he had left, before stepping up on the parapet and turning his back on the city. He frisked himself again and double-checked the Ruger in its shoulder rig. It wouldn't do to drop it right now.

Was he ready? He checked the rope bag to ensure it was clear. The harness was tight. His personal equipment was safe. Getting his testicles caught in the harness would be very distracting and something he always tried to avoid. With everything in place, he clipped in and leaned back until the rope was taught. He spread his legs and flexed his knees twice, before pulling his arm from behind him and kicking off into the void.

He let himself fall six feet, before his shoes hit the slick glass. He absorbed the impact and kept his feet still, so as not to make any noise. It was like walking on the surface of a drum, any impact would be broadcast to those inside, and it wasn't time for that yet. The part in the curtains was only a foot to his right, so he adjusted until he was straddling it.

He secured his break to free his hands and

pulled out the stethoscope. After planting its bell against the glass, he was rewarded with the voice of the president of the United States speaking. His familiar baritone vibrated the glass and told Carl he had the right room. With a smile, the stethoscope went back into his pocket. Carl replaced it with the Ruger.

He looked below. It was thirty-eight stories to the parking garage's roof and another three stories to the ground. He had debated his options for several weeks. If he ended up on the other side of the building, he might have BASE jumped it, but the height was right at the limit, and he couldn't afford to be injured after carrying out the mission. Besides, a jump would only save him a few seconds at best. He'd developed a new plan, one that Dayton had approved after a raised eyebrow. Now Carl looked for what he needed and saw it: the two items on the roof of the garage, and the crowded sidewalks of the Las Vegas strip. Everything was in place.

He tapped the Ruger on the glass.

Nothing.

He tapped again, this time louder.

The curtains parted, and the man's face appeared. He had time to develop a look of astonishment when he saw the black clad figure hanging outside his penthouse window, but it was erased a second later with a pull of the Ruger's trigger.

The glass cracked in a spiderweb pattern but held, and Carl was treated to the neat hole of the .22 round as it punched through the man's forehead. The man seemed to be thinking about it for a second, before his legs failed and he sank to the ground, pulling the curtains down with him. Carl watched his feet jerk twice before deciding a second round was unnecessary. He holstered the Ruger and replaced it with the envelop. Peeling off the double-sided tape, he stuck it firmly to the glass. The letters TTS were on the inside and clearly legible by anyone standing in the room. How they were going to get it down, he really didn't care. He had his own priorities. The first was to release the break on his line.

He made the repel down in four long intervals and landed softly next to a parked Lexus. He squatted to get some slack and then quickly stepped out of the harness. The rope was abandoned as he reached in a pocket and thumbed a key fob. The trunk of the Lexus opened, and he dumped every piece of gear he didn't need inside. Still clad in black, he grabbed an equally black helmet from inside and slipped it on his head.

Two spots to the right of the Lexus was a

Ducati motorcycle. The keys started it, and he soon had it rolling down the exit ramp. He ignored the vale and the many security people at the entrance and goosed it out into the traffic on the strip. He found a spot behind an impatient cab and followed him for several blocks, before breaking away and entering the side streets. From there, he found his way through the city to highway 15 heading toward Utah. He had plans to do some mountain biking for a week in the boonies.

At the last red light, he paused long enough to send a coded text to William. He waited for a full minute and got no answer, but that was okay; he was sure the man was busy tonight.

THE J. EDGAR HOOVER BUILDING

"CAN YOU BELIEVE THIS?" Sydney spoke.

Nobody answered, their attention focused on the man on the TV and the unbelievable words he was saying. All around them, the ops center had gone quiet. Only the traffic of the radios and the whispered answers of those attending them could be heard.

"What's going on at the Capitol Building?" Jack asked the room.

Deacon nodded to the watch commander for an answer. He spoke into his radio.

"Sierra One, what's the situation there?" he asked a sniper team stationed on the roof of the Capitol Building.

"Sierra One. We're seeing no change here, other than the crowd growing in size. So far, they're staying behind the barriers and not giving us any problems."

"Sierra two?"

"Sierra Two. We're seeing the same on our side. Some fires are visible to the north and east."

"The crowd?"

"Bigger. But no issues."

"Roger." The watch commander turned to Jack. "What were you thinking, Jack?"

"The President's speech, if the crowd is watching it—"

"The cell towers are jammed with traffic."

"Exactly. What if it's them all watching? What are they going to do when they hear this?"

"Shit." The man put it together and began shouting orders. "Get me the reserve force to the Capitol Building, now. Cancel all nine-one-one response until they are in place. Tell HRT to get their birds in the air. I want—"

"Sir!"

The commander spun to the operator addressing him. "What?"

"I'm on with a guy at the *Post*. You better hear what he has to say."

"The *Post*? I don't have time for reporters right now, I—"

"No, sir, he's not asking questions. They've received a communication."

"From who?"

The operator looked from his commander to Jack.

"The Twelve Shepherds."

The room went silent again. Jack looked to Deacon, who waved him toward the phone. Jack took it from the operator and raised it to his head as the room watched.

"This is Jack Randall. Who am I speaking with?"

"It's Danny, Jack. We just got a ton of email here. I mean every employee is getting it. Hundreds of files. All of it on current and past congressmen, senators, Wall Street guys, it's just—"

"Danny! Slow down. What's in the files?"

"Uh, not sure what we're going to call it yet, but you guys would probably call it evidence."

Jack paused and shared a look with his boss. Danny had been speaking loud enough for the whole room to hear. Deacon held up two fingers.

"Okay, Danny. I'm going to send over two guys. Can you wait for—"

"How you plan on doing that? Have you looked outside lately?"

"Yeah ... Okay. I'll send them on foot. I need you to hold on to what you have until—"

"Not a chance, Jack. We're not the only ones getting this stuff. *New York, Denver, LA*, all have it too. I'm sure there are a dozen others. It's out. Like toothpaste. Listen, I'll watch out for your guys and all, but I was just giving you a heads-up, so you know what's coming. I..." Danny's voice dropped to a whisper, "I gotta go."

The line went dead. Jack handed the receiver back to its owner and turned to face the group. He saw Sydney frantically punching the buttons of her phone. She looked up, and he caught her face.

"What?"

"Larry isn't answering."

New York City

The sound of the arrival chime stirred him, and he glanced at the tiny screen to see who was boarding. It was him, and he was on the phone.

"... don't care if he's not answering! Somebody find him and get his ass on the phone! I want to know how this happened! And I want to know now!"

Stephen waited while the man punched the down button and listened to whatever the reply was.

"Well, call me when you fucking know something!"

The man stabbed the screen and fumed as the elevator started its decent. Stephen gave it a count of six before touching the button on his phone. The elevator stopped immediately and went dark.

"Now what!?" the man voiced. Stephen saw the glow of the cell phone and heard the man punching the elevator's controls repeatedly. He donned the night vision goggles and silently powered them up. In the gray-green glow, he could make out the man's frustrated face through the ceiling grate. He silently lifted its hinged door and quietly passed an object down through it.

The man was punching buttons of the cellphone again, so he didn't see the device reaching out for him. The phone rang once, before his body was hit with several thousand volts. He collapsed to the floor and twitched, his muscles trying to make sense of the sudden contractions. In the dim light, he could just make out the shape of a man as he lowered himself to the elevators floor.

"Who ... are you?"

"More like 'what,' actually," Stephen replied. "But it's much too late for questions."

The banker watched in horror, as the man reached behind him and extracted two items from his belt. One was a large envelope. The other a large knife. He struggled to move, but his body refused to respond. The two items impacted his chest one after the other.

"So, WHERE IS HE?" the guard asked.

"I don't know. He's not on any of the screens. Did you see him come off the elevator?"

"No. Odd that he'd just call and hang up though. You s'pose I should head up and check?"

"Better you than me. You know how he hates being interrupted."

"Yeah, still, maybe we should try calling again, and—"

The ding of the arriving executive elevator cut him off, and they both turned toward it.

"There he is. I ... What the hell?"

The guard at the desk looked up to see that their boss had indeed arrived through the open doors. He rose from his position, and they both walked until they were at the door of the elevator and looked on in horror.

"Shit! Call the damn police!"

Inside the elevator, their boss swayed in tiny circles, his feet only inches off the marble floor. The noose around his neck was tight, yet his hands were free.

"He do this himself?"

The answer was provided for them as the man slowly rotated. The knife holding the envelope to his chest was planted deeply, but the letters on the outside could still be plainly seen through the blood soaking it.

TTS

"I don't think so."

THE HOUSE CHAMBER

"WHEN ANY SOLDIER falls into the hands of one of the most ruthless and barbaric foes we have ever faced, our immediate reaction should be to rescue him from their clutches. Our code of never leaving a soldier behind is written in the blood of many who have lived those words. It is a contract that should never be broken or debated. We bring our men home. To ask them to sacrifice so much without the guarantee that we in return will never abandon them. This should stand without question.

"But there are those who see opportunity in such situations, and they have been allowed to have too much power. They tug at the strings of our elected representatives in order to further their own gain, and the life of an American soldier is reduced to that of a bargaining chip, one that is used for their own personal profit. Their influence is limitless. Reaching even that of the highest office in the land."

A wave of murmurs traveled through the assembly and several glanced to the congressman whose son the president was speaking of. He sat frozen, his eyes glued to the man on the dais. His hands gripping the arms of his chair tightly.

The president picked up the device in front of him and held it up.

"One of these men called me a few days ago. I would like to play for you that conversation." With a cold glare at the nervous men before him, he held it to the microphone and pushed PLAY. There was a slight pause before the voice of the president's secretary was heard.

"Sir, he's on line two."

"Thank you."

The President watched them as they all leaned forward. He hoped the man they were about to hear was also watching. He took some satisfaction knowing that he and his brother were. The elder of the two's voice was heard next.

"Charles?"

"Yes, Mr. President. How are you, sir?"

"It's been a busy day. How's the family?"

"All very well. David still insists on staying in Kansas for some reason; I still can't get him to join me here in the Big Apple."

Two men in the chamber abruptly stood. They were pulled back down into their seats by their colleagues.

"Can't blame him; I prefer the country myself, as well."

"I manage to avoid it as much as possible."

"You'll never change, either one of you. Wish I

could chat, Charles, but I have a budget meeting in ten minutes. Is there something I can do for you?"

"Well, there is. I'm told we have some action being taken in Syria and I wanted to check in with you on that."

"It has to be done, Charles. I can't leave the boy hanging."

"You realize this will jeopardize many things."

"I do. But the choice was a clear one."

"Are you sure?"

"What are you suggesting, Charles? That we leave the man in place?"

"We'd like you to reconsider the rescue. The pilot serves a purpose, one we can profit from greatly."

"We can deal with that afterwards."

"We don't feel the same, Mr. President. The pilot needs to stay on the ground. He's one man. We lose that many a day to training accidents. If the people are to be convinced to keep this war going, then certain ... sacrifices need to be made."

"I don't—"

"He's a catalyst! A rallying cry that we can use for the next five years and beyond. Opportunities like this must be seized when they present themselves! If he dies at their hands, we'll have the justification we need to extend and escalate the campaign in the middle east. Not even the Russians would vote against it. You have to look beyond what's in front of you."

"He's the son of a congressman."

"All the better."

A wave of shocked gasps traveled around the room. But most were struck dumb by what they were hearing.

"Call the SEALs back, Mr. President."

"And if I don't?"

"We cannot ignore this. If you cannot see the situation as we do, re-election will become ... most difficult."

There was a long pause before they all heard the President's reply. The silence in the chamber was palpable.

"I'll give it some thought." A dial tone followed as the connection was severed, and they heard the voice of the president stating the time and the date and who the person he had been speaking to had been, followed by a heavy sigh.

The president stopped the playback and, once again, faced the room. The tone had changed. Men who had been ready to protest now sat quietly and averted their gaze. Many of them glared at their colleagues across the aisle in both directions. A few squeezed the shoulder of the soldiers' father as he stared at the floor.

The cameras caught every second of it and broadcast it to the world.

15

"America was not built on fear. America was built on courage, on imagination and an unbeatable determination to do the job at hand."

—Harry S. Truman

BRIGHTON BEACH, NEW YORK

A block away from the restaurant, Vasily reached the darkness of the alley and stripped off the waiter's uniform before throwing it in the nearest dumpster. At the alley's end, he found the car still waiting and was soon on his way north, its heater struggling to clear the fog from the windshield. He took a roundabout route through the borough until he arrived at the bridge over the creek separating the island from the mainland. Once across, he turned left and made his way past the golf course and on to the basin marina. The combination of winter cold and the late hour had resulted in a deserted dock, and he doused the headlights as he rolled the car past the treatment plant at the dock's entrance. The many boats up on their racks and the few still in the water cast odd shadows in the moonlight, and he kept to them as he made his way to the end.

His boat was modest. A sailboat of only twenty-two feet, it looked out of place among the larger boats. But it was all he needed. He wedged the car in between two large powerboats covered in blue tarps, before exiting and covering the car in one as well. He left everything behind except the gun in his belt, and moved directly to the stern, throwing off the line and then doing the same to the bow. The boat drifted calmly in the cold water and bobbed only slightly as he jumped aboard.

While outside the boat looked run down, inside it was anything but. Everything was in its proper place and ready for departure, and he wasted no time in moving to the helm and starting the small engine. Despite the temperature, the Yanmar diesel fired up without hesitation, and he gave it a full minute to warm up, before advancing the throttle and moving out into the harbor.

He kept his speed low, and because of it, the sound of the engine was minimal. The prop gave him just enough forward speed to give him steerage and depart the tiny slip without calling attention to himself. He kept all lights off until he was well out into the river. He headed dead away from land and toward Hoffman Island until the GPS told him he was in the sea lanes. There, he turned on his navigation lights, executed a sharp turn to port, and headed for open ocean. As he passed out of the bay and into the Atlantic, he produced a phone and sent a quick text message. Confirmation of the message from William came within a minute, and the phone promptly went over the side the second he finished. The lights of the city faded away behind him, and he rose to set the sails.

A half hour later, he was making a steady seven knots through moderate swells. The radar was clear and the weather report good. The last light faded behind him as he adjusted his course to the south.

It had been worth it, he decided. The pain of his parent's death and his flight from the Russian mafia in St. Petersburg had come full circle. He had come a long way since then. First hiding by joining the US military with forged papers, he had volunteered for repeated deployments to stay out of the country and off their radar, only to be re-cruited by the Twelve Shepherds when his real identity was discovered by William. He had en-dured the facial surgery and then overcome the fear of discovery to get himself back into their midst.

Watching the man who had ordered the death of his family eat and drink and laugh with his mafia cronies had been a slow torture. But tonight, that was over. Mixing the man's last drink had not only brought him closure, it had ended the rage in him he had carried for years. The man was dead, and those he had called friends had all been there to see it. Now they were the ones filled with fear. There was nowhere to hide. No place they would be safe. He had just proven it, and he took pleasure in them knowing it for the rest of their lives.

He glanced behind him to see the top of the great tower disappear over the horizon. Turning away, he exchanged its lights for the stars overhead and let out a contented sigh.

"For you, Papa," he spoke to them.

It was the last land he would see before hitting Bermuda.

THE CAPITOL BUILDING

"WAIT HERE."

She nodded and continued her shouting, along with the others. Despite the temperature, she was warm. The closeness of the crowd around her and their physical activity had served to ward off the falling temperature. Their accumulated breath fogged the air over them and reflected the lights of the city. The signs poking through the gray layer served to mark their depth and growing numbers.

Her husband leaned his sign against the marble and pulled himself up to stand next to the statue. He scanned the area over the heads of the protestors and smiled beneath his face mask. It was huge now. The size usually seen for inaugurations. They were ready.

He turned to check on the building before them. The Capitol police had formed a ring around the building with the usual portable barriers. The protestors outnumbered them a hundred to one. Farther up the stairs were more serious men with automatic rifles. And then there were more just inside the doors. On the roof there were snipers, and he feared them most of all.

It would come down to speed and numbers. That and justified rage. Rage that was growing. He looked down at the crowd and saw many of them on their cellphones. Watching the tiny screens in two and threes as the news of the files hit. His eyes found his wife. She was watching herself. As if feeling his gaze, she turned to him and nodded.

It was time.

He examined the front row of protestors. It, and at least the first four rows back, were occupied by people with heavy coats and hats. All of them bundled up tight against the freezing temperatures and wearing face masks.

He climbed down and found his way back to her side.

"The files hit the news," she shouted over the noise. "All the networks are running with it."

"I can see the crowd lit up with cellphones. They're all seeing it. The front looks ready, and the crowd fills half the mall now."

"Now?"

"Now."

She reached into the pocket of her coat and pulled it out. It was a simple can with a push-button on the top. Hardly what one thought of as the trigger for such an operation.

With a deep breath, she closed her eyes and pushed.

NEW YORK CITY

THE LOUD CURSING of the older brother prompted the door to be flung open, and Tommy saw the green glow of the man's body heat fill the doorway. He centered the suppressor on the man's chest and fired twice, the loud coughs echoing in the small space as the man staggered back and fell to the ground. Tommy watched him, the gun never wavering, but the man stayed still.

More cursing sounded from down the hall,

and Tommy looked that way to see the glow of the man's phone illuminating his face as he frantically punched the tiny screen. He dismissed the man on the floor and moved to cut the older brother off as he fled the small study for the hallway.

But the goggles robbed Tommy of his depth perception, and he stumbled into a large potted plant as he moved to pursue him. His feet slipped on the marble floor, and he landed hard. It gave the older brother enough time to run down the hall and slam the door to the master bedroom behind him.

Now cursing himself, Tommy pushed himself up and followed. He stood aside and tried the door, only to have two shots from inside the room punch through it. He dropped to a crouch and examined the holes in the wall across from him. Based on their paths, he sent two rounds back inside before moving back down the hall the way he had come.

The man was locked in and armed. Some kind of handgun that Tommy was unaware of. He had to hurry. He ran past the entry with the two men on the floor and out to the guest room, tossing the goggles aside when the lights of the city flooding in through the window overloaded them. Planting his face against the glass of the balcony, he scanned the one next to it.

Empty.

He opened the door and leveled the Ruger in that direction, before sliding down the wall to get closer. The door to the master bedroom suit was open, and he could hear the man inside.

"Somebody's in here! They shot my guards, and now they're gunning for me! Get up here, now!"

Tommy inched forward and craned his head around the corner. Through the glass he could see the brother crouched by the bed, the phone in one hand and a nickel-plated six-shooter in the other. The gun was in perpetual motion as the man panned it around the room while he barked into the phone.

"I don't care! Just get up here!" the man screamed.

Tommy looked around. The only thing close by was a small table. He lifted it silently and hefted its weight before flinging it across the narrow gap and into the group of chairs on the other side. The crash was loud.

As he predicted, the man turned and fired, snapping off three rounds in rapid succession without even aiming.

Not enough. Tommy fired a pair of rounds of his own, the bullets snapping through the plate glass and sending it crashing to the ground. The six-shooter barked again, and the round snapped past Tommy's head to travel off across the city's skyline. He immediately vaulted up onto the railing and jumped across the gap, landing and rolling free of the shattered glass to his feet, the Ruger aimed at the man inside.

Click-click-click.

The man stood not five feet away, his finger rapidly squeezing the trigger of the empty pistol. Tommy let him until he stopped.

The man struggled for breath against his racing heart. Words gushed forth.

"Money. I'll give you whatever you want!"

"We're not here for that," Tommy told him.

"It's always about that!"

Tommy shook his head at the man. "You're eighty years old, with just as many billions, and it's still not enough. What makes you think any amount is enough for me?"

Charles had no reply to that. He backed away for every step forward the man in black took. Eventually, his back hit the door. There was nowhere else to go.

"Security will be here in a few seconds," the man tried to warn him.

"They won't be fast enough."

"God dammit! Don't you know who I am!?"

"We know exactly what you are."

"We? What the hell are you—"

The envelope impacted his chest and fell to the floor in front of him. Charles looked down to see it illuminated by the city outside. The letters were large and unavoidable.

TTS

"You ... you have no idea the war you've just started. My brother and I will hunt you to the ends of the earth. We'll park you in an overseas prison, and the pain will last for decades! My people will—"

"The Trust?"

"How ... how do you—"

"There is no Trust anymore, not after tonight."

"My brother and I—"

"Your brother's dead, and so is your Trust."

The words cut him off. Tommy watched as they sank in, and the man's lip began to quiver.

"You'll never win."

"We'll see."

Tommy fired until the gun was empty. Each

shot another knife of pain traveling from the man's ample gut and up to his chest. His face contorted with each impact, and Tommy watched as the message was driven home.

The echoes of the shots had barely died when Tommy felt the phone in his pocket vibrate. He palmed it and checked the screen. The elevator was moving, with what looked like several men. Many of them armed with shotguns. His planned departure was cut off.

He thumbed the controls, and the elevator died. He watched the men in the red glow of the emergency lights. One of them punched the button a few times before gesturing at the door. Another pulled a crowbar from his belt and stuck it in the gap. Fingers followed and soon the men had the door open. Tommy watched as they crawled out and onto the floor several flights below him. His last sight of them was their booted feet running away down the hall.

The stairs. They would enter the stairwell and make their way up to him. He had no way of stopping them, and he was very outnumbered. The sound of sirens approaching reached him through the shattered window. Within minutes, the building would be surrounded.

Thinking quickly, he reached out and yanked Charles' body away from the door before walking through it. He estimated that he had about four minutes.

VICE PRESIDENT HANEY'S HOME

"TRAITOR! You'll be dead before the week is over! God damnit, I'll—" He cut himself off and snatched up the cell phone. Like most men in his position, he had priority access to the cell phone network, something they had gained after the 9-11 attacks and refused to give up. He now used it without thinking twice.

"Harper! Where are you!?"

"I'm in position."

"That idiot we put in office just sold us out! Get going! Do it now! We have to cut this speech off at the knees before he can run his mouth any longer! We have to implicate the Shepherds now! Blow the damn Hoover Building! Do it now! I want that damn thing—"

The line went dead, and he seethed in fury before rapidly punching the buttons again. It rang and rang without answer, and he barely stopped himself from throwing it across the room. He checked his anger just in time, and the brief moment cleared his head enough for him to realize what he was doing.

This wasn't a secure phone. In his rage he had used his own personal one to call Harper's. It was a break in tradecraft, and Harper had wisely ended it.

What had he said before the line went dead? He couldn't remember now, but he was confident his order to move had gotten through. He set the phone down and rose to pace the room as the man on the TV spoke on. Broken glass and aged scotch crunched under his shoes, the first casualty of his anger, and he ignored it as he listened. He expected the phone to ring any second, and he was confident it would not be Harper on the other end of the line. The man on the screen stared him right in the eyes as he spoke, as if he were taunting him.

"You fool! You could have had everything! Now you'll have nothing! I'll see you dead!"

Outside the door, the security men all slunk away. They had heard the man's words and now huddled together in small groups having quiet conversations. Guarding the man was one thing.

Looking the other way was a bit more. But this? Many of them found a reason to move downstairs, away from the man in the study.

———

A FEW MILES AWAY, Harper palmed the phone in his gloved hand and snorted.

"You fool."

The man had lost it. So had the Trust leadership. Haney would no doubt be replaced after this. By who, he didn't know, but nobody was indispensable. Results, that's what assured that you stayed in the game. And no one could deny the results Harper produced. Despite his employer's mistake, Harper would still get them results. It would give him a better position to negotiate his place and compensation with whomever the Trust made their new operations man.

And why could that not be him? Hadn't he always delivered? He entertained the thought for a moment before setting it aside. Later. To apply for such a position, one needed leverage, and by completing tonight's mission, he would have it.

He started the engine and dropped the truck in gear. The J. Edgar Hoover Building was only a few blocks away. He thumbed the light bar on as he pulled out and onto 10th street, and the traffic parted for him as best it could. Thick crowds of people watched from the sidewalks as he weaved the truck down the street. The large white letters on the front and side serving as a warning to anyone who might delay him.

A few blocks later he was at the roadblock three blocks shy of Pennsylvania Avenue. It was the path the president traveled to and from the Capitol Building, and they would keep it clear until he was safely back in the White House. The guard there checked his ID without a word and then waved him through before returning his nervous gaze back to the mob of people all around him.

A block later, Harper could see the Hoover Building. Its distinct overhang marking it on the left side of the road. A line of white bureau cars appeared along the curbs on both sides of the street, and he threaded the truck between them. People scrambled across his path to get out of the way, but none stopped to impede him.

It was a dead end. Pennsylvania avenue was just ahead and blocked by a pair of DC police cars. There was only one way to go.

Harper swung the truck into the entrance to the Hoover Building's underground garage. There were two cars ahead of him, and he stewed behind the wheel as the guard examined their drivers' ID.

His right hand reached into the box and found the timer. He had set it an hour ago and made sure to allow himself plenty of time to get a safe distance away. As soon as the barrier came down and let the first car in, he activated it. The box was quickly locked, and he checked his watch before placing both hands on the wheel.

He didn't want to make the guard nervous.

LARRY PAUSED for a moment to catch his breath. The protestors on the mall were dense, and while they served to block the wind, they also were making his trip a slow one. He couldn't travel more than ten feet without having to alter his path to navigate around a small knot of them. The ones traveling in his direction never did so for very far and often paused before doing so. It was like navigating a bumper car arena. He gaped at them all now, their half-covered faces leaving small clouds with every exhale. It gave the crowd an eerie look, as the fog hovered over them for as far as he could see.

Closer to the Capitol Building, the fog was

denser. Signs poked up through it with several colorful slogans. Among them, he saw quotes from many former presidents, but also a few from Malcom X, Howard Zinn, and even George Orwell.

"Orwell?" Larry asked himself. But he then admitted that the quote fit.

But he had no time for that now. The Hoover Building was just a couple blocks away now, and the crowd looked like it thinned a bit once he got off the mall.

He was just adjusting the grip on his bag, when the horns sounded. The crowd around him stopped their movement. They first looked toward the Capitol Building and then to the protestors around them. The distant horns were joined by others and began to travel closer. Larry watched in wonder as the blare approached and then engulfed him before moving on and spreading across the mall.

"What the hell?"

A roar sounded, and he watched openmouthed as the crowd surged up the steps of the Capitol Building en masse. The building was soon covered in the bodies of the protestors, and he heard the rattle of gunfire for a moment before it stopped. The crowd around him surged forward as well, and Larry fought to keep his place against the tide.

Seeing a gap in the crowd, he took it, dragging his bag as fast as he could for the street.

The Hoover Building was only a block away now. Despite his current shape, Larry broke into a run.

16

"You're not supposed to be so blind with patriotism that you can't face reality. Wrong is wrong, no matter who says it."

—_Malcolm X_

KANSAS CITY, KANSAS

The lights of the ATV drew his attention, and he watched them closely as they moved off into the trees. Another patrol, this one no doubt being done by the guard he had lost track of. At least now he knew where they both were. The fact that one was out of the house was a problem: There was no way to watch them both and the man he was here for at the same time. He zeroed the volume of the tiny speaker in his ear so he could follow the progress of the ATV as it circled the property. If the guard kept pace with his last trip around the home, he would be directly behind him in about thirty minutes. That was not good. The CheyTac was not suppressed. Its roar would announce his presence to everyone in a half-mile radius, and if the people who heard it were outside, they would have a general direction in which to look for him. He would have to be very careful. The guard by the pool had an ATV of his own, and there was no way Lee could outrun him.

The man in his scope was still in the chair before the TV, watching it intently. The look on his face betrayed his thoughts; he was obviously not happy with what he was seeing. He suddenly got up and began pacing the room, the phone held to his ear. His free hand began to gesture as he spoke into the device, whoever was on the other end getting an earful. Lee tracked him through the scope as he walked about, the thick glass distorting his view.

And then it happened. The man thumbed the phone silent and flung it at the chair he had vacated, before snatching up his glass and draining its contents. He cursed a few times before leaving the room, and Lee adjusted the scope to center on the kitchen window.

His target appeared a few seconds later. Lee took three slow breaths, and the crosshairs centered on the man's chest as he added ice to the empty glass. Lee's finger tightened on the trigger as he took a half breath and held it.

The man reached for the bottle of amber liquid and began pouring its contents into the glass. Lee saw and approved of the name on its side, just as the trigger broke.

The CheyTac bucked comfortably back into his shoulder, and Lee rode the recoil back on target in time to see the bottle in the man's hands shatter as the round traveled through it and his chest. Lee was surprised to see the man stay upright, and Lee watched the man's face as his blood poured from the wound and soaked his crisp white shirt.

"Take your medicine," Lee muttered as his target sank out of sight.

———

THE DING of the alert drew William's attention to the screen, and he saw the icon for the flagged call. He punched keys and soon had it playing back to him. The voice of Haney was immediately recognized, and his jaw dropped at what he was hearing.

"Warn them," the General spoke.

"Yes, sir. But the lines are jammed—I may not be able to get through, and even if I do, it could get lost in the noise."

"You have to try. Warn Mr. Dayton, as well. He may be close to the location."

William's fingers scrambled to comply.

———

THE CAPITOL BUILDING

SGT. MASON HAD BEEN on barrier duty for a few hours now, and was wondering when he might use a bathroom next. The crowd was loud and larger than he had expected. Much bigger than last year or the year before. But they had been well behaved —at least here, at the Capitol Building—and he had endured their shouted protests with a stoic face and a set of earplugs.

His partner wandered over and nudged him. Mason pulled an earplug free.

"Break in five, when Haynes gets back. There's coffee inside."

"Got it."

They both paused and looked out over the crowd. From their post halfway up the steps, they could see all the way to the Lincoln Memorial.

"Big crowd this year."

"Yeah, I was just thinking that. Fired up, too. You'd think the weather would have kept them—"

The blare of an air horn sounded right in front of them. Air horns were not allowed and would get its user arrested. Neither one of them wanted to be the one tasked with doing so, though. Their eyes searched for the guilty party when another sounded off to their right. And then another to the left.

"What the hell is this?" Mason asked.

Another air horn joined in, and another, multiplying until the crowd was drown out, and all that could be heard was the wail of the multiple canisters.

And then they died.

"That was—"

The crowd roared, and the police manning the barrier seemed to all drop and contort on the sidewalk below. The crowd were immediately over the barrier, swarming the downed men. They disappeared as the people broke into a run straight up the steps at them.

Mason saw them now. Tasers. Everyone seemed to have one. He was frozen in place by the sight as the mob stormed their way up the steps on a broad front, taking down officers and swallowing them up in their numbers as they moved.

"Inside!" his partner yelled.

They both turned and ran for the building, but the crowd were on them just as they reached the doors. The men inside slammed them shut, and they bounced off the glass, before the crowd pulled them away.

Mason struggled, but there was little he could do. His wrists were seized, and he was thrown down onto the ground. In seconds, he was stripped of his weapon and belt, zip-tied around the ankles and wrists, and shoved through the crowd to land against the concrete wall of the building. Seconds later, another officer joined him, and then another, all of them similarly tied.

"You got this one?"

"He's mine. You take the fat one!"

The police men braced for a beating but instead were stood over by large men—one for every officer—each masked and armed with a Taser or baton of some kind. They faced the crowd and pushed away anyone who got too close. Mason shared a bewildered look with his partners.

What the hell was going on?

ON THE OTHER side of the glass, the officers sounded the alarm. The snipers on the roof and the surrounding buildings began all talking at once, and it was difficult to sort out what was happening.

But they knew what was going on right in front of them. They watched as several of their fellow officers hit by a Taser or overwhelmed by numbers before disappearing into the crowd. The people now beat on the glass and screamed loud enough to penetrate its thickness.

An agent appeared with a submachine gun and leveled it at the crowd.

"No! You'll break the glass!"

The agent hesitated and then lessened his

pressure on the trigger. If he shot, the glass would shatter, and then there would be nothing stopping the crowd from pouring into the building.

The officer grabbed his radio and keyed the mic.

"I need every man available to the south entrance!"

"The crowd's attacking the building on the north side! They're at the doors!"

"East side. We're trapped inside!"

"What the hell is going on?" the agent yelled to him.

"They're at every entrance. I don't..."

"What?"

"Look."

The people at the glass had ceased their pounding and were now stepping back. In their place stood men and woman with shiny objects in their hands. He recognized them. Spring loaded punches. He'd kept one in his old unit for breaking into cars. He reached out and grasp the arm of the agent with the machine gun.

"I'd think real hard about what you plan to do with that, if I were you."

The man blinked and then realized what was going to happen. He took a step back and lowered the gun.

The glass began shattering one by one. The crowd kicked at the glass until it fell inside.

"They're inside."

He managed to broadcast the words a second before the mob was on him. He heard one burst of automatic fire from the other end of the lobby before it too stopped. He and the agent next to him were quickly cuffed, gagged, and flung into a corner, where they were stood over by masked men.

His only other sight was the swarm of people rushing past in every direction. Their stampede echoed off the tall ceilings and their travel shook the floor like a herd a passing buffalo. The vibrations were felt by everyone, and he watched as the discarded submachine gun of the agent move across the slick marble next to him.

Why hadn't they picked it up?

The question went unanswered as the crowd filled the building. Snow-covered boots left dark streaks across the marble floor and kicked the glass fragments and shell casings about at random. He heard yelling and the splintering of wood as doors were forced open.

The crowd parted for a moment, and he caught a look at a protestor across the hall, his shoulder bloody from a gunshot wound. Others were taking care of him, and the agent who had delivered the shot was bound and gagged and un-moving next to him, his own head bleeding and joining that of the man he had shot in a common puddle. He lost sight of them as the room filled with more bodies.

KENSINGTON, MARYLAND

DAYTON HAD JUST GRABBED the door handle when his phone buzzed. Anna's followed a second later and they both paused to grab them. With William's partial control of the local cell phone system, they had priority access, and he wouldn't call unless it was important. They each read the text at the same time.

"We're too far away," Dayton said. "The FBI is on their own." He tapped out a reply to William before tossing the phone back in the cup holder. "We've got our own mission to perform. Stay here while I check the trail. If it's clear, we go for the weapons as soon as I return. Okay?"

Anna nodded. "Okay."

She watched as Dayton left the SUV and immediately took up a jogging pace on the trail toward Haney's home. As soon as he was out of sight, she pulled her own phone out and tapped out a text. Without hesitation, she hit SEND and held her breath. Would the message go through? Would William see it? She shoved the thoughts aside. It was why she had hurried, so there was no going back.

With a polite ding, the phone confirmed her message had been delivered, and she let out a breath.

"Whatever happens, you deal with it later," she told herself.

THE J. EDGAR HOOVER BUILDING

"WHAT THE HELL?"

Jack stared at the TV screens with the other agents in the room in disbelief. The crowds surging forward and into the building were moving as one, converging from all sides and overwhelming the police at the barriers in seconds. The steps of the Capitol were soon covered with the bodies of the protestors as they met the barrier of the doors.

"Those won't hold long. What do we have?"

The Hostage Rescue Team commander was

already on it, speaking rapidly into the radio in a hushed but controlled tone. Jack fidgeted until an operator answered his question.

"We've deployed the backup force at District PD headquarters and alerted the rapid response force at the armory."

Jack nodded to the man for an answer, but his eyes never left the screen. The camera feed was from Homeland Security, who had saturated the DC mall years ago with the most high-tech surveillance system devised. He watched cameras that had a high view of the mall first and quickly saw a pattern emerge. The crowd that had packed the mall earlier had now moved, with half of their number joining the assault on the Capitol Building and the other half moving into the streets on all sides. Traffic came to a stop and the people could be seen on street level cameras disabling the cars in place. A few were now burning at intersections, and the rest sank to the pavement on deflated tires.

"It's coordinated!"

"What?"

"It's organized! Look at the pattern!"

The commander stopped giving orders long enough to see what Jack was saying. He keyed the mic again and issued another order.

"Get your team inside the Capitol and secure the president!"

He moved from the screen he was at and walked to Jack's spot before the multiple smaller screens. He quickly saw it too. Jack stepped back to let the man work and was tapped on the shoulder by Sydney.

"Says it's priority." She held out his phone.

He read the text twice before recognizing he number at the bottom.

"848 ... shit!"

"What?"

"We're under attack. Get people on every entrance!" he yelled, before bolting from the room. Sydney scrambled to follow.

Outside, they ran into Eric as he was making his way to them.

"Hey, boss. I was—"

"You armed?"

"Yeah?"

"Come with us!"

Eric knew better than to ask more questions. He set the laptop down on the nearest flat surface and bolted after them.

The House Chamber

A FEW WHISPERED CONVERSATIONS BEGAN, but the president's voice cut them off.

"As you have just heard, not even the president of the United States is outside the reach of these men. I, too, have been ensnarled in their net of corruption. I, too, am a party to this. I, too, am guilty."

He reached into this coat and pulled out an envelope. The chamber stared at it in silence as he removed a piece of paper and then signed it. Returning it to its envelope, his eyes located the secretary of state seated in the front row. He beckoned him forward, and the man reluctantly rose. The president handed the document over without fanfare and returned to the lectern.

"I would like to speak to the citizens of this nation with my next remarks. The solution cannot start with me. It must come from you. If we are to survive as a nation we must join together and fight this cancer from within. I have proven myself unworthy of this task and of this office. It is up to you now. I urge you to root out this corruption and purge it from our system. There is an election on the horizon; let your voices be heard."

He paused and took one long look at the room and the people in it before speaking again.

"It is with great regret that I hereby announce my resignation as president of these United States effective immediately. I see no other alternative than to—"

The crowd had rumbled with the words and then got louder as the Secret Service agents all moved as one, converging on the president from every direction and tearing him away from the dais. The congressmen and senators all stood in shock as the man was carried off the stage and through a nearby door. The door slammed shut and was quickly followed by several others around the chamber.

The cameras panned around, in a futile effort to broadcast it all. The last shot seen was of serious men in dark suits standing in front of the doors. Many of them now held submachine guns, which had appeared in their hands as if by magic. The congressmen and senators all stood, craning their necks around.

Except for one. He sat quietly amid the chaos around him. His hand found its way to his wallet, and he removed a picture. It was of a young man standing in front of a fighter jet. His helmet held in his hand and his sweaty hair mussed by the ocean breeze. The grin on his face spoke of a man who had found his purpose, and his father stared at it now with pride. The sounds of the chamber were pushed aside, and he was alone with his thoughts.

But then the sound changed. The voices in the chamber died, only to be replaced by new ones from outside.

THE WHITE HOUSE

THE MAN SAT QUIETLY in the Roosevelt room with his wife. He was the designated survivor, a practice put in place back in 1947. It was a relic of the cold war, when the threat of nuclear attack had prompted the creation of the Presidential Succession Act. With the events of 9-11, and the growth of terrorist organizations, the act had taken on new meaning. So now, one of the cabinet members—usually one deemed junior by the president, or whomever he delegated the decision to—would sit somewhere the others from the line of succession were not. Tonight, the President had invited him to the Oval Office, and he had of course accepted. With nearly everyone around glued to the TV, he had used the opportunity to bring his wife. She had gotten a tour from a staffer, and then a handshake from the president himself, before he had departed. Now they reclined in the leather seats and ate sandwiches from the White House kitchen under the steely gaze of Teddy Roosevelt from the wall.

"You don't want to wait in the oval?" his wife asked.

"No, it seemed a bit ... I don't know ... intrusive."

"Humph."

"What?"

"Just a picture in my head," she replied with a grin.

He knew what the grin meant.

"You're bad."

Her grin stayed.

"Maybe next time, when we don't have an audience." He nodded toward the door.

His wife looked for the hundredth time and saw the man sitting outside at attention. The leather case sitting on the floor next to him and shackled to his wrist by a short chain. The chain looked polished, like it was part of the uniform he was wearing. She found it odd.

"He goes everywhere he goes?"

"Everywhere. Except for tonight."

She examined the young man. He looked so serious. But then he had a serious job. It was hard to imagine that in that tiny case was the ability to end life on earth. She shuddered at the thought.

"And the others?"

"I'm sure they're lurking around here, somewhere."

She had enjoyed the tour she had gotten earlier, that is until she noticed the group of agents shadowing them. While security was something she had gotten used to, her husband, in his capacity as secretary of transportation, had never needed it to this level. It was a little ominous.

"Did he tell you what to do, if something did happen?"

Her husband chewed and swallowed before answering. It was not the answer she expected.

"Nope." He took another bite.

"Seriously? No DEFCON 1 or anything like that? No run to the bunker or to Air Force One? There is a bunker, right? In the basement somewhere?"

He shrugged and continued to chew. She waited.

"No idea."

"Well ... does *he* know?"

"The kid with the football? I imagine." He shrugged again.

"Well, what if something—"

People running past the door stopped her next question, and they both turned to see another race past.

"What's going on?"

"I don't know. Did you see—"

The door opened, and a pair of agents swept into the room.

"Sir! We need you to come with us."

"I—"

Before he could stand, the agents had grabbed him by both arms, and he was being propelled from the room. His wife scrambled to follow, and an agent grabbed her arm long enough for the young man in uniform to jump in front of them, before dragging her along after. They passed the shocked faces of the West Wing staff, half of them watching, the other half glued to the televisions, before they were out of the room and traveling down a stairwell.

They packed into an elevator and the door was immediately closed. Her stomach rose into her throat as the car descended.

"What is going on?" the secretary asked.

The agent in charge answered without turning.

"There's been an attack on the Capitol Building ... sir."

17

"Never in the field of human conflict was so much owed by so many to so few."

—Winston Churchill

WASHINGTON, D. C.

T he men and women who had been sitting at their desks or in various break rooms were now scrambling to put on riot gear and helmets. Shouted questions went unanswered and only added to the chaos. Nobody knew anything, only that they had all been ordered to the Capitol Building. Some paused to try and call their families, only to find the phones useless. Others cursed their cell phones as the connections were cut off or answered by apologetic recordings.

"What the hell is going on!" someone yelled.

It was the question of the hour, and no one had an answer.

But they did have orders. As soon as they were properly dressed and armed, they streamed from the building and out into the lot. Several paused to open the trunks of their police cruisers and extract rifles and vests. They quickly paired up and started their engines, revving them up to warm them, before dropping them in gear and moving toward the exit. The bottleneck slowed them only slightly, and they fanned out in both directions after clearing the gate. The first car to exit was greeted by an unusual sight.

"Where the hell did all these people come from?"

Her partner wrestled with the wheel as he eyeballed the crowd lining the streets. The crowd was a few rows deep and watching the cars as they exited with calm expressions, not one member of the crowd doing so much as raising a hand or waving sign in the cars' direction. It was a startling change from what the cops had endured over the past several weeks.

"Creepy."

It was the only reply he had time for, and even then, he had to shout it over the wail of his siren and those of the multiple cars behind them. But the people on the sidewalks didn't matter at the moment; what mattered was getting to the Capitol Building—as long as the people stayed out of the streets, he had no issue with them. They reached the next intersection, and he spun the wheel into a high-speed turn.

They both felt it immediately, and the driver cranked the wheel to counter, but it was too late. The rear end broke loose, and the car fish tailed a few times, before the driver got control. The cruiser slid to a stop and lightly impacted a parked car. Other than stepping back a bit, the crowd did nothing but watch.

"What the hell?"

"The tires?"

"Take a look."

She grabbed the shot gun from the rack mounted to the dash and eyeballed the crowd before getting out. They watched her without moving. She got a look at the rear tire and saw that it was flat, a large spike protruding from the tread.

The sound of an impact reached her ears, and she jumped away from the cruiser by reflex. Turning her gaze behind her, she saw other cruisers skidding on the icy streets and impacting the parked cars on either side. The sound of further crashes traveled on the wind back toward the station.

With a start, it hit her, and she spun around with the shotgun aimed. But the crowd had not moved. They seemed content to watch as the fleet of cars came to a sudden stop in the middle of the road. Only when the last crash was heard, and the sirens had died one by one, did they move out into the street and form a barrier several lines thick. Behind them, the dome of the Capitol Building could be seen in the distance. To get to it now, they would have to go through the people, and even then, it would be a journey of several blocks, one they would have to make on foot.

With nowhere to go, she got back into the car.

"They spiked the tires. Both of the rear ones."

"Seriously?"

"The whole fleet is out. It looks like they got every car. We're not going anywhere."

Her partner gripped the wheel with both hands and stared out the windshield at the line of people. They were bundled up in thick coats, and all with hats and face masks on. With the weather as cold as it was, he had thought nothing of it—he was dressed the same, himself. He now saw the true meaning for it.

"Call it in. Tell them they'll have to find help from somewhere else."

With a shaking hand, his partner reached for the mic.

THE WASHINGTON POST, WASHINGTON, D. C.

DANNY STARED up at the screen in shock. As the cameras tried to capture it all, the feed from the Capitol Building became one of chaos. One by one, the options died, and soon he lost his view of the inside of the building completely. The producers quickly switched to the studio, and the two political correspondents were caught with their mouths hanging open. One of them flinched, no doubt due to the director screaming into his earpiece, and he turned to the camera as if just noticing it. He stammered a few words, and Danny immediately dismissed him. He obviously didn't know any more than he did.

Ignoring the screen, he glanced around the room. Everyone was on their feet and staring at the screens as he had. Phones rang and went unanswered. Nobody moved. All of them shocked into inaction. He turned to find Steve frozen in place as well, his hand resting on his head.

"Steve?"

Steve snapped out of it and faced his colleague. "Yeah?"

"What do we ... I mean, do we go there?"

"I'm not sure."

Danny glanced at the screens again but saw only the talking heads offering speculation. There was only one way to know what was happening. He tossed the TV remote aside and reached for his coat.

"Danny, that's a bad idea."

"You got a better one?"

"The roads are blocked."

"The mall isn't."

"They'll never let you get close."

"It looks like someone found a way to. If they can, so can I. You coming?"

"I can't keep up with you. Besides, it's ten degrees out there."

"Where's Sean?"

"Kazakhstan."

"Crap." Danny pulled on his boots and pocketed his phone, before searching for his gloves. Steve watched him, shaking his head. If he were twenty years younger and twenty pounds lighter, he might join him, but those days were long gone.

"You sure? You might not like what you see."

"Somebody has to see it," Danny shot back.

Steve looked away and raked his hair back again. The motion brought his head up, and he spotted Ed leaving his office and headed their way, his eyes on the paper in his hands.

"If you're going, you better do it now. Ed's coming our way."

"Shit." Danny gave up looking for his gloves and ducked down before moving out of his cubicle and slinking away.

Steve watched him out of the corner of his eye, and Danny made it around the far corner just before Ed rounded the nearest one. He seemed surprised to find Steve standing and waiting for him.

A glance in Danny's cubicle revealed it to be empty.

"Where'd the kid go?"

"I ... uh."

Steve was a lousy liar. Ed looked again and saw that Danny's coat and hat were missing as well. He shot Steve an accusing look.

"Don't tell me he—"

"I tried to stop him."

"Damn it, kid."

Ed looked at the TV. It was now showing long-range shots of the Capitol Building. The mob occupied every square inch of the steps and surrounding grounds. It ebbed and flowed like water and stretched for hundreds of yards in every direction. The building was several blocks from the building they were in—Danny could be there in a matter of minutes, if something or someone didn't stop him first.

But then what?

QUANTICO, VIRGINIA

"SAY THAT AGAIN?"

"I said the Capitol Building has been breached.

Every entrance has been compromised, and the protestors have taken over the building. The broadcast of the State of the Union has been stopped, and the president is unaccounted for! I've called for every cop I have, but the response has been stopped by roadblocks and sabotage of the fleet. I need you to get every marine you have there, and send them to the Capitol Building, now!"

"It'll take us at least fifteen minutes to arm up and get on the trucks. Is it just the Capitol Building?"

"I'm not sure. The nine-one-one system has been flooded with calls. They've got the Arlington, Roosevelt, and Scott Key bridges all blocked, and the 14th and 395 bridges full of burning busses. Same with 695. There's reports of other roadblocks too, but I can't confirm. The White House is locked down, and so far, the crowd seems to be leaving it alone, but I haven't talked to the Secret Service yet. I need men, and I mean everyone you got. Get them armed and get them here now!"

The Colonel shook his head at what he was hearing. The man was the Chief of Police in DC, and they had even met on one occasion. But he had no pull at all with the military, and as such, the Colonel had no reason to do what he was asking. But if what he was saying was true...

"Are any of the joint chiefs available? I—"

"They're inside the damn building! Are we going to sit here arguing technicalities, or are you going to do something?"

The Colonel glanced at the TV in his office. Like most of the nation, he had been watching when the man went off the teleprompter. As shocking as his words were, they were nothing compared to seeing the Secret Service agents swarm him and carry him off the dais and out of the room. Less than a minute later, the signal had been lost. He'd been waiting for it to reappear when the phone had rung.

"I'll grab every man I can and be on the way in fifteen minutes."

"Make it ten!" the man hung up.

"Holy shit," Colonel Hurst whispered. He thought for three long seconds, before storming out of his office. Outside, the duty NCO and his runner stood waiting, the TV behind them showing nothing from the senate chamber.

"Alert the base. I want every marine we have to get their rifle and be out on the street and ready to deploy in ten minutes. Tell the motor pool to have every troop carrier ready. It's not a drill—draw live rounds. We're going to DC in fifteen minutes."

The sergeants face fell, but he recovered quickly. "Yes, sir!"

Hurst watched him snatch up the phone and spun to reenter his office and do the same. Stopping at the door, he turned back around when the picture on the TV caught his eye. It was a shot of the bridge between them and the Capitol. It was a log jam of burning buses and cars. Swarms of people were gathered at both ends.

"Johnson!"

The man stopped dialing.

"Add some armor to that order."

"Yes, sir."

"Go." King whispered the word into the mic.

The response was deafening. The tube behind him gave off a muffled thump as the round was dropped down its mouth, only to be spit out a fraction of a second later to arch up over the trees on its way to the mansion.

The explosion was bright and threatened to rob him of his vision through the binoculars. He blinked the spots away as the rumble of the impact reached them and the shockwave wrinkled the snow before him. The man next to him spoke a correction into his own mic, and a few seconds later, another round followed. This one impacting the stone wall and showering the area with boulders.

King let the men with the mortars work while he watched and listened for a response. He was sure there was one in store, but he did not know from where yet. He watched another round impact the wall, and this time a full section gave way and fell into the snow, throwing up a large cloud and masking his view.

It was enough.

"Cease fire. Cease fire."

"Copy cease fire."

"Assault team. Go."

"Roger."

King switched his focus to the tree line, where the assault team was hiding. A pair of flashes marked the location of the grenade launchers, and the smaller rounds traveled the distance quickly but gave no immediate sign of impact. As planned.

A second later, a thick cloud of smoke welled up and began to blanket the open area of snow between the assault team and the wall. It traveled on the slight breeze and was almost back to the trees when the men appeared. Dark shapes emerged from the trees and struggled through the snow toward the gaping hole in the wall.

"Too slow," King muttered, watching the men struggle in the deep snow. One of them faltered and collapsed, and a second later, the report of the shot reached King's ears.

"That sniper! He's still out there!"

The two men scanned the tree above the target, and King was lucky to see the flash of the rifle's second round. He froze on the spot and hit the button on the binoculars and read out the direction and range to the man next to him. He whispered the numbers to the crew behind them.

The J. Edgar Hoover Building

Harper pulled the truck up to the barrier. He'd been tempted to ram the truck through behind the car in front of him but had hesitated when the sound of the air horns had reached him. What they meant, he didn't know, but they had distracted him enough to miss the opportunity. The orange barrier snapped out of the ground much faster than he had expected, and he was sure the guard had a button just for that purpose. If he had tried to follow the car in front of him, he was sure the truck would have ended up pinned to the concrete ceiling of the garage before he could get through. It would not stop the mission, but it might stop his escape. He quickly discarded the thoughts and focused on the guard.

"What are you doing here?" the guard asked.

"They told me to come. It's crazy out there."

The guard examined the windshield and saw the stickers. The laser had already read the barcode and approved it. There was only one problem.

"There's no trucks allowed in the garage; you guys know that."

"The rules are being broken tonight. I'm not even sure why they want it here," Harper answered while he gazed over the man's head at the controls inside the booth. They were just out of reach.

The guard saw the look and didn't like it. He knew every agent in the building and every member of the Hostage Rescue Team, and this guy was a stranger.

"So, you're saying Fitzgerald called for the truck?"

"Yeah. I just go where they tell me."

The guard just nodded. "Okay, hold on."

Harper nodded but saw the man's expression change before he was fully turned. There was no Fitzgerald. He'd just screwed up.

He reached for the gun, as the door to the booth slammed shut. The man slammed his fist down on a button, just as Harper fired.

The thick glass shattered under the impact but held. Harper continued to pump rounds into it, one after the other.

Bullet proof glass is not forever. It has a major enemy. Sunlight. Sunlight slowly eroded the glass's integrity until it was no longer serviceable. Because of this, it required frequent replacement. The booth the guard stood in every day faced east, and as a result the sunlight hit it full force for several hours a day. It was changed monthly and was scheduled for its next replacement in two days.

Despite this weakness, the glass held for the first few rounds, but by the time the fourth round from the .44 Desert Eagle had fired, it was failing. The fifth round punched its way through and hit the guard in his right side. He collapsed against the opposite wall, and his own gun fell from his hand.

Harper fired at the glass twice more, before sending his foot into it. It required two strong kicks, but he was soon through. He switched hands and reached inside to punch the buttons.

Nothing moved. The gate stayed up.

He punched some more, before returning to the original. This time, he held the button down and was rewarded by the barrier slowly sinking into the ground.

"C'mon!" he screamed at it, but it continued to move at a snail's pace. Harper revved the engine in frustration and was about to yell at the leisurely pace of the barrier again, when the windshield shattered. A round zipped through the cockpit of the truck, barely missing his face.

The sound of the shot did not come from the building, but from the street to his right.

Harper spun to return fire.

THE MANSION

CATER SMILED as he worked the bolt. The assault team were hampered by the deep snow, and the first shot had been an easy one. He'd taken out a man with a light machine gun and then another with a M203 grenade launcher. He slammed the bolt home and looked for his next target, but before he could find one, he was forced to duck behind the tree next to him.

The mortar round impacted only a few yards away, and if not for the tree and the small depression he was in, he'd have been shredded by the flying shrapnel.

"Son of a—"

The branches above him shivered as machine gun fire raked them, dumping their load of snow on him and destroying any visibility he had. They had his location pinned. It was time to go.

He rolled to his right twice and found the long depression in the snow under a fallen tree. He used its overhead cover for as long as he could to leave the area. He was fifty meters away from his sniper position when the machine guns stopped, and he waited a few seconds for a coming mortar rounds.

"No? Saving them for the house?" he asked his adversary.

Whatever their reasons, he was not one to look a gift horse in the mouth. He scrambled up and headed deeper into the trees, following the map in his head to the spot he'd been pointed to.

If he hadn't been looking for it, he would have run right by. But the stump was prominent, and the flat area next to it drew his attention. He stomped it until he got a hollow sounding return, and then quickly swept the snow aside.

A steel plate painted in woodland camouflage. One with a door in it. He worked the mechanical lock using the number Charlie had sent to him, and the door gave. He yanked it open with a loud screech, to reveal a ladder leading down.

"All right, Charlie. Here I come."

18

"All tyranny needs to gain a foothold is for people of good conscience to remain silent."

—*Edmund Burke*

THE J. EDGAR HOOVER BUILDING

J ack bounded down the stairs three at a time with Sydney and Eric in tow. They had just reached the third floor when the alarm sounded, and by the time they hit the ground floor, several agents had joined them. They burst out into the lobby with guns drawn but were met with nothing but an empty room and con-fused front desk personnel.

"Did it say where?" Sydney asked.

Before Jack could reply, a second alarm sounded, this one followed by a recorded female voice calmly informing them of a triggered alarm at the main parking gate. The agents dispersed, half of them heading out the front doors, the other half heading back into the stairwell. They had just burst out the steel door, when the first shots rang out. Jack ran toward them, the Glock pistol locked in his fist. Eric and Sydney followed his lead and produced their own weapons just as the truck came into view.

"Spread out!" Jack ordered.

Agents moved left and right and used the cars as cover as they converged on the truck. Jack ig-nored the cover in favor of speed. He now saw the windshield shatter, and the flash of a handgun from inside the truck fire back. He dove across the hood of a car and spun to look for its source. He spotted Larry, an ancient .357 Magnum in his hand, on the sidewalk just as a bullets impact spun him to the ground.

"Larry!"

Sydney's yell was the only thing that saved Larry from his own fellow agents. Jack spun back to the truck and began pumping rounds into it as fast as his finger could stroke the trigger. Several agents followed him and soon the truck was being shredded by multiple rounds from several directions. Jack emptied a magazine and quickly slammed another home, before pausing to take a new look at the target.

"Cease fire! Cease fire!"

The cry was taken up and repeated until the last weapon went silent. Jack exchanged a look with Eric, and they both moved forward under the watchful eyes of their fellow agents until they reached the door of the truck. Jack gestured, and Eric grasped the handle. With a nod from Jack, Eric flung it open, and Jack swiveled into the opening, his weapon tracking left to right.

Nothing. The opposite door was open, and there was nobody there.

"Stay put!" Jack yelled to everyone behind him. Entering the cab, he stuck his head around the corner over the barrel of the Glock and scanned the back of the truck. What he saw made the blood leave his face.

"Bradford!"

NEW YORK CITY

"YOU AND YOU, stop once we're inside and secure the door!" the man hissed before crouching down before the door. The two men nodded at the command and raised their shotguns to point at the ceiling while the three men in front of them made ready to burst through the door.

The leader gave them ten seconds to catch their breath from the run up the twelve flights of steps, before turning the nob and diving through. The men were well-trained, and they passed through the door and into the marbled entryway and moved left and right. The body of a guard siting in the corner distracted them for only a moment before they moved to the inner door. The light from the one window was barely enough to light their path. The leader positioned the two men at the rear before the rest of them stacked up at the door.

On his signal they moved through and began

clearing the rooms on their way toward the back. Their shotguns panning left and right and their fingers tense on the trigger as they moved with leapfrogging movements deeper into the penthouse, each of them seeking a target.

"Clear."

"Clear."

The word was hissed repeatedly as they moved, until they reached the master suite.

"In here!"

The leader entered the room to find his man down on a knee over their boss. The man's shirt was soaked a crimson red. He'd been shot several times.

"Is he dead?"

"Very."

"What about him?"

14TH STREET BRIDGES, WASHINGTON, D. C.

"GET the hell out of the way!" Colonel Hurst screamed at the traffic.

He had assembled a convoy of deuce-and-a-half trucks, a half-dozen Hummers and a pair of Bradleys, before driving the streets of the base and loading as many armed Marines as he could. When the count had reached a hundred, Colonel Hurst had labeled it enough and directed them out into the streets. A pair of police cars lead them to the highway, and they straddled the centerline as cars bailed out the way in both directions. His marines had experience on the streets of Bagdad and Kandahar and didn't hesitate to bump the civilian vehicles off the road when they refused to move fast enough. Throwing up chunks of asphalt behind them, the Bradleys raced toward the city center.

"What the hell is that?"

"It's the bridge, sir."

What had once a faint glow had now become a column of flame as they approached the bridge. A roadblock of firetrucks and civilian traffic stopped the convoy cold, and Hurst scrambled out and onto the roof of the hummer to see what was ahead.

It was not what he had expected.

The bridge ahead was blocked by at least three busses. Each planted sideways across every lane and throwing flames into the air. There was no way across that he could see, and the fires were only getting bigger.

The reason for that was the hundreds of

people standing between the bridge and the firemen. Row after row of civilians stood locked arm
in arm, across the wide expanse of the road. Their
backs to the flames, they seemed to be waiting
calmly for whatever happened next. He scanned
their hands and saw no weapons.

"Holy shit, look at that!"

Hurst followed the soldier's pointed finger and
saw the Arlington Memorial Bridge to the west
also engulfed in flames. The dancing light reflecting off the river's cold water, drowning out the
moonlight.

"What the hell ..."

A fire chief appeared out of the maze.

"You in charge?"

"Yeah," Hurst yelled back. "What's the
situation?"

"They've crashed the busses into the barriers
on both sides and lit them up. All the tires are
blown. Even if they weren't on fire, I'd need some
heavy equipment to move them. And I can't get
close because of the crowd."

"Are they armed?"

"I haven't seen any guns."

"Where's the cops?"

"Everywhere. Nine-one-one has been jammed
for hours, and the reserve units we called for all

went down when they tried to respond. Somebody sabotaged their tires. Same thing at the armory. A group attacked it and disabled all the vehicles. You guys are it."

Hurst absorbed the information while he examined the line of people. What the hell was this? A protest? A coup? A riot? It didn't look like a riot; they were just standing there.

"They got a leader?"

"Not sure."

"Well, shit. Hold this." He handed his driver his sidearm and then walked toward the crowd. He could feel the heat from the flames as he got closer and examined the faces of the men standing by with hoses. It gave him an idea, but he didn't want to go there yet. He stopped several feet short of the line.

"Who's in charge?"

The people exchanged looks but offered no response.

"Talking beats the alternative, people! Somebody better speak up!"

A few more nervous looks traveled among them. Hurst watched their general direction and centered his gaze on the older man in the middle of the line. He took two steps closer to the man and fixed his gaze on him.

"If nobody wants to talk to me, it's going to be tear gas and firehoses pretty quick. What's it going to be?"

An old woman spoke up. "You can shoot if you need to, Colonel. I'm not scared."

Hurst hesitated and then examined the line closer. Most were dressed for the weather, and they all had their faces covered, but there was enough showing for him to see they ranged from all ages, races, and economic levels.

"What is this? Why are you here?"

The man finally spoke.

"We don't wish anyone any harm, Colonel. But we can't let you through yet."

Yet? Hurst thought. What does that mean?

"I don't want to hurt anyone, either. But I have my orders, and that requires us crossing this bridge, and I'll do what I have to do so. If that means—"

"What? That you'll shoot us? Unarmed civilians? We're just standing here, Colonel. Do what you have to do. Like this woman said, we'll hold still."

Hurst tried to stare the man down, but it was no use. The man met his gaze with tired but determined eyes that showed no sign of backing down. The lights of several cell phones were now shining as the people filmed the exchange. Hurst had no doubt he was being broadcast live via some social network.

"This is not how we do things here!" Hurst said.

"It is today."

"You leave me no choice, here."

"We understand, Colonel. We didn't have one, either."

Hurst spun on his booted heel and stalked back to the line of firemen. The cold wind chose that moment to travel up the river and enter his coat, and it chilled him as he examined the men and their hoses. Each of them charged and ready to douse the flames still engulfing the busses. The chief joined him.

"What do we do?"

Hurst turned and examined the people again. None of them had moved. The fog of their breath showed in the frigid temperatures and traveled on the wind to the west.

Maybe that was the way. He turned to the chief.

"Hose them down. But do it gently."

The chief frowned but quickly saw the wisdom of the decision. He pulled out his radio to address the men he commanded. Hurst returned to his hummer.

"Sir, they've lost communication with the Capitol Building."

"Okay ... tell the Bradleys to move up to the front here ... and call the base. Have them get ahold of every ambulance they can and get it here."

"Sir? Are we going to—"

"I hope not. Just a lot of very cold people."

"Yes, sir."

Hurst turned back around in time to see the hoses come to life. The multiple streams of water arched skyward and met the freezing temperatures of the night air before falling on the crowd below. They all shielded their faces from the icy blast but remained locked arm in arm across the bridge. Behind them, the fires, just out of range, looked like they were lessening.

How long their resolve would last against the onslaught, Hurst didn't know. He hoped it would not be long.

The noise of the Bradley Fighting Vehicles brought his head around. He pointed left and right, and the vehicles stopped where all could see them. Hurst used his radio.

"Pan your cannon around and let them get a good look at it. While you're doing that, figure out the best way to shove those busses out of the way. And whatever you do, don't run over any of their fire hoses!"

"Yes, sir. But what if they won't move?"

"I'm giving them some time to move. After that, we use the gas."

"Sir? I ..."

"You got a better idea?"

"... No, sir."

WASHINGTON, D.C.

HARPER SHED the jacket as he ran and turned it inside out before donning it again. The FBI hat went into the nearest storm drain, and the new one was on his head a second later. By the time he entered the street, he was just another protestor.

Dodging the bottleneck gathered around the burning car at the intersection, he moved further north. The street was clogged with disabled cars and people, and he cursed them as he traveled. If they had done this for the next three blocks, he was going to be forced to find alternative transportation.

A car appeared at the curb. A young man sat in the driver's seat with his phone on the steering wheel. He ignored the people all around him in favor of what was happening on the screen. Harper left the curb and circled around him, examining the door from a different angle.

It was unlocked. Exhaust fumes fogged the air behind the car. The engine was running. The man was taking a break from the street and warming himself up while he checked on what was happening.

The street was full of people but looked free of disabled cars. His own was several blocks farther away.

It was an easy decision.

19

"Experience hath shewn, that even under the best forms of government those entrusted with power have, in time, and by slow operations, perverted it into tyranny."

—Thomas Jefferson

KANSAS CITY, KANSAS

The roar of the ATV's engine brought him out of the scope, and he looked to his right to see the ATV's headlight aimed right at him. He spun and fired at it, but its bobbing beam kept coming. The light was quickly doused and replaced by the rapid-fire flashes of an automatic weapon. Lee rolled behind the tree and abandoned the rifle, triggering the timer and rolling away from it, before getting to his feet and unslinging the submachine gun. His legs were stiff from laying on the cold ground for so long, and he stumbled once as he sought better cover.

He had just ducked down behind a thicker tree when rounds impacted the branches over his head. He spun to return the fire from the guard by the pool, before realizing the man was hopelessly out of range and only shooting in Lee's general direction. He saved his ammo and moved again, this time seeking out the ATV's location.

It was between him and his planned path out. He paused when the guard did, and Lee thought he heard a shouted voice. The man was on a radio or a phone of some kind, calling for help.

That would not do.

It would soon be three against one, with more on the way. Lee needed a way to even those odds. He bolted back the way he had come.

The rifle was where he had left it, and the timer was down to seconds. He stripped off a glove and thumbed the device off, before resetting it and tossing it away. The submachine gun was tossed over his back on its sling, and he took up the rifle again.

Ignoring the man behind him, he ran toward the house, counting down the seconds in his head.

The trees were now whistling as the wind moved through their upper branches. It distorted the sound of the ATV behind him, and he could only guess at its direction as it searched for him. Lee forced the man from his mind and focused on the house. Its lights would silhouette anyone between him and it, and Lee knew he would only have a second or two to capitalize on that when the time came. He scanned with both eyes, waiting.

The man appeared suddenly from behind the pump house, ducking low and running for the ATV parked off to one side. An M4 held firmly in his hands. Lee swung the rifle right and centered the crosshairs on the ATV. A second later, the man leaped aboard and reached for the ignition. Lee's finger stroked the trigger.

The round slammed into the man, who rolled off and onto the snow to land flat on his back. He twitched once and then no longer moved, and Lee dismissed him. He rolled left twice before rising to his knees, his ears still ringing from the shot.

Splinters showered his face as the tree he was behind absorbed rounds from the other guard's rifle. Lee fired off a shot in the man's direction without looking, before bolting for thicker cover. He traveled thirty meters and found some thick brush, before pausing to look and listen.

The ATV was now silent. The man was not an amateur—he had quickly gotten within range and then abandoned the noisemaker in favor of moving silently on foot. Lee scanned the trees with his eyes, and then again with the scope, and saw nothing. He opened his mouth wide until his ears popped and his hearing improved. All he heard was the wind, but that lasted for only a few seconds.

The distant sound of a turbine engine began to scream, and Lee realized that the helicopter was firing up.

"Starting to get interesting."

He scanned the area again without seeing his quarry. What would he do? He would wait, Lee decided. If the helicopter pilot had night vision goggles, he could find him and report to the man on the ground. He was no doubt waiting to see what the pilot found. Either way, it was time to move. Lee had less than a minute left.

As he had predicted, the helicopter circled left to find the trail left by the ATV. Lee followed it long enough to confirm this and tracked the bird as it flew lower. It was moving toward the area Lee had shot from, and he wondered how close the guard from the ATV was to that spot. If he was there in the next thirty seconds, he was in for a surprise. Lee moved the scope from the bird to the ground and back, waiting. The bird suddenly stopped and pulled into a hover. Lee moved the scope along its shape and centered on the section right below the rotor.

The explosion of the small charge he had left behind was an expected surprise, and Lee flinched only slightly when it happened. He stroked the trigger three times in rapid sequence, and was rewarded by a high-pitched squeal as the heavy rounds tore into the bird's transmission. The aircraft immediately began to spin and throw out smoke.

But the pilot was a skilled one. He cut the power and bottomed the pitch of the rotors enough to salvage enough lift for him to set the aircraft down. The skids pranged loudly on impact, and one crumpled, throwing the bird on its side. The tail and main rotors destroyed themselves on the hard ground and nearby trees, showering the area with steel and fiberglass as the bird spun in place. It came to a halt in a shower of dirt and pine branches.

The rifle fell from his grip as the round tore into his shoulder and flung him to the ground. He rolled on impact and clenched his teeth as the arm went numb. He was back on his feet and running before the pain hit, and he used his good arm to feel his way through the trees. Another round zipped past his ear, and he ducked into thicker vegetation trying to conceal his escape. After a hundred meters, he took cover behind a large tree and inspected the wound.

It was bad. A through and through, the round had entered his triceps from the front and taken a good chunk of meat with it as it left. The pain was really spiking now, and he bit his lip as he struggled to wrap the wound up. He shoved a glove into the wound and tied a bandage over it with his teeth, before putting it out of his mind and taking up the submachine gun. He made sure the safety was still off, before hoisting it and looking behind him.

Was the man still following? His boss was dead, so he had no reason to. But he would, as

Lee admitted that he would if he were in his position. Professionalism? Or maybe he was just pissed? Either way, Lee had to leave. Cursing the trail of blood he was leaving behind, he moved on.

The J. Edgar Hoover Building

JACK STOOD FROZEN between the seats as he stared into the back. The rocking of the truck made him cringe as Bradford came aboard.

"Is that what I think it is?" Jack pointed.

"Holy..." Bradford said. "Get everybody out of the building."

Jack moved out of the way, and Bradford carefully crawled over the center console and into the back.

"I need light."

Jack padded down his pockets but found nothing. He was about to leave and find a flashlight, when they were both dazzled by a bright light. Eric had activated his cell phone. He took in the barrels and the wires leading to them and asked the question of the night.

"What the hell is going on?"

"Get everyone out of the building," Jack told him.

"They're on it already," Eric replied.

Bradford was now on his belly, examining the wiring beneath. He traced it to the center console and then examined the lock.

"I need tools!" he cursed.

Eric slid his backpack from his back and dug inside. He pulled out a small tool kit and offered it.

"I was building a new server, so it's not a big kit."

Bradford cracked it open and looked inside, before selecting a screwdriver.

"It'll do. Jack, leave."

"I—"

"No, you don't. It's a two-man job. Get out of here."

Bradford had a command voice of his own when it was needed, and Jack did as he was told, leaving the two men behind. He stepped outside to find an agent waiting.

"They're evacuating the building and the ones on both sides. But, Jack, all these people. I don't—"

"We do what we can. What's going on at the Capitol Building?"

"I don't know. I ... Is that Larry?"

The agent turned and saw a man slumped

against the building. He was clutching his chest, a pool of blood spreading out on the cold concrete below him. Sydney was bent over him.

"Oh, my god."

THE HOUSE CHAMBER

THE HUSBAND and wife followed the small group in front of them as they moved into the building. So far, they had lost three, but they had the momentum. The agents seemed split as to what to do, the majority retreating while others had wisely surrendered their weapons. One had required the use of a shotgun, and after the round lifted the man off his feet, he was quickly surrounded and subdued. His vest and the bean bag round saving his life. Like the others, he was assigned a keeper and left in place.

"There!"

They followed the direction indicated and came to a large set of double doors. No doubt, there were armed men on the other side. But they had a plan for that.

The lock was merely a suggestion, but it had been thrown anyway. The Husband watched as the men produced a rope and slipped it through the handles. With a team effort, they yanked the doors open and then stepped aside, waiting for the expected fusillade of bullets.

The Husband waited.

Noise from inside sounded, as other doors were forced open. He held the radio to his ear.

"Door three, we're in."

"Door five, in."

"Door two is open."

When it was announced they had access to the last door, The Husband stepped forward.

"You, inside! I wish to speak to the chairman of the joint chiefs."

"Who are you?"

"That is not important. You have thirty seconds, before we take the chamber by force."

The people inside spoke at once and were quickly quieted by someone inside. The Husband waited for his answer. It was not long.

"Wait."

"This is the Chairman. Who am I speaking to?"

"Who I am is unimportant, General. I asked for you, as I am sure you can understand the tactical situation. We number in the thousands and hold every entrance. Let's avoid a costly battle."

"And then?"

"We will be heard."

The general shared a look with the Secret Service agent next to him. The man shook his head, but the general was a man who had seen many battles and understood when he was beaten.

"Is the president away?" he whispered.

The agent spoke into his sleeve for a few seconds, before nodding to the affirmative.

"Tell your men to hold their fire. No shooting. You understand?"

The agent was junior to the general by two decades, and the salad bar of medals decorating his lapel contrasted sharply with the dull gray suit the agent wore. It only served to give strength to the general's command voice. The agent did as the man said.

THE GENERAL STEPPED BACK, and the Husband entered. He took one long look around as the world stared back. The people stood, even those in the balcony. The vice president and the speaker of the house stood behind their chairs on the dais, each of them behind a Secret Service agent. Despite the general's order, numerous guns were trained on him, but he dismissed them as his people filed in behind him and spread out.

"They will surrender their weapons," he spoke.

It was not an order; he said it as if he were merely stating a future event. The general watched as the crowd continued to swell, several of them breaking away to gather in circles around each agent.

"Put them down," the general loudly ordered.

The agents looked at one another. They had never trained for this. Their first mission—safeguard and remove their principals—had been thwarted in the first minute of the attack. They had been forced to hold in place, and now they had nowhere to go. The agents recognized what the general had already seen: They had no options left.

One agent lowered his gun and placed it on the floor. Then another. And soon, they all did. The Husband let out a sigh of relief. The agents were carefully approached and restrained, each receiving a keeper who led them out of the room.

"With me, please, General," the Husband said.

The Husband walked the center aisle, and the general followed a step back and one to the left. It was ingrained—he did so without thinking. His thoughts were elsewhere, as he searched for a way out. The Husband had said he wished to be heard. The general wasn't sure what that meant, but he would play along until an option presented. He exchanged looks with his fellow joint chiefs as they climbed the dais. None of them offered any ideas.

The Husband stepped to the microphone and listened to his radio briefly, before reaching out and adjusting it. When he spoke, his voice was calm and measured, but it brooked no argument.

"Remove them."

The general watched as the crowd moved. It was soon apparent to his trained eye that this had been well-planned. What he had thought was a spontaneous attack by a protesting mob had revealed itself to be a coordinated effort. He now watched as the balconies were emptied, and the non-government people were escorted out. The TV stations' crews were also removed, and several of the initial attackers went with them. As they exited, the doors were slammed shut, one by one.

The most ominous sign were the ones who picked their way through the seats behind the representatives. It was as if they knew where they were going but had never been there before. Each of the politicians, man and woman alike, now had a two-person shadow. Others walked the spaces in front of them with newly liberated submachine guns. The movement stopped once everyone had their new keepers. No one was spared, including the joint chiefs of staff and the entire presidential cabinet. The justices of the Supreme Court nervously eyeballed the masked people standing over them. The balcony was now empty and lined with faceless people.

The vice president broke the silence.

"You'll never get away with this! We'll find you! We'll find all of you! It's just a matter of—"

"Time, Mr. Vice President? You've had enough time," the Husband answered, before turning to face the room. "All of you have. Now it is *our* time."

He was joined on the dais by a woman. One who held a large envelope in her hand. He turned and faced the chairman.

"The president?"

"They took him away. I won't tell you where."

"I would not expect you to, sir. No matter. Thank you, General." He signaled to the two men behind him, and the man was escorted back to his seat.

"Take them!"

With some cries and a few physical protests,

the legislatures were quickly bound hand and foot, their mouths were covered in tape, and their heads hooded. When it was complete, the Husband turned to his wife.

"I'll find him. Are you okay, here?"

"We'll be fine."

He left the dais and walked down the center aisle. He met a group of men on the other side of the door, just as his wife called the first name. They shut it firmly behind him, before speaking.

"We found him. He's trapped in a room, in the basement."

"Outside?"

"No response yet. The plan is working. But..."

"What is it?"

"Did you hear the man's speech?"

"No, I was in the crowd. I saw the news release, and I had already seen a copy."

"That's not the speech he gave. You better watch this, then. I queued it to the beginning."

He produced a phone, on which the Husband saw the frozen image of the President on the dais he had just left.

"Take me to him, first."

20

"Anywhere, anytime ordinary people are given the chance to choose, the choice is the same: freedom, not tyranny; democracy, not dictatorship; the rule of law, not the rule of the secret police."

—*Tony Blair*

D espite the cold, Bradford was sweating. He'd forced everything out of his mind, except the device before him. He'd done this before, sometimes while under fire. First as a SEAL and then with EOD. He'd dismantled countless IEDs in Iraq and Afghanistan, only to come home and do so again with a homegrown terrorist. Now they were here, at his own building.

Seeing no anti-tamper device in place, he unscrewed the hinges holding the box shut. With Eric holding the phone, Bradford pried the box open a fraction of an inch and peered inside. Wires. A circuit board. A timer. He examined the lock on the other side and saw nothing attached.

"Good."

"What?"

"Nothing. Grab this lid here and here, and when I say, pry it up," he instructed.

Eric did so, and Bradford watched carefully as the gap increased. The lock protested, and Eric moved his feet for better leverage, before applying his back to it. The lid bent some more. When it was enough for Bradford to get his hands inside it, he stopped him.

"Gimme that phone."

Bradford took it and activated the camera, before snaking it inside the box. He took several pictures of what he couldn't see and then examined them with a critical eye. Eric caught the reflection of the timer counting down in the phone's shiny surface and swallowed. Under a minute. Bradford showed no sign of moving.

"Uh ... Brad?"

"Hold on."

The timer continued, mocking him. Eric started to sweat.

"Brad?"

He was ignored. With less than thirty seconds left, Bradford dropped the phone.

"Pull!"

Eric followed the order immediately, and Bradford snaked his hand in the opening to grasp a wire. With a solid yank, he pulled it free, and the timer stopped with fourteen seconds remaining.

He held up the wire and grinned at Eric.

"Fourteen seconds? Aren't you supposed to wait till there's only one?"

"A movie star, I am not," he replied.

They both had a short nervous laugh, before collapsing on the metal floor.

NEW YORK CITY

"WHAT DO YOU THINK HAPPENED?"

"I don't know; looks like somebody got in here. I ... Holy shit!"

"What?"

The man moved away from the window and to the body of the guard on the floor. The man had just raised a bloody hand.

"This one's still alive! Get EMS up here!"

The security man stared wide-eyed as his partner pulled the man free of the corner. The man groaned as his head hit the marble, and the bloody trail left behind him made the guard step back.

"Stop staring and call them!"

He fumbled with this radio.

"Yeah, uh, this is Johnson. I'm upstairs, and we got a man down. Looks like one in the chest. Yeah...Yeah ... I don't know—just get EMS up here, now!"

———

DANNY FOUGHT his way through the crowd, but it was hard to make any real progress. They all seemed determined to move slowly and crowd the path as much as possible. Due to his height he couldn't see much, as the crowd averaged well above his 5'8. So when he finally broke free and emerged out into the wide-open expanse of the mall, he stopped to gather his bearings.

People. Thousands of them. They crowded the mall like he hadn't seen since the inauguration. But something was different. This crowd was masked. They would look like normal winter wear in any other setting, but here they took on a different meaning. The people moved past him in twos and threes, and he found their eyes examining him as they did. He was not masked, and therefore out of place. It made him a bit nervous. He fumbled in his coat for his press pass. A laminated card that announced his occupation to all who would need to know. He hoped it would work here.

Another sight caught his attention. The benches. They were all bare. No one was sitting. The cars were all moving at the same slow, deliberate, zombie-like pace as the crowd on the sidewalk. It was unnerving, and he searched for an explanation. The one his mind produced sent a shiver down his spine.

Gridlock. That was their goal. They were shutting the city down with their own bodies and glacial pace. The masks kept their identities hidden from the thousands of cameras in the city, and the constant movement denied the police an excuse to arrest them. If that was the case, then ...

Danny jumped up on one of the empty benches and gazed out over the crowd. It was like a single living organism. A giant amoeba pulsing and flowing in and around the city, with the Capitol Building in its center. He could see the roofs of police cars and broadcast trucks which had been swallowed up by it and the denser areas which crowded the access points in every direction. Even at its thinnest, there was only a matter of feet between the people. Fires burned in the distance down some streets, and the wail of sirens could be heard coming from multiple directions. Danny stared at it in awe and then cursed himself for not bringing a camera. He shot a few pictures with his phone, but after getting several looks from the passing crowd, quickly thought better of it, and stowed it away in his coat.

Making sure his press pass was showing, he jumped back down and faded into the crowd again. He began moving toward the capitol dome as fast as the crowd would allow him to.

He'd gone only a few yards when a helicopter roared overhead.

KENSINGTON, MARYLAND

HARPER TURNED another corner before slowing down and finding a dark spot to back into. After assuring he had a clear view back the way he had come, he turned on the car's radio and began cycling through the local stations.

Nothing but chatter and speculation. And commercials. It was the greatest crisis the United States had seen since 9-11, but the commercials still had to go on, as if anyone was thinking about asking their doctor about the latest drug from Big Pharma tonight. If he wasn't so pissed off, he would have laughed at its absurdity.

Time. Only six minutes. It had seemed like forever. But he knew periods of intense activity and adrenaline often seemed to last longer. His own heart was still racing, and he forced himself to relax. The heater had been set at high and had blasted him with cold air the second he had taken the car. He'd been too busy to adjust it, and it now hit him at its maximum output.

But Harper was warm enough. Sweating, even. He thumbed the fan down to a lower setting, before sitting back and checking the time again. One minute. An odd whistle caught his attention, and he found its source in a neat bullet hole punched through the passenger door. The wind gave it a voice when it gusted, and he could feel the stream of cold air on his hand when he held it up. Whoever had shot at him had missed, but he gave them props for trying.

A helicopter flew overhead and roared off in the direction of the Capitol Building. The helicopter's path might even take it over the building he had just left.

"Might want to gain a little altitude," he told it. The helicopter ignored him, of course, and flew on, its spotlight now probing the ground below. He dismissed it and checked the clock again.

Any time, now. He sank lower in the seat and watched the gap between the buildings. Normally, he would exit the area after a job like this, but not this time; this one, he wanted to see.

"Goodbye, Jack."

WASHINGTON, D. C., AIRSPACE

"THE ROOF?" the pilot asked.

"Negative," was the answer from the back. "All the units on the roof have gone quiet. Find a spot near the entrance."

The HRT pilot was good. A former pilot with the Delta Force, he had flown missions in nine different counties, several of them under fire. He could thread the tiny helicopter down the narrow streets, with the buildings only feet from the rotors on both sides and drop the team off wherever they pointed.

But today he was being defeated. Not by terrain, or architecture, or even enemy fire, but by people. And not combatants, but his own countrymen. It was a dilemma he had never given any thought to, and he was stymied as to how to deal with it.

"There's no clear area."

"Make one."

The pilot grunted and spun the tiny bird into a banking turn. The men in the back were dressed for the weather. Thick underwear insulated them from the biting cold under their fatigues and armor. Fingerless gloves made of leather did little to protect their exposed skin, so many were having a hard time maintaining their grip on the handholds.

Spotting the street in front of the Capitol Building, he picked a spot between two police cars and settled the bird down slowly. The blast of wind and the temperature would surely be enough to drive the people back and allow him to land.

But the opposite happened. The crowd surged toward him from every direction and planted themselves under the sinking aircraft. Hands reached up to meet it, and the men in the back yelled over the din of the spinning rotors.

"They aren't moving!"

The pilot peddle-turned and saw the same thing in every direction. He let the aircraft sink a few feet more and felt a jerk as a member of the crowd leaped up to grab the skid. The aircraft rocked and threatened to tip.

"What the hell?"

The pilot increased the power to the main rotors, and the bird climbed, dragging the weight of the man with it. Several members of the crowd grabbed his legs, and the bird struggled to stay upright as they were slowly pulled skyward.

"Get them off us!"

The HRT operators kicked at the man's hands, until he finally let go and fell back into the waiting arms of the crowd. The bird surged skyward when the load was jettisoned, and the pilot let it before slewing it around for another look. He spotted masked men cheering the crowd on from the roof of the Capitol. Men in dark clothing laid tied at their feet. Their numbers were in the hundreds.

"Fast rope?"

"They'd just drag us down."

"Well, then what?"

"I don't know! Come up with something!"

The HRT leader gazed out at the passing crowd and saw no clear spaces. Even if he did, the crowd would quickly fill them if they tried to land. There was only one way to get into the building, and it would require an action he was not willing to take.

He felt the eyes of his men on him and looked up to see them all reading his face. First one and then the rest, all shook their heads.

They were not going to fire on their own people.

"Damn it! Circle around the other side!"

The pilot did as ordered, and the team watched the lite-up dome of the Capitol Building rotating beneath them. But the view on the other side was the same they had seen. People. Thousands of them. Even if they found a place to land, there was no way they would ever get to the building. The fires burning in the distant intersections only drove the revelation home.

"RTB."

"Say again?" the pilot asked.

"Return to base. They'll have to find another way to them."

"Roger." The pilot banked left and flew over the crowd again on its way to the Hoover Building. The roar of the mass below them reached them, claiming victory. The HRT commander set his jaw and stewed, the icy wind not even felt as they retreated.

"What the hell is going on?" he muttered.

His men had no answer. With a sigh, he switched frequencies to inform them of their failure, knowing he might be ordered to do the unthinkable.

He already had his answer to that.

Instead of the rebuke he expected, he was told to vacate the area. No explanation. He relayed this to the pilot, and he did as ordered, flying them higher and circling the area.

"Now what?"

One of his men tapped his arm and pointed. The bridge over the Potomac River drew his attention. It was covered in burning vehicles and hundreds of people. The lights of several fire trucks reflected off the water. A column of military vehicles was stopped behind them.

"Are they spraying those people?"

New York City

THE HEAD of the Security team was still trying to piece together what had happened. What he did know was that his boss was dead, and he wasn't looking forward to what lay ahead for him because of that.

"Looks like one guy. Don't know how he got in. The boss's gun is empty. Looks like he connected at least twice. Must have been one hell of a shootout."

"You sure there was only one?"

"We checked every room twice. There was just him and the two guards we found. Plus, the masked man here."

"How's the other guy? Can he talk?"

"Dunno. He's on his way to the ER."

The Capitol Building

"MR. PRESIDENT?" the Husband called.

"The president is not here," a voice called back from inside.

The masked man next to him held up a cell-phone. On it was a picture of the room around the corner, obviously done in haste and without aim. It showed him a group of six men, all well-armed and surrounding one man in a tight circle. The man's face could be seen between two shoulders of his security detail.

"I have a picture that says otherwise, young man. Mr. President, must we play games like children?"

He waited patiently for a reply, taking in the surroundings while he did so. The basement was tight. A far cry from the expansive halls of the upper floors. The exit sign at the end of the hall told him much. They had been so close. A few more meters and the man would have been in his armored limousine. A few bloodstains adorned the wall and floor, and he grimaced at that.

"Is anyone wounded, sir? Are you all right?"

"I'm fine. One of my agents needs a doctor," the president answered.

The Husband's heart raced. The man had chosen to speak with him.

"Please, send him out. He will be taken care of."

"I don't know you."

"That is true. We have never met. But let us try this, and get started."

"These men will not allow that."

"I see. A trade perhaps. Myself for your man? Perhaps, then we can talk?"

Silence.

"Very well."

"Sir!" an agent objected.

"Do it." the president ordered the man, before calling, "You come in first."

"Agreed."

The Husband shed his coat and handed his tools to the nearest man, before raising his hands and entering the room. He took two steps in and then stepped to the side. The president was hidden by the men, only his shoes were visible behind the wall of steel and muscle.

"Go," the president said.

An agent detached himself from the group and stumbled forward. His shirt soaked a crimson red due to a chest wound. He stumbled in the doorway and was caught by several gloved hands. They carried him away at a rapid pace.

The Husband surveyed the room. It seemed to have several purposes, chief among them storage for custodial supplies. Several shelves occupied one half, while the other seemed to be a small break area. To his right was a table and few folding chairs. He pointed with a raised hand.

"May I?"

Without waiting for an answer, he walked to the closest one and sank into it. The barrels of several weapons followed his every move, but he gave no indication of acknowledging their presence. He kept his hands slow and out, where the men could see them, grasping them in one another and resting them on the table.

"I have a cell phone in my pocket. May I retrieve it?"

The president's face appeared from out of the circle, and he slowly moved the agent further aside so he could see the man. They sized one another up over the small gap between them.

"What do you want?"

"To talk. I'm currently conflicted. I'm told I need to watch your speech. Evidently, it was not the one I was told to expect, and I wish to see it now. So, again, my cell phone?"

The president sized the man up further. About fifty. Educated by his speech and choice of words. The mask hid his face, but not the skin around his eyes or his wrists. The clothes were just clothes. The boots warm and still wet from the snow outside. He was of average height and showing a bit of spare tire at the waste. The President decided to meet him half-way.

"Lower your weapons."

"Sir, I—"

The president reached out and slowly pushed the barrel of the closest agent's submachine gun down. The president waved the others down, as well, and they reluctantly followed. The man then pushed his way out of the circle and walked to the table. The lead agent waved two men to the door, and one at the man on the other side of the table. The weapons found new points of aim.

The president offered his hand.

"Walter Preston."

"John Citizen," the man answered back, and they both smiled.

The man pointed to his shirt pocket, where a cell phone could clearly be seen. The president held up a hand in the direction of the agent and nodded. The Husband retrieved it with two fingers and then set it on the table. After a flick of his finger, they were watching the speech together.

21

"There is no week nor day nor hour when tyranny may not enter upon this country, if the people lose their roughness and spirit of defiance."

—*Walt Whitman*

WASHINGTON, D. C.

Harper cursed when the clock ticked past the allotted time with nothing happening. Had the timer failed? Had someone defeated it? Short of having an EOD tech standing right there, he couldn't see how they could. He waited another full minute to be sure but finally accepted that the truck would not be exploding.

With another curse, he reached for the phone.

"What happened?" Haney asked.

"I'm not sure. I parked it right at the gate, but they drove me off. It should have gone off a full minute ago. Somehow, they defeated the mechanism."

"Then do something!"

"What? Go back and try again? I don't think so."

"Finish the mission!"

"I aim to. Jack Randall's house is close. I'll be there in a few minutes. But he's at the Hoover Building; I saw him."

"So, wait for him."

"I aim to. With his wife."

The connection broke, and Harper pocketed the phone. His boss was operating under a thinly controlled rage. He could hear it in his voice. Whatever else was going on tonight, it was bad. But Harper had no choice but to set it aside. He had a mission to complete; he would deal with the rest later.

With one last look toward the mall, he dropped the car in gear and pulled out onto the street. The Randall home was only a couple miles away. He nudged the car through the traffic as best he could.

TOMMY KEPT his boot on the man's back. He'd been lucky to get a small one, and as soon as they had traveled a block, he'd unbuckled the straps holding him to the gurney and subdued the man while his partner struggled with the traffic. Now he held the knife to the man's neck while his partner drove where he was being told.

"Two more blocks, then find a place to pull over."

After a glance at his partner on the floor in the back, the EMT in the driver's seat did as instructed. Whoever the guy was, he was fast. The driver realized now that the head injury had most likely been self-inflicted, and the Taser barbs planted so they could not be missed. At this point, he no longer cared; he'd just followed the man's instructions and hoped for the best.

"Stop here."

Tommy watched as the man pulled the unit to a halt under the bridge. He then put the rig in park and held up his hands.

"Toss me the keys, your phone, the portable, and the mic. Very slowly."

The driver did as he was told, and Tommy pocketed them before slicing through the mic's cord with one swipe. He then handed the man two zip-ties.

"Your hands, to the wheel. Use your teeth."

The EMT did as he was told.

"Listen up. I'm a good shot. If I hear the horn sound before the five-minute mark, I'll be pumping rounds through this tin box a second later. Understand?"

"Y-yeah."

"Good boy."

Tommy dismissed them and exited out the back, slamming the door behind him. He pulled the bloody suit coat around him and walked off in the direction of the river.

After a few blocks, he pulled out the phone.

"Stephen? Yeah, I'm okay. Change of plans though—I need a ride."

"LARRY!"

Larry groaned as they sat him up. His entire arm and left side were numb. He felt Sydney's hands on him as she probed his body for injuries and opened his eyes in time to see them both come away bloody.

"I need an ambulance!"

The click of a switchblade sounded, and Larry was startled to see it in Sydney's hand. The blade made short work of his coat and shirt, and the cold felt good when it hit his wet skin.

"Damn it, Larry!" she scolded him, working. "Shoot from cover? You may have heard of that in training? I think it was the first week."

"No time," he managed, before grunting in pain.

Sydney's blade made short work of the shirt and soon she had his chest exposed. The round was a big one, and it had entered Larry's chest at an angle, tearing through the right pectoral and then exiting to catch the right bicep. The chest wound was shallow, and she was relieved to see it rise and fall evenly with Larry's breathing.

The arm was a different story. The blood flowed freely and was bright red in color. Her brain screamed in alarm at her as it identified the source.

Brachial Artery.

Larry was bleeding out.

"A belt! Give me a belt!"

The agent standing over her yanked his free and offered it. She looped it around the arm above the wound and cinched it down tight. But here was no hole. The switchblade worked to make one. She held it in place and examined the wound. Both the entry and exit were bad, but the bleeding slowed to a trickle.

"Larry? You still with me?"

Larry groaned. The numbness was leaving, and the pain was making itself known. She grabbed his face with a bloody hand and looked him in the eye. They were glassy and unfocused.

"Larry!"

But he was fading. His face grew even paler, and his eyes closed.

"Larry!"

THE 14TH STREET BRIDGES, WASHINGTON, D. C.

"THEY'RE NOT MOVING, sir. Your orders?"

Hurst glowered at the junior officer but had to admit he was right. Mission first, welfare of the men second. That was the rule. But what if that mission required you to trample your own countrymen?

"We have four men with CS ready, sir."

"Ours or theirs?"

"Ours, sir."

Hurst frowned at that. The police had their own riot-control gas, but what most people didn't know was that it was a far weaker formula than the gas utilized by the military. If he used it on these people, the fallout would be great—not only end his career but impact the people's view of the military for decades to come. It was Tiananmen Square, in America.

"Damn you," he muttered.

"Sir?"

"Nothing."

The captain stewed next to Hurst as he gazed at the crowd. They had been under the assault of the freezing water for several minutes now, and while a few of the elderly had been carried away, the majority had hunkered down and withstood the onslaught. He watched their faces as the water passed over them repeatedly, each of them closing their eyes and gripping the person next to them that much tighter until the hose moved on. They were going nowhere.

"Stop the hoses," he ordered.

The captain replayed the order and then switched mics, ready to order the men to fire the gas. But the colonel had another idea.

"Move the Bradleys up slowly. See if they move."

"Yes, sir."

The Bradleys' engines roared, and they both jumped, before moving slowly toward the line of people. The crowd stood their ground.

Hurst sought out the gaze of the man he had spoken to. He was still in the center of the line, his face and hair now locked in place by the frost that had formed on him. As the treads of the APC rolled across the road, the ice on the road popped and cracked, bringing up the heads of the shivering crowd. Hurst ignored it and kept his eyes on the man until he saw him glaring back. Hurst silently mouthed one word to him.

"Please?"

The man seemed to consider the request, only to then shake his head. Hurst cursed him under his breath for what he was making him do.

"Captain."

"Yes, sir?"

"Tell the men to don their masks. I—"

He was cut off by the sound of air horns. A distant drone sounded from across the river, and soon traveled closer and closer, until the occupants of the bridge joined in with air horns of their own.

"What the hell is that?" Hurst shouted.

Before the man could answer, the crowd parted like the red sea before them. Hurst and the young captain watched with open mouths as the people broke ranks and moved to the side. Several dropped their signs and began making their way down the sidewalks, leaving the scene entirely.

"What the hell? Some kind of signal?"

Hurst didn't care. All he saw were the still smoldering hulks of the busses blocking their way. The people continued to walk away, many of them moving through the gathered firemen and soldiers as if they weren't even there.

"Ignore them and get those damn busses moved!" he ordered.

WILLIAM'S EYES traveled the screens to ignore the muffled impacts of the mortar rounds outside. Several stories below ground, he was not affected by them, but the sounds promised more to come and served as a reminder that time was short.

The ding of an alert drew his attention, and he

saw another communication from their unknown soldier to his boss. He clicked it and quickly read the transcribed call.

"What do I—?"

"Send it on," was the General's immediate reply.

William did so with another series of clicks.

22

"Corruption is just another form of tyranny."

—*Joe Biden*

Capitol Building

"Quite a speech," the Husband said. He was examining the paper copy now.

They had finished watching his performance on the small screen. He
seemed perfectly calm, not caring one bit about
the half-dozen guns aimed at his head.

The president nodded.

"It's not what was prepared. When did you
write it?"

"My wife and I started on it a few minutes after
the phone call was made."

"I see." The Husband had suspected and then
confirmed it by the date scribbled at the top. Al-
though the speech had been printed out, it was on
the first lady's letterhead, and her handwriting was
in the margins here and there along with his. She
was a lawyer, he recalled, and they had the habit
of dating everything they wrote.

"How long?"

The Husband was confused by the question,
and his face showed it.

"I'm sorry, sir?"

"How long have you been planning this? This
was no spontaneous action. You. The people with
you. The protests over the last few weeks. This was
set in motion long ago."

The Husband carefully folded the speech before placing back in its envelope. He set it on the

table between them, but the president chose to leave it be while he waited for his answer.

"Yes, sir. It was. By who, exactly, is hard to say. There were several people, really. Snowden. Manning. Shepherd. People who brought the actions of the government, and those that manipulated it, out into the sunlight. They showed us a fraction of what was really happening, and it prompted others to look deeper. By now, even the most amateur of users knows that there is no such thing as a secure computer, and people with the skills and the knowledge of where to look found their way to us. Many of them were former members of the very agencies that they were exposing. They armed us well."

"I've seen no weapons here tonight."

The Husband smiled and gestured to the many guns in the room aimed at him.

"Not with guns, Mr. President, but with something far more powerful: information. Without it, a gun has nowhere to aim. And this—" he once again gestured to the firepower in the room "—this becomes secondary."

"This information you speak of. Does it occupy envelopes? Ones with letters on them?"

"You're referring to the Shepherds? I assure

you, I am not one of them. But we have received information from them, information that has helped us make many important decisions."

"Nobody elected you." The president stated.

"Or you." The Husband shot back.

The president grimaced at the remark. The truth of it biting deep. The man was right: He'd been chosen. Selected. Shopped for and then bought, trained, and then operated by others.

An uncomfortable silence filled the room. The man, whoever he was, was in no hurry. It was if he was waiting for something and had decided to have a chat with the president while doing so. What he was waiting for dominated the president's mind, and he was caught off guard by the next question.

"I'm curious, sir. What about tomorrow? What did you plan to do?"

"My wife and I were going home. We have a farm in Vermont. The kids are there already."

"You had to know that your words would require action. Investigations. Charges. By resigning, you lose presidential privilege—you could go to prison."

The president met his gaze with a calm shrug. The Husband saw it now. The president knew his future and had accepted it already. He was now a man resigned to his fate, whatever it might be. The two men contemplated each other, now with a new understanding.

Outside the room, a cellphone rang. The two men waited in silence until the whispered conversation was over, and the man relayed the message to the Husband in two words.

"They're finished," his voice told them.

"Yes." The Husband acknowledged the message before drumming his fingers on the table. The president watched in silence as the man churned a thought in his head—what it was, he could only guess.

"If your men would refrain from shooting me, sir, I have something in my coat I would like you to have."

The president turned to the lead agent. "Lower your guns."

"Sir, I—"

"It's okay."

The president waved the barrels down until first one, and then the others slowly did so. The Husband opened his coat, so the men could see inside, and extracted a large envelope with two fingers. He set it on the table and slide it toward the president. The words on its front were plainly clear.

President Walter Preston.

The president contemplated it with dread. It was similar to other envelopes he had previously seen in pictures. Case files. Pictures with evidence markers attached. It was an envelope from the Twelve Shepherds.

"My misdeeds?"

"Yes."

A nod. "What happens now?"

"That, sir, is not up to either one of us."

The Husband slowly stood, so as not to alarm the agents, and the president stood with him. Neither offered their hand.

The Husband looked down and reached for his phone on the table lying next to the two envelopes.

"May I keep this?"

The president followed the pointed finger and saw it resting on the envelope containing his speech. He looked from it to the man's eyes and back. The speech had been broadcast. He had a copy of it on his phone. There was nothing different about his copy other than ...

"Yes."

"Thank you."

The president and his security detail watched closely as the man pocketed the envelope and phone before turning to leave. He paused at the door for one last message.

"Sir, I would need you and your men to wait a few moments before departing. The sight of all these weapons might result in actions we would both regret."

"Very well."

"I would also like to say, well done, Mr. President. Well done."

The president could not bring himself to accept the compliment, and the man smiled behind his mask in approval before turning and departing. The men with him soon followed, and the president put out an arm to stop his lead agent from moving to the door.

"Give him the time he asked for, John."

The President stared at the empty doorway for some time before voicing a question.

"My wife?"

"She's secure in the Senator Lamar's office. They didn't try to enter."

"The chamber?"

"It's gone quiet, sir. I have nothing."

The president nodded at the news and sat back down at the table. The envelope mocked him. It was thick. Like the others he had seen, it strained to hold its contents. Part of him wanted to toss it in the nearest trashcan and then set it ablaze, but the newly awakened part of him overruled. He instead reached out and picked it up with both hands. It was his to own, and own it he would.

The distant sound of an air horn reached them. Several others soon joined it. An agent stuck his head out the door and checked in both directions while his detail commander spoke rapidly into his sleeve.

"They're leaving, sir. I need to get you to the car. We can—"

"No."

"Sir?"

"Take me upstairs, to the chamber."

Ignoring the man's protesting look, the president got to his feet and walked out. The detail scrambled to follow and take up their positions. They found the stairs they had run down earlier unoccupied and climbed them with weapons pointing in every direction.

The hallways of the main floor were eerily quiet. Save for the occasional bound and gagged Capitol police officer or Secret Service agent, they were empty. The only evidence of the crowd that had filled them was the multiple scuff marks on the floor and the puddles of melting snow. The president ignored the sight and pushed on, his mind on the chamber he had left only a short time ago.

The detail men now ran ahead, releasing their fellow servicemen and dragging them to their feet as they traveled. Unarmed and slightly ruffed up, they fell in behind the entourage until they reached the chamber doors.

"Open it," the president commanded.

KENSINGTON, MARYLAND

ANNA AND DAYTON stopped when their phones vibrated. They were in the wood line and examining Haney's home. A plan had been made, and they had been about to implement it.

"Inside your coat," Dayton instructed.

They both pulled their coats up over their heads and then stuck the phones inside from the bottom. It was the only way to see the bright screens without giving away their location. They both read the text and then emerged to face each other.

"What do we do?"

Dayton stewed for a moment, and she almost repeated the question, but he moved to get up. When she started to follow, he waved her back down.

"Jack's house is only a mile away. I can be there in five minutes on this trail. I'll take care of this guy and then come back. Haney can wait a little while longer."

"You sure?"

"Jack's not the enemy, neither is his wife, and I'm not going to let them get used by Haney to discredit us."

"So, what do I do?"

"Stay here. I'll be back."

With that, he was gone.

Anna stared into the darkness where he had disappeared. What more could they do?

She couldn't call Debra—she didn't have the number. But she did have Jack's.

She yanked the jacket back over her head and fumbled with the phone.

THE 14TH STREET BRIDGES, WASHINGTON, D. C.

HURST SNAPPED his fingers to get the Captain's attention. The man, and several of his troops were watching the civilians walk away. A few made eye contact, and many walked right in front of the rifle barrels the troops had aimed at them, but they never slowed. It was as if they had just suddenly lost interest.

"Tell them to hold their fire. No shooting. Let them pass."

Ten seconds later, one of the Bradleys struck the first bus with a shriek of tearing steel. The axles ground deep grooves in the concrete as the engine of the Bradley roared. First a few inches at a time, and then with a steady gait the bus was shoved aside. The crowd backed off, and the driver planted the smoldering hulk up against the concrete wall of the bridge. No one moved to stop him or the soldiers behind it, so the driver repeated the action on the rear of the bus until a gap appeared. He widened it further with a sideswipe, and the way was clear.

"Single file!" Hurst ordered over the net. "Keep your weapons on the sky and be careful but get us to the Capitol Building as fast as you can!"

The Bradley roared through the tight gap, and Hurst shielded his face from the heat as they followed. What appeared in front of him was the low skyline of Washington DC. He spotted several fires glowing in a multitude of directions, but he ignored them and focused on the lighted dome of the Capitol Building. Barring any more roadblocks, they should be there in a few minutes.

JACK STARED at the message on the tiny screen, reading it twice before looking up. He spotted Larry leaning against the wall of the building with Sydney attending him. The streets were clear around him as agents pushed the people back. He spun in every direction, looking for options, but none presented.

"Jack?"

Jack turned to see Eric standing before him with a concerned expression.

"You all right, boss? The bomb is stopped. Bradford just yanked a—"

"Your bike, Eric! Where is it?"

"Just inside the ramp? You need it?"

"Yes!"

Eric had barely gotten the keys free of his pocket when Jack grabbed them and ran for the garage. A few seconds later the bike roared to life, and Jack guided it past the barrier without even acknowledging Eric. Jack pointed to the north and raced off.

"Where the hell is he going?" Eric asked.

———

DAYTON RAN.

The path was clear of snow, and the moon provided enough light to see clearly. This was no jungle path or mountain trail, and he stopped worrying about noise after clearing the area around Haney's home. He'd left the equipment and heavy firepower behind in favor of speed, and it now allowed him to cover the distance in near record time.

He emerged from the trail and out on to the street without stopping, confident he would appear as just another evening runner in the affluent urban neighborhood. A few hundred meters later, he was rounding the curve on which Jack's home sat.

A car. One that had not been there earlier, and a bit too low-cost for the area. It was parked a few houses away from Jack's, and Dayton slowed to examine it. A four-door sedan of Japanese heritage, it was still warm. He squatted down and examined the grass of the nearby lawns. The driver's tracks could barely be seen traveling off into the manicured landscaping.

Dayton's hand traveled to the small of his back and came back full of steel. He flicked the safety off as he followed the trail.

———

KANSAS CITY, KANSAS

THE BREAK in the trees told him he was close. The ground had gently slopped down for the last half mile, and Lee had slowed his pace some while looking for landmarks. He'd only stopped once to tighten the bandage, and had not seen nor heard any sign of his pursuer. The river was close. He just had to find it and then the boat.

But he was tired. The two miles had been exhausting, and the blood loss had only added to that. He needed the boat.

Pushing off the trees, he made his way through the last stand of pines to the shore. The water was black and cold, and he examined the far bank to get his bearings. Left. He had to go left. He moved on, the grip of the submachine gun now sticky with blood. A hundred yards later, he found it.

It was a john boat. Fourteen feet of aluminum

with a flat bottom. It could float in only a few inches of water. Lee had powered it with the largest electric motor he could find, and the boat would be virtually silent when moving through the water. He cut it free and pushed it out into the river before clumsily getting aboard with his one good arm.

The boat drifted, and he let it while he caught his breath. The current was taking him away from the house, and the moon told him he was alone on the water. He waited until the boat moved too far out for his taste before thumbing the motor on. He had just guided it back into the shadows of the riverbank trees when three flashes erupted from the bank.

The rounds tore into his chest, and he gunned the engine as his muscles reacted, sending the boat right at his assailant. The submachine gun fell away into the water, and Lee lay in the bottom of the boat looking up at the stars until the craft softly impacted the bank. A few meteors chose that moment to travel across the night sky, and he smiled at their glowing paths. It was a beautiful night to be out among the stars.

A face appeared over him. The guard from the ATV. *Persistent bastard*, Lee thought. He managed to suck in enough air to voice a question.

"Is he dead?"

The man looked down and considered the question before answering.

"Yes."

"All right, then."

Lee let the darkness take him, a smile on his face.

23

"When scrutiny is lacking, tyranny, corruption and man's baser qualities have a better chance of entering into the public business of any government."

—*Jacob K. Javits*

WASHINGTON, D. C.

Jack squinted against the cold onslaught of winter air as he weaved the bike through the traffic. It had been a few years since he had ridden a motorcycle, but his worry of being unable to handle the bike had soon dropped away. With every twist and turn he gained confidence, and the speed of his travel increased.

Ignoring the shouts and honking horns of the people he cut off, he pushed the bike faster, his hands growing numb on the grips. The Ducati responded to his every input and asked for more. Jack kept it moving, jumping curves and threading the smallest of gaps to get clear of the traffic that threatened to stop him.

A burning bus appeared ahead, but he slowed only long enough to search for an alternate route. The crowds were rapidly breaking up, and he now had more options. He spotted an alley off to the left and pointed the bike toward it. Racing up its wet pavement, he slewed his way around dumpsters and piles of pallets. A homeless man and his shopping cart nearly cut him off, and Jack's hand scraped the side of the cart as he darted past. The blood was stopped by the cold only after gluing his fingers to the throttle.

And then he was free. The alley deposited him back on the street, and he planted a foot down in time to keep from being hit by an approaching car. He gunned the engine and leaped away as the car occupied the space he had been in a fraction of a second earlier. Jack blinked the moisture from his eyes and read the street sign, before twisting the handlebars and heading north again.

"Debra," he breathed.

THE CAPITOL BUILDING

THROUGH THE SAME entrance he had entered, the Husband left the building, and the men and women with him quickly melted away into the re-treating crowd. He paused only for a moment to look out over the mall and witness the sea of people melting back into the surrounding streets. Behind them was a litter of protest signs and other debris, broken here and there by the bound and gagged body of a capitol police officer or Secret Service agent. He ignored them and walked down the steps.

She was waiting where they had agreed to meet, and he examined her eyes behind her mask. In them, he saw the same determination. The same steadfastness. The same resolve they had

had before they'd both entered the building. But now there was a sadness, as well. A profound wretchedness that spoke of a task, which, while required, there was no pride in carrying out.

"Are you okay?"

"I think so. It was hard, but nobody faltered. You?"

"I'm not sure. We'll find out soon if I made the right decision, I think. But I'm hopeful."

He offered nothing else, and she didn't ask. Slipping her arm in his, they walked the rest of the way down the steps and off to the east, following the crowd as it dispersed. The streets were now free of obstacles, and several vehicles cautiously made their way down them, their occupants attempting to look in all directions at once. They left them behind and found their way to one of the wide sidewalks stretching all the way to the Lincoln Memorial at the other end of the mall, just over a mile away.

She shivered now, and he pulled her closer. The adrenaline was subsiding, and the cold was now able to make itself felt.

"Do you think the schools will be open tomorrow?"

He shrugged. "I don't know. If not, my students will be happy."

"So will mine. Have you thought about how tonight will change your next lecture?"

Her remark produced a short laugh. "Well, I still teach civics, so I imagine it will come up. Come on, let's go visit Abe for a bit before we head home."

THE RANDALL RESIDENCE

LIKE MOST PEOPLE around the world, Debra had been watching the State of the Union address, and was first puzzled by the president's words, and then even more by his rapid exit. She now gapped in wonder at the footage from the streets outside the capitol building. She had tried Jack repeatedly with her phone, only to have it respond with a "System Down" message. Eventually, the battery had died, and she had placed it on the charger in the bedroom. They still had a landline; Jack would call her on that if he needed to.

She now lay on the couch with the remote in her hand. She been shuffling through the stations, but all of them had lost the camera feed from inside the capitol. They now moved from views of the mall to shots of the White House and other government buildings. It looked like ... She wasn't sure what to call it. Orderly chaos?

A pair of talking heads came on and began discussing a slew of emails someone had sent to the station. Debra quickly got lost in all the speculation and rose to refill her wine glass. To her dismay, the bottle was empty, and on her way to the garage to deposit it in the recycling bin, she considered opening another. She'd only had one glass —the rest had been consumed the night before by her and Jack. And judging by what was happening on the television, it was going to be a long night of worrying and tension. She'd open another, she decided. A good one. She left the glass on the counter and hefted the empty bottle, heading for the garage door.

She pushed the door open and tossed the bottle in one motion into the dark. The bin was big, and she had never missed it before, but this time the bottle hit something, fell to the ground and shattered.

"Shit." She reached for the light switch and flicked it on.

His large shape was all she had time to register before a fist slammed into her jaw. A blurry kaleidoscope of lights and shapes followed until her head hit the tile behind her. She winced and raised her head in time to see his face.

"Hello, Debra. Is your husband on his way?" Harper asked.

Not waiting for an answer, he backhanded her hard, and taking advantage of her momentary daze, he slapped a length of tape across her mouth before wrapping her wrists and ankles. She could only whimper as he dragged her back inside and deposited her on the kitchen floor.

"Stay," he ordered.

Debra shook her head to clear it and then followed him with her ears as he roamed the house turning off lights and checking doors. He paused briefly at the TV and watched the action outside the capitol building, before moving to the kitchen again. He examined the layout and the doors and windows, before pulling a chair from the table and placing it where he could see all the entrances at once, as well as the TV.

Sitting back, he watched the coverage and cursed.

"You know who's going to have to clean up this mess?" he asked her. "Me."

He chuckled at the absurdity of it all. Politicians just screwed up everything they touched.

Haney was the worst. He debated what he was going to do after he was done here.

He pulled the gun from his belt and examined it before placing it on the table and running both hands through his hair. He watched some more TV and cursed some more.

He spoke to her again. She was a captive audience.

"This," he pointed at the TV, "this is just the inevitable. A swing of the pendulum. Nothing ever changes."

Debra stared at him wide eyed. Who was he? What did he want with Jack? Whatever it was, it wasn't good. She forced herself to calm down. Visions of the control room at the dam flashed through her mind. She and Sydney trapped with terrorist. What had Sydney told her then? What had Jack instructed her to remember? Think dammit!

Opportunity. It always came. You had to ready for when it did. You had to have a plan and be ready to execute it at a moment's notice, as it might be all you got.

But what could she do? She was taped hand and foot. Gagged. Her eyes traveled the room, searching. There had to be something. Anything.

And then there was.

The wine glass. It looked down on her from the edge of the countertop. She could see her reflection in its curved surface. Only three feet away, it may as well be a mile.

Or not.

A plan began to form.

WASHINGTON, D.C.

HURST ORDERED the Hummer he was in to pass the Bradleys, as they roared down 14th street. The lights of the city that normally drew his gaze were now ignored in favor of what occupied the sidewalks.

People. Every size, shape, age, and color crowded the sidewalks in every direction. Gone were the signs and raised fists of protest, and in their place was now a quite walk. Many looked up at the soldiers as they raced by, but Hurst could tell little from their masked faces. They never stopped moving, not even when the Bradleys' engines roared and the asphalt was flung skyward as they rounded corners at high speed, did the methodical march of the people slow. They simply plodded on. If not for their breath fogging in the cold night air, Hurst would have thought them zombies right out of one of his wife's favorite TV shows.

"Anything from the Capitol Building?" Hurst barked at his radioman.

"Nothing, sir. The White House is secure, as are all the other government buildings. They are telling us to continue to the capitol and then make contact."

Hurst didn't bother to answer. His eyes had caught the sight of an elder couple, standing arm in arm on the curb, patiently waiting as the convoy passed them. Hurst watched them in the mirror, as they stepped off the curb behind them and walked on toward the Lincoln Memorial. If was as if they were simply out for an evening stroll on the mall.

"Check it out, sir!"

Hurst turned to find a set of binoculars in his face. He accepted them from the gunner up in the hatch and trained them on the building they were now speeding toward.

"Holy shit."

The steps were littered with bodies. Or so he thought. Several seemed to be moving, and he realized they were restrained. Disregarding them, he trained the lenses on the building's entrance. The glass was absent from every door. He could see no movement inside. He snatched up the radio just as a small helicopter landed on the grass in front of the building. Several men leaped off and ran toward the entrance. They would catch up to them in a few seconds.

Hurst snatched up the radio.

"That's HRT! I want the first three trucks to unload right in front, the rest fan out and cover all the other entrances. No one in or out without my order!"

A series of acknowledgements came back, and he ignored them in favor of pointing his driver where to go. The young man pulled the Hummer right up to the heavy balusters circling the building, and the marines poured out and followed Hurst up the steps. The HRT men had taken up positions at the doors, but were waiting for the marines before moving in. Hurst used the pause to pull his knife and free a man laying at his feet.

"What the hell happened?"

THE RANDALL RESIDENCE

HARPER STOOD and walked toward the TV to get a better look. His reflection showed in the window, and he saw a tear in his sleeve. Was he injured? He probed the opening, and his hand came away with blood. A cut. Its source was a mystery, but it was not the first time it had happened to him. With the adrenaline pumping, wounds went often unnoticed. He'd seen men in combat try to run on obviously broken legs, only to stare at them in confusion when they refused to function. Harper flexed his hands and then worked the arm in a circle. A little stiff. Whatever the wound was, it was not impairing the function of his arm too much. He glanced at Debra and saw her watching him.

"Sorry about the carpet," he told her, shaking the blood from his hand. The drops splattered on the floor and nearby couch. A little DNA evidence, but it was nothing for him to worry about. He'd been removed from every database years ago.

Still, he needed to stop the bleeding.

He had the jacket halfway off, when a sound reached his ears.

The Mansion

Carter shucked off the heavy coat and stamped the snow from his feet before gazing down the tunnel. The concrete was smooth and the floor dry. A lightbulb in a metal cage illuminated it every ten meters. It led in one direction. At the foot of the ladder was a sled with a harness. Some snowshoes. A cabinet. He opened it to find some cold weather gear and a pair of shotguns. He swapped the rifle for one and added rounds to his pockets before moving off down the tunnel.

A couple hundred meters later, he came to a door. One made of steel with a heavy lock. He pulled the paper from his pocket and punched in the code. A light blinked a pleasant green at him, and he gave the handle a pull. The massive door swung open with a screech, and he froze.

Hefting the shotgun, he stuck his head around the corner for less than a second. His eyes took a snapshot of the space beyond, and he blinked hard to interpret it.

A voice called to him.

"Come in, Mr. Carter. We've been expecting you."

24

"It is not my nature, when I see a people borne down by the weight of their shackles—the oppression of tyranny—to make their life more bitter by heaping upon them greater burdens; but rather would I do all in my power to raise the yoke than to add anything that would tend to crush them."

—Abraham Lincoln

The House Chamber

The chamber was silent as he entered, and the president's footsteps echoed on the floor as he strode forward. The men around him followed obediently, but all thoughts of outside threats vanished from their minds when they saw the horror that awaited them.

The bodies hung from the balcony everywhere they looked. Some of them still grasping the ropes around their necks while others appeared to be quietly sleeping. Many turned in small circles with the opening of the doors, and the creak of ancient oak balusters could be heard as they labored to hold the men and woman up. A shoe dropped from one, and the men flinched, but the president moved on.

As the bodies slowly turned, they all revealed one thing in common. An envelope. One with their owner's name on it in bold handwritten letters. Each of them easy to read from his position on the floor. They were exactly like the one he now held in his hands. He matched each one to the face of its owner. There were no mistakes.

The action of the people set in with vivid clarity. It had been a cleansing. A removal of a cancer by the people themselves. Over their heads hung the guilty, tried and judged by the people they had been elected to represent. Their sins worn on their chests for all to see. The men were all struck mute by the sight of the body's twisting at the ends of their ropes. Most were still trying to make sense of it, but Preston realized with a jolt that he was not shocked. The people had reached their breaking point, much as he himself had, and their actions were simply the result. Preston gripped the envelope tighter as he gazed up at their contorted faces. He was supposed to be among them. Why wasn't he?

"Over here!" An agent shouted from near the front, and the men broke out of their daze.

The group moved forward to find a pile of people on the floor. All hooded, hogtied, and gagged. The agent produced a knife and freed the first. The hood came off to reveal the face of Remington Lamar. The president hurried forward and waved the agent to the rest of the pile of people. The others joined in.

"Rem, you all right?'

"Mr. President?"

"It's okay, Rem. It's over. They're gone."

He untied the man's hands and feet, while Lamar gazed up at the swaying bodies.

"Oh, my god. What did they do?"

The president followed his gaze and thought of the man he had spoken with in the basement. He had been so calm. So patient.

The president helped his friend to his feet, and they were joined a moment later by Senator Bunker. He waved away their questions, and they stared up at the corpses. Lamar covered his mouth and pointed to the last few bodies off to the right.

The vice president and the speaker of the House slowly turned in tiny circles at the end of the row. A pair of Supreme Court justices hung next to them.

The congressman spoke, "Our own people, how could they do this?"

"I imagine Louis asked himself the same thing," the president remarked. The remark jolted them, and they both unconsciously rubbed their necks.

"What now?" Lamar asked.

The president returned to look at the dangling bodies of his vice president and speaker of the house. The line of succession was complete.

"That ... would be up to you ... Mr. President."

Lamar's eyes went wide at the statement. Preston reached out and gave his arm a squeeze before turning and heading for the door. He didn't look up again, and he didn't look back. The Secret

Service agents wavered, unsure what to do. Lamar gave them an order.

"See that he gets home safely."

"Yes, Mr. President."

He turned to his friend. "Senator Bunker, I need a judge, and a book, and a few friends."

"I think we have that here, sir."

They both turned and watched the man leave the room from where he had addressed the entire world only minutes ago. Head down, hands in his pockets, he was walking with ease, as if a great burden had left his shoulders. A pair of Secret Service agents led him front and back, but the rest remained in the chamber around the senator. Just as Preston reached the heavy doors, a young man burst in. He was shoved aside, long enough for the president to leave, and wisely did not protest. The Secret Service agent ignored him as soon as they were past, and he stumbled into the room to stare at the bodies. A press pass dangled from his neck.

"Let's include that young man, as well."

"Yes, sir."

THE RANDALL RESIDENCE

DAYTON HAD SLIPPED the gun down to the floor to use both hands on the door. He had been following the tracks to the garage door but had stopped there in favor of a look through the windows. The form of Harper standing in front of the TV had presented, but he didn't know where Jack's wife was. The gun had come up and centered on Harper's chest, but the thick glass and movement of Dayton's target had made him withdraw. Was the man alone? Until Dayton knew that and exactly where Jack's wife was, it was best to use stealth.

The garage door was open, so he moved inside without resistance. The inner door to the house was found a moment later, and he tried the knob. A small click made him cringe, but he held on and gave the door a tug. It was sticky. He applied more pressure and felt it give. He held it in place and reached for the gun on the floor.

The door splinted outward in a shower of splinters where his head had been a split second ago. He shoved the door open and somersaulted into the room, bringing the gun up and firing a round into the ceiling before impacting the far wall.

The sound of a body hitting the floor with a loud grunt reached his ears, and he aimed the gun through the doorway. In the limited light, he could make out two shapes struggling on the floor. He jumped up to enter and promptly slipped on the slick tile, falling into the mealy on the floor.

Another shot rang out, and he spotted a bloody hand holding a gun. He kicked at it.

THE CAPITOL BUILDING

DANNY'S HEAD was on a swivel as he ran through the crowd. The closer he got, the more their numbers thinned, and his breath clouded his view of their masked faces. None of them moved to stop him or even slow him down, and the reason for that was something he hoped to find at his destination.

His heart threatened to explode from his chest as he struggled up the marble steps. He saw the bodies, now. Several police officers lay in every direction. All of them tied at the wrists and ankles. A few blood stains could be seen on the walls and floor of the entryway, but whoever had produced them was now gone. The sight of the shattered glass of the multiple doors made him stop, and he sucked in lungfuls of air as fast as he could, until the cold made him cough.

The roar of diesel engines and the rattle of rotor blades made him turn. A column of army vehicles, including two Bradley tanks, were roaring up the street. On top of that, an FBI helicopter was landing on the street below him.

"Go, Danny," he told himself.

His boots crunched on the broken glass, as he stepped through the opening in the doors. He knew the way and now followed a trail of glass, melting snow and bullet casings down the hall to the house chamber. There was no one manning the door, so he pushed it open and walked in.

The sight before him stopped him cold. A Secret Service agent planted a hand in his chest and pushed him up against the wall. Danny didn't resist, and silently watched the man walked past. The president didn't even acknowledge him as he walked out, and the Secret Service man released him as soon as he was through the doors.

Danny hardly noticed. His gaze was now riveted on what he saw inside the room.

KENSINGTON, MARYLAND

JACK SLAMMED ON THE BRAKES, and the bike threatened to flip him off over the bars, before both tires broke loose on the icy pavement and planted him into the driver's door. The man yelled at him through the fogged glass, but Jack ignored him and picked himself up off the pavement. The Ducati was undamaged, and Jack soon had it threaded around the careless driver and on across the intersection. The man's protest followed him, but the traffic stopped him from doing anything further.

"Screw it," Jack muttered and angled the bike left.

The Ducati handled the curb with ease, and Jack gunned the engine. The sidewalk was now mostly clear of protestors. They seemed to be melting away in every direction, and he only had to steer around a few for the next block until the street became clear enough. Jack jumped the curb and only skidded a little, before steering the bike back into the middle of the street.

He threaded the gap between the traffic, and the bike glued itself to the double line.

Despite the frigid temperatures, Jack was sweating. Taking a corner caused the coat he was wearing to open, and the wind chilled him to the point he let off an involuntary shiver. He forced the physical reaction away and ignored his numb fingers as well. He'd have time to be cold later.

With every fiber of his being, he willed the bike faster, pushing it to the limits of the road conditions and his own skill. His only thought that of Debra.

THE RANDALL RESIDENCE

DEBRA'S EYES had widened at the sound of the knob turning. Its disfunction had been on Jack's to-do list for months, but he had never gotten around to it. She sometimes had to use both hands to turn it, especially when it was humid.

The click of the knob had not gone unnoticed by her captor, either. He appeared over her and leveled the gun in a bloody hand at the door. The knob was turning. Jack?

Summoning all her strength, she kicked at the gun just as it went off. A split second later the door burst open, and a man came tumbling inside. She kicked at her captor's knees, and he fell on top of her. The man joined them on the floor, and they became a tangled knot of arms and legs. Another shot went off, followed by the grunts and impacts of hand-to-hand fighting. The two men rolled over her, and she heard the sound of a gun sliding across the tile.

The fight moved away from her, and she scooted up against the refrigerator.

THE MANSION

"WE'RE INSIDE. It's room to room now."

King barely let the man finish. "The General?"

"No sign. The place is a maze and mostly stone. Lots of good cover. I estimate less than a dozen of them left."

"Keep moving in. If I know the man, he'll have a safe room or a bunker somewhere. Look for basements and stairwells."

"Roger that. I could use more men."

"I'll send in the perimeter."

The man's reply was cut off by the rattle of rifle fire, but King didn't need to hear it. He shouted an order to the man next to him instead.

"Move the men on the perimeter inside to back up the assault team."

"That'll leave them exposed to—"

"It's too late for that!"

The mortar man frowned but did as he was told. King turned back to his binoculars. A few seconds later, the machine gun crews could be seen running through the hole in the wall.

"There's no escape now," he whispered.

THE RANDALL RESIDENCE

CHAIRS TUMBLED, and the sounds of fighting filled the room. Debra struggled to see who the men were, but the light was too dim. The blue glow of the TV reflecting off the windows gave her little to go by.

She needed to get free. But how?

Then she remembered. The glass.

After rolling across the floor, she reached the spot below it. It mocked her now, sitting on the edge of the countertop just feet away. Squirming around, she got herself under it and kicked out with both feet.

Short. She tried again, and this time the glass wobbled. Another kick.

And it fell. The slight *tink* of it breaking was lost in the sound of the fight taking place just feet away. She rolled and searched behind her with her bound hands. There. She grasped the broken glass and promptly cut herself. Ignoring the sticky warmth of her own blood, she turned the shard in her hand and attacked the tape.

A foot impacted her temple, and she saw stars for a moment, but she somehow kept her hand on the glass. The tape was stubborn, but she felt it give a little more with each stoke.

The fighting stopped. She craned her head around to see her captor holding the other man from behind, his arm encircling his throat.

"Time to finally finish what I started in Iraq!" he yelled.

The other man's eyes only got wider at the statement, and he punched and elbowed repeatedly on hearing it. His eyes met hers as he struggled to breath. But the man had him. The two of them rolled on the bloody floor as they continued. Harper laughed as Dayton's blows became weaker and weaker.

The shot was deafening.

25

"There is nothing permanent except change."

—*Heraclitus*

Dayton's eyes opened, and he pawed at his throat as he rolled over. His breath was ragged, and he sucked in the air several times, before looking around.

Warm. Something warm on his back. He

shoved the still form of Harper off him and saw it was blood. His shirt was soaked with it, and he watched the man take his last breath as the flow slowed. A large pool was slowly spreading. He swallowed twice, pushing himself away.

"Who are you?"

He looked up to see Debra standing over him, a large handgun in her hands. Lengths of tape hung from her bloody wrists, and he saw more on the floor.

"I'm ..." he coughed, "a friend."

The gun didn't waver. He slowly stood, careful not to make any sudden movements.

"You have to do better than that."

"Sorry. I can't."

"Who's he?"

Dayton looked down at the dead man. He recognized the face. It had been altered, but he still knew it. He'd thought the man was dead, but there had been rumors for years stating otherwise.

"He works for Haney. Or at least he did."

"Haney? You mean the former Vice President? That's insane."

"I wish it were." Dayton rubbed his neck and arm and inspected himself for damage. Deciding he'd live, he searched the floor for his gun.

"Are you okay?"

Was she okay? Debra hesitated. The man didn't seem to be worried about her at all. Still, she kept the gun on him.

"I'm ... okay. Who are you?"

"Like I said, I'm a friend." He reached down and retrieved his weapon from the floor and slipped it in his belt, before standing and facing her. She backed away, but the gun didn't waver.

"I need to leave. Listen ... tell Jack ... tell him he won't have to worry about this, after tonight. Okay?"

Debra hesitated. The gun began to waver, and she lowered it.

"You know Jack?"

"No. Well, we've met once before. Just tell him that I'm taking care of it." He turned and walked for the garage door, his boots crunching on the glass. He paused for a moment and made a last remark without turning.

"Sorry, I was late. And thanks."

Debra watched him go and then slowly sank to her knees. She stared at the still form of Harper on the floor across from her. The gun was now glued to her hand by her blood. Despite the shaking, she couldn't let go of it.

A minute later, the sound of a motorcycle reached her ears.

The Mansion

"General Marr?"

"Yes, Mr. Carter. My aide, Charlie. And you know William already."

Carter took in the room and the three men. An underground bunker full of computer hardware, it was not what he had expected. He scanned it quickly and then returned to the three men watching him. His eyes met Charlie's.

"You sent the drone?"

"Yes."

Carter moved his eyes to the General. "You sent Dayton?"

"And another Shepherd."

"To rescue me, or kill me?"

"I think you know the answer to that already," The General calmly voiced.

Carter's hands gripped the shotgun hard. How could he have ever thought...

"I thought—"

He was cut off by the silence. They all looked up at the ceiling.

The mortar rounds had stopped.

"They're coming," Charlie whispered.

The Randall Residence

Jack let the bike fall in the snow and leaped clear. Throwing all caution aside, he pulled his Glock and stormed inside. His mind noted the tracks in the snow and the open garage door as he moved, and he managed to keep the gun out in front of him, but he didn't slow his pace.

What he found was unexpected.

The body of the man on his kitchen floor was still. The size of the pool of blood he lay in told Jack he was dead. The shaking form of his wife on the floor across from him, a gun locked in her bloody fist quickly took over.

"Deb!"

She sobbed and pawed at him, and he gathered her in his arms while his eyes searched for threats.

"Are there—"

"Just him. There was another, but—"

"Where?"

"No. No, it's not what you think."

"I don't understand."

"The other man. He saved me. That one had

tied me up, and they were fighting. I ... the glass, and—"

"Slow down, slow down. Are you hurt?"

"No. A cut. But it's nothing. You have to go after him. He needs you."

"He knows me?"

"He said you'd met once before."

"I don't ... Where? Where did he go?"

"Vice President Haney's house. He said he was going to finish it, that you wouldn't have to worry about this anymore."

Jack's mind raced. The blurred image of a man in overalls and helmet standing on a rural California road came to his mind.

THE J. EDGAR HOOVER BUILDING

"LARRY!"

Larry's eyes snapped open, and he saw the concerned look of Sydney only inches away from his.

"Stay awake!" Sydney said.

But I'm so tired, he thought. His head bobbed as she jerked on his coat. A sharp pain woke him further, and he grunted.

"My arm."

"What?"

"I can't ... I can't feel my arm."

His head fell back to strike the wall, and he stayed awake only a second longer before passing out.

Sydney shook him once, and then gave up, concentrating instead on the jacket. She soon had it free and was working to stop the bleeding.

"Eric!"

"I'm right here." He spoke from behind her.

"Get me an ambulance!"

"The phones are out. I don't think—"

"Then get a car!"

Eric sprinted away to do so.

Sydney gave up on trying to stop the bleeding with her hands and attacked Larry's shoes instead. She freed a lace and then wrapped it around his upper arm. A yank on it brought a spike in the pain and woke him.

"Syd ..."

"Stay with me, Larry!"

Eric pulled up with an FBI car and opened the back. With the help of a pair of agents, they loaded Larry in.

"George Washington!" Sydney yelled at Eric.

The car pulled out onto Pennsylvania and

knocked over a barrier. Eric found the lights and siren, and they were off.

"ARE YOU OKAY?" Anna hissed.

"I'm good. So is Jack's wife. Tell you later."

Anna took in the cuts and bruises and the blood and then looked him in the eye. Dayton was telling the truth; he was alright. There was something else, though. It was hard to label. Happiness? It was only there for a second, before he adopted his game face. He slipped the vest on and picked up the grenade launcher. He pointed at hers with his chin and fired a question.

"What do you have loaded?"

"High-explosive incendiary, alternated. Same as you. What's the plan?"

"Guards?"

"I think we have less of them."

"Less?"

"Yeah. I'm not sure why, but a few of them had a little group talk, and then they walked away. I think he's down to a skeleton crew at best now."

"Somebody was watching what was happening at the capitol and put two and two together. Haney?"

"No sign of him, but I saw his driver earlier."

"William would have told us if he had moved. You ready?"

Anna swallowed hard and hefted the launcher. "Yes."

"No change. You start at the top left on that side, and I'll go from the top right on mine. Meet you in the middle. Listen for me to start, and don't miss."

"Got it."

He refused to look at her before moving off into the trees, but she watched him until he was gone before moving herself. What he would be after tonight, she didn't know, but she thought she had caught a hint of it a moment ago.

There was no time to peruse it now though; she had to get in place. She eyeballed the tracks he had left in the snow coming from the trail, before dismissing them and moving off into the trees. The snow and the darkness let her travel stealthily to the position she had mapped out earlier. She found a spot next to some good cover and took a knee.

The sights of the launcher found the upstairs window, and she centered them there before taking a few deep breaths. The sights stopped wavering and settled down.

Her wait wasn't long.

The dull thump of Dayton's launcher was barely heard, before the upstairs window on his side exploded outward with a rush of orange flame. The night became day, and she blinked away the spots in her eyes only to discover herself still on target. She squeezed the trigger.

Her position behind the launcher allowed her to see the round as it traveled, and it punched a forty-millimeter hole through the glass only inches below her aiming point. A white flash erupted from inside, and the room was engulfed in flame a second later.

More explosions sounded from Dayton's side, and she followed his lead, quickly cycling through the remaining rounds in the magazine and sending them through the remaining upstairs windows. When the launcher was empty, she reloaded it and then set it aside before unslinging the submachine gun from her back. She aimed it at the front door and waited.

It wasn't long. A pair of men stumbled out, their bodies silhouetted against the flames. One of them was on fire, and he batted at his jacket in a futile effort to douse the flames. She stroked the trigger twice, and they went down under the three-round bursts. Another man appeared from the garage door, and she put him down as well. His body painted the door behind him in crimson, before he fell against it and smeared it on his way to the ground. A pair of burst from the other side of the house told her Dayton was doing the same. She waited for a count of five, and when no new targets presented, she switched back to the launcher.

Five more rounds entered the house, and the flames leaped higher. She set the launcher aside again and examined the doors and windows over the sights of the submachine gun.

The car. She sent a pair of bursts its way and took out the tires and then the engine, before returning her attention to the house.

Movement. She saw the shape of Dayton, as he broke free of the trees and ran toward the house. She scanned the windows for anyone who might fire on him, but he reached the house unchallenged. She sprinted forward as well and joined him as he went about flipping over the bodies of the men they had shot.

"He's not here!"

"Then he's still inside!"

Dayton spun and kicked the door in. A blast of heat rushed out, and they both ducked it until it subsided. Anna gazed inside and saw the main floor relatively untouched. The fire and explosives had obliterated the top floor, and would soon travel downward, but for now the house was still standing.

Dayton walked in without hesitation.

KENSINGTON, MARYLAND

JACK RAN.

The tracks in the snow only served to confirm the man's destination, and Jack followed them down the jogging trail. Haney's house was well-known to Jack, as he had passed it several times during his own runs. The handgun in his fist went cold in the night air, and the blood on it only hardened his resolve to find the man.

Jack was still a half mile away when the sound of the first explosion reached him. A tongue of flame rose over the bare trees ahead of him and was then followed by several more. He used the light to quicken his pace.

Another explosion, followed by the rattle of an automatic rifle.

Jack ignored the cold air burning in his lungs and pushed himself on.

26

"It takes but one person, one moment, one conviction, to start a ripple of change."

—*Donna Brazile*

K ing watched as his men disappeared through the hole in the wall. The sound of a breaching charge reached him, and he knew they were forcing their way inside. How many men did the General have here? King didn't know. He considered joining them but then thought better of it. It was hard to spend money if you were dead.

Beside him, the mortar man spoke freely into the mic—there were no more worries about making noise. The mortar tube went silent and crackled as it rapidly cooled.

"Report!" King demanded.

His assault team leader answered him with the rattle of automatic weapons fire in the background.

"We're on the main and second floors! It's room to room now and they have good weapons! We're pushing our way in!"

"Remember what I said! I want him alive!"

He got two clicks of the mic for a response and fumed. But the man was busy. Despite Haney's orders, King had chosen to change them. He wanted the General alive. Such a prize was priceless. Haney and his owners would pay handsomely for him, whether to assure his silence or simply to enjoy his death, King really didn't care. It was the zeros he was sure they would hand over without thought that were foremost in his mind.

King lay in the snow and watched the flashes of light coming from the mansion. He couldn't help but grin.

THE HANEY RESIDENCE

JACK STOPPED at the tree line and gazed out over the open space at Haney's house. The flames engulfed the top floor and the fire roared as it fed on the wooden structure. He could feel the heat on his face as he examined the front and then ignored it as his eyes found the bodies. He was about to move forward when two people appeared out of the dark, their bodies silhouetted against the burning structure. He watched as they examined the bodies and talked briefly before entering the burning house.

Jack moved to follow.

THE HANEY RESIDENCE

"IN HERE!"

Dayton moved slowly toward the shouting. He could barely hear it over the sound of the crackling flames. Behind them, an upstairs window shattered and showered the entrance with glass. Dayton could feel the heat stinging his face as he slowly made his way inside. Behind him, Anna followed, fighting hard not to cough and give their position away to those they were looking for.

Dayton rounded a corner and found a man on the floor, who was struggling to breathe as he crawled forward from the foot of the stairs with a gun in his hand. He'd obviously been upstairs and been blown down by one of their rounds. His clothes smoldered as he moved forward, and Dayton examined him long enough to determine he wasn't Haney, before dispatching him with a single round. Dayton moved on without hesitation.

"In here, damn it!"

Dayton waved Anna to the left as he reached the doorway. The flickering light on the opposite wall told him the fire had breached the ceiling inside the room. As soon as she was on the opposite side, he spun into the doorway, his weapon tracking left to right.

It was the study. The ceiling had collapsed

under the force of the explosive rounds, and a pile of burning timbers now occupied the room.

Under them was the pinned body of Vice President Haney.

"Get this off me! What the hell—" he cut himself off when he saw who was standing over him. "You."

Dayton stepped forward and stood over the man. Under the smoldering floor joist, Haney's leg was bent and twisted.

"Did you think I was gone, that I would never come for you?"

Haney's face took on a mask of evil.

"You're a fool! You think this will stop anything? My men will find you! There's no place you can hide!"

"Mr. Harper? Is that who you mean?" Dayton showed him a bloody hand. "He won't be doing anything for you anymore."

"Harper was a tool. I have many more. More than you and Marr could ever hope for. We will—"

"Your Trust is gone!" Dayton shouted at him. "We killed them all!"

Haney's face twisted again.

"You lie! We control everything! You think the FBI can stop us? Or your Shepherds? We have the true power! You have nothing."

"Not after tonight."

Haney started to laugh. "Harper was right—I should have let him finish you in Iraq. So convenient were the IEDs. So handy. If only Harper had used something bigger. No matter. Marr is gone, just like your wife, and you will be, too, very soon."

Anna flinched at the news and then scrambled to find her phone. Haney watched her.

"Yes, I had a few men visit him tonight. Experienced men. Ones who know how to finish a job."

The sound of a distant firetruck pierced the roar of the fire, and Haney smiled.

"Time to run along Mr. Knox. I ... Hello, Mr. Randall."

Dayton turned to see Jack standing in the doorway, the large handgun in his fist was leveled at his head.

"Don't," Jack ordered Anna without looking away. "You'll never make it."

The three of them froze. Dayton knew that, if he moved, Jack would beat him, but Anna would then beat Jack. It was a standoff.

"Who are you?" Jack asked

Dayton exchanged a look with Anna. It seemed like a good time for the truth.

"We're Shepherds. We've met before."

"On the road," Jack stated.

"In California," Dayton confirmed.

Timbers fell behind them, and Jack ignored them, but there was no doubt the fire was getting closer.

"Why?'

Dayton knew what he was referring to: Debra.

"They were going to kill you and blame it on us. I couldn't let that happen."

Jack excepted that without speaking. Nobody moved.

"And him?"

"The leader of it all. He works for the Trust. He's their fixer."

"Don't believe them, Mr. Randall! They're the Shepherds! Shoot them, now!

Jack ignored him, but his gun didn't waver.

"We're not your enemy, Jack," Dayton said.

"And how do I know that?"

"I have no way to prove it. I just—"

"I do."

Anna spoke quietly, barely heard by the men over the flames. Dayton turned his head to look at her, and she refused to meet his gaze.

"What—"

"I can prove it!" Anna spoke.

Jack turned his head slightly to meet her gaze.

"I don't—"

"848262."

"What?" Dayton asked.

"848262. I sent that to you months ago. I sent it again tonight," Anna spoke to Jack.

"What are you talking about?"

The words came in a rush now, and Anna spoke them for both men.

"I ... I wasn't sure. I wanted a way out if I needed it. I called you when they first recruited me. But then..." she deflated. "It was my husband's badge number."

Jack's jaw dropped. It was her. The person who had been sending warnings. The person who had warned him tonight.

"We're not your enemy, Jack," Dayton repeated.

Jack looked him in the eye. His face was bloodied and bruised. His hands, too. The shirt was soaked in blood from the man lying on his kitchen floor. He pictured his wife, the bomb in the truck, Larry.

The gun came down.

"No!" Haney screamed.

Jack turned and walked away.

Haney stared at Jack's departing shape as he disappeared into the smoke. The fire was burning faster now and would soon be upon him. The sound of the approaching siren was closer.

Unless ...

He gazed up at Dayton, as the man opened the breach of the grenade launcher. He removed two rounds and set them on the floor, just beyond his reach. The letters HE were stenciled on their side.

"I'll see you in hell," Haney hissed.

"You first," Dayton replied

27

"Change means movement. Movement means friction. Only in the frictionless vacuum of a nonexistent abstract world can movement or change occur without that abrasive friction of conflict."

—Saul Alinsky

THE MANSION

"We need to leave." Charlie said.

"Not yet. There's still the matter of PRISM," the General spoke.

"As soon as our people are away, I can activate the virus."

"How long?" the General asked.

"I don't know, sir." William shot a look at Charlie. The virus was queued and waiting on a separate screen. A progress bar that read zero, its prompt blinking its readiness.

"We need to go, sir," Charlie said again.

"Not yet."

The rattle of an automatic rifle traveled to them over a speaker, and the voice of the security team leader broke through their conversation.

"At least a dozen inside, now! We're holding them, but they have more firepower."

The general reached out and grabbed the mic. "We need more time. Get your men out but slow them as much as possible!"

"Yes, sir!"

William and Charlie shared a look. The fighting upstairs would reach them soon. They both knew it. William mouthed a silent command to Charlie, one that Carter saw as well: *Go.*

Charlie spun and grabbed the General's chair.

He released the brake and had it rolling before the man could react.

"No! Not yet, we have to finish!"

"William can finish! We have to get you out!"

The General grabbed the wheels of his chair with an iron grip, and Charlie struggled to move him. They wrestled for a moment, before the sledgehammer fist of Carter entered the fight.

Charlie jumped back and pulled his gun, only to see Carter swing the shotgun onto his back and stoop down to pick up the unconscious man in the chair. Carter slung him over his broad back with little effort and turned to Charlie.

"Where to, son? You do have a plan to get out of here, don't you?"

Charlie holstered the gun and pointed to the tunnel which Carter had arrived through.

"This way."

Carter set off without hesitation, and Charlie paused only long enough to look back at William.

"I'll activate it soon but know that it will shut down all communication for hours, including the nine-one-one service."

"What about—"

"I'll be fine, Charlie. It was my invention, so it's only right that I be the one to destroy it."

Charlie offered his hand, and William grasped it. They shook once, before Charlie spun and raced down the tunnel after Carter and the General.

He caught up to them at the end. Carter spun in a circle as he waited.

"What now?"

"We use this."

Charlie grabbed the sled and the harness and shoved it up the ladder, forcing the door open and tossing its plastic form out onto the snow.

"Put him in the bag, and then get him on the sled," he ordered.

Carter saw the plan and quickly complied. He had the general zipped into a sleeping bag a moment later and then carried him up the ladder to deposit him on the sled. Charlie emerged shortly later clad in winter gear and slipped on a pair of snowshoes before grabbing the harness.

"I have some transport about a mile away, and—"

"I'll get William out," Carter cut him off.

Charlie opened his mouth to protest, but after one look at Carter's face, and Charlie knew it would be time wasted.

"Okay."

The rattle of gunfire broke the silence, and Carter punched Charlie in the arm before descending the ladder again. Charlie checked on the general before grabbing the harness and pulling. It was difficult, but his adrenaline level was high, so he soon had the sled moving over the snow at a steady pace.

Behind him, the tunnel entrance slammed shut.

"Hurry, Mr. Carter."

28

"What I've learned is that real change is very, very hard. But I've also learned that change is possible—if you fight for it."

—Elizabeth Warren

C arter ran down the tunnel to find William pecking furiously at the keyboard. He looked over his shoulder to see a map of D.C. Two blue dots blinked at him. One of them was moving, the other was not, but they soon were both at the same location.

Dayton had found Haney.

There was nothing more William could do to help Dayton.

With a deep breath, he reached for the mouse and clicked the waiting prompt. The screen turned read and flashed a message: PRISM VIRUS ACTI-VATED. The progress bar began to move.

"What's PRISM?"

William smiled at the question.

"A surveillance program I wrote for the NSA, years ago. It was intended to locate and counter terrorist cells, but then they decided to use it on our own people. It's more valuable to them than any weapon ever made. Aircraft carriers. Stealth bombers. Nuclear weapons. They all pale in com-parison."

"And this program?"

"It destroys it."

Carter's eyes bulged at the information. His follow-up question was cut off by the speaker.

"They're at the stairs, William! We can't—"

The man was cut off by the sound of an ex-plosion.

"Jacob's?" William shouted. He got no reply.

Carter gazed at the progress bar and then at William.

"How long do you need?"

"Another five minutes, give or take." He reached under the desk and retrieved a submachine gun. Carter couldn't help but smile as the nerd before him racked a shell into the chamber. He then proceeded to speak while he loaded his pockets with magazines.

"You see the white boxes mounted over our heads, Mr. Carter?"

Carter had but had dismissed them as firefighting devices or simple wiring.

"Yes?"

"The servers in the next room. This computer here. It cannot be allowed to be compromised. I've taken certain ... steps, to ensure that would not happen."

Carter examined the boxes again and smiled.

"I see."

"Perhaps you could invite our visitors in?"

Carter's grin got wider. The nerd had teeth.

"REPORT!" King shouted into the mic.

There was no response. Either the man was dead or the thick stone walls of the mansion were blocking the signal. Any rifle fire they now heard was muffled, which told him that the battle was now deep inside the structure.

"Damn it! I'm going in! Nobody leaves!"

The mortar team knew better than to reply and watched silently as King sprinted through the snow toward the mansion. His voice however still reached them through the microphone strapped to this throat, and they listened in as he repeatedly called the team leader somewhere inside the giant structure. A few minutes later, King disappeared through the ragged hole in the wall.

"What now?" a crewman asked.

"We wait."

WASHINGTON, D.C.

"LARRY!"

Sydney shook him and got no response. She felt for a pulse in his good arm. It was there, but faint. The belt wasn't working. No matter how tight she cinched it, a trickle of blood still poured forth to run down the seat and pool on the floor. The arm was growing cold.

"Is he okay?" Eric asked from the front seat.

"I don't know. Just hurry!"

Eric tapped the brakes and put the car into a drifting turn around the next corner. They were detouring around the White House, and Sydney had almost yelled at him to go through the barriers but then decided that would be a bad idea. The Secret Service and D.C. police would be on high alert, so even with their FBI car, they would probably be fired on if they didn't stop. Eric now worked the streets and sidewalks to get them around the roadblocks.

"Syd?"

Larry was awake.

"I'm here Larry."

"I'm cold."

"I know."

"So cold."

"I know, Larry. Hang on."

He faded back out, and she cursed under her breath. There was nothing more she could do. She felt helpless. She had no equipment. No tools. Not even a decent tourniquet. She stroked his hair and willed the car faster.

Outside, the lights of the city raced by in a blur. The car bumped over curbs and weaved around slower vehicles. She ignored it all and continued to stroke his hair.

"Don't you leave me," she told him.

Eric slammed on the brakes, and the car slide into the curb. Sydney looked up to find them a hundred yards short of the ER, its red sign lighting up the clogged street. Eric bailed out and whipped the door open.

"We need some help!"

A pair of medics standing outside saw them and grabbed their gurney. Eric didn't wait for them. He yanked Larry free of the car and threw him over his shoulder. Sydney scrambled out and ran after him, amazed that Eric could handle Larry's weight. The medics met them halfway, and Eric dumped him on the cot. It threatened to tip over on the snow-covered walkway, but they grabbed both sides and ran for the ER.

"What happened?"

"He's been shot in the chest and arm!" was all she had time to say before they hit the doors.

They pushed through the doors and entered the chaos of the Emergency Room.

WASHINGTON, D.C.

CARTER PLANTED his back against the stone and listened. There was at least a dozen of them, and from the sound of it, they had eliminated all the opposition. The security team was dead, so there was only him and William left. He now heard shuffling feet and fresh magazines slamming home. As soon as the noise stopped, Carter counted to ten and executed.

The shotgun was still slung across his back. What occupied his hands were hand grenades. He had pulled the pins minutes ago and now held the spoons down with his fingers as he counted off the seconds. The squeak of a wet boot on the stone floor told him of their progress and made him cut that count short.

One long and one short. The grenades went around the corner and down the hall. The first hit the opposite wall and banked twice, while the other rolled down the center without opposition. Carter was back around the corner and slapping his hands over his ears before the four-second fuses timed out.

The screams and warnings of the men were snuffed out as the grenades exploded within a split second of one another in the tiny space, and the whistle of high-speed steel was heard as it zipped past Carter's head.

With his ears still ringing from the blasts, he slung the shotgun around and rounded the corner pumping rounds downrange. The first two did nothing but announce his presence, but the second two found targets before the men not hit by the grenades could return fire. One slumped in a doorway, while another crawled away on a shredded leg. A rain of rifle fire pushed Carter back around the corner.

With no cover, he quickly fled down the stone tunnel to the entrance to the stairwell. These men were pros. They were spread out and would not allow themselves to be fully compromised in the tight space. Carter had no doubt that the men had grenades of their own, so he needed to get somewhere to mount a defense against them.

But where? And for how long?

"C'mon, William," he muttered as he took the stairs three at a time.

He was three flights down when an object passed by in his peripheral vision. He immediately threw himself down and against the far wall as the grenade traveled past him for two more flights and then detonated.

The stairs shielded him from the blast, but he

screamed in mock pain, before descending further. He kept to the wall and out of sight of anyone above him, traveling past the damaged section and onto the floor.

The elevator had already been jammed shut, and the door fought the screwdriver he had wedged in the track as he ran past it. The airlock was open, as well, and he sprinted through it to find William already on his feet.

"Two minutes!"

"This will be over in one!" Carter informed him.

"I have a plan!"

William hobbled past him and reached for a panel on the wall. He removed two gas masks and tossed one to Carter.

"Put it on!"

Carter gapped at him as William put on the gas mask and then reached for the handle inside the panel. With wide eyes, Carter caught on and scrambled to put his mask on. William didn't wait for him. He yanked the handle with all his strength.

Halon gas immediately poured from the pipes overhead and flooded the room. Carter got his mask on just in time for it to engulf them both. The cloud spread across the server rooms and into

William's workstation, before expanding to the stairwell, where it began to climb with the updraft.

Shouts of warning were quickly followed by coughing and the thump of boots on the stairs.

The gas system was designed to snuff out a fire in an enclosed place. William had released it from the server room to occupy the entire chamber. As a result, it would dissipate quickly, but until then, it would rob the room of oxygen and buy them some time.

Carter gazed at the screen across the room. The progress bar was still short of its goal but climbing fast. He ignored it and ran for the tunnel entrance.

"Can we lock the door behind us?"

"Maybe. But they can always go around and catch us outside."

"The trigger?"

William handed him a remote. A simple button with a safety cover. Carter palmed it and looked toward the stairwell. The cloud was already sinking to the floor. He turned to look down the tunnel. The lights stretched into the distance. It looked like miles.

"Will the tunnel hold?"

"I don't know."

"Get going. I'll catch up."

"I—"

"What? Run faster than me? Get the hell going!"

William grimaced, but turned and moved off as fast as his leg would allow.

Carter watched him for moment to make sure William was moving and then turned his gaze back into the room. The progress bar was closer to its goal now, but so were the men from the stair-well. He felt the door with his free hand, telling himself the inches of steel would be enough. If he could get it closed in time for—

A grenade bounced into the room. Carter glared at it as the progress bar turned blue across the room with a pleasant ding. He pushed the button just as the grenade detonated.

The Haney Residence

More of the ceiling fell around him as the fire worked its way through the house. The pain in his leg was now secondary to the goal of reaching the two rounds. His manicured fingernails scrapped the hardwood floor as he tried to pull himself toward them.

A burning section of the ceiling fell and ignited the Persian rug the rounds sat on. Haney felt the fire singe the remaining hair from his head as he stretched out for the rounds. If he could just get ahold of them and toss them away. The fire department might still reach him.

His shirt caught on fire as the rug quickly succumbed to the flames, and he roared in frustration and pain as it defeated his effort. The pain climbed up his arm and across his back, and he screamed along with the dying siren outside.

His last sight was of the stenciled markings of the high explosive rounds distorting from the heat, before they both exploded.

THE MANSION

CHARLIE HELD his breath as he advanced the throttle. The plane eased forward to the edge of the hangar, and the skis met the edge of the snow he had just rapidly tapered with a shovel. The General stopped rubbing his jaw and grabbed the edge of the instrument cowling as they bumped their way up onto it. The prop immediately stirred up a cloud of ice, effectively blinding their way forward.

Instead of tapering off, Charlie opened the throttle more, and the small plane punched through the cloud to emerge on the other side and into the star-filled night. Charlie's rapid breathing only slowed a slight bit. After leaving the tunnel, he had strapped the General on the sled and towed him through the trees to the hangar without stopping. The physical exertion had just about depleted him, but he had rallied when they reached the hangar at the far end of the lake. A quick lap around the tiny building had revealed it to be untouched. Evidently, the attackers had dismissed the building as irrelevant.

Good.

The General had woken as he was being loaded onboard, and he stayed quiet as the rumble of mortar rounds now reached them. Flashes of light came from the direction of the mansion, but Charlie forced himself to concentrate on the task at hand. He had to get the General to safety; everything else was secondary.

He kicked the pedals and turned the plane out and onto the ice of the lake. It was several inches thick and would handle the weight of the small plane with ease. But there was always the danger of a hidden ridge of ice under the snow—or worse: a thin patch caused by the moving water underneath. If either were present, he would know it very soon.

"Throttle up," he muttered, going through the mental checklist. A glance at the General showed his eyes fixated on the mansion. Charlie glanced that way as well, just in time to see another explosion.

"William," the General whispered.

Charlie shut it out and focused on the ice ahead. The angle into the wind was away from the mansion, hopefully out of range of whatever weapons the attackers had brought. He set his jaw and advanced the throttles to the stops. The plane responded by leaping forward.

Loud cracks and pops sounded as they traveled over the ice. The plane bounced and rattled as the uneven snow fought them. The trees on the far side cast long shadows directly at them now, as if they were reaching out and ready to grab them the second they strayed into range.

Then a new sound. Charlie saw the flash in the mirror, and his heart leaped as a column of snow and ice erupted skyward from the surface of the lake behind them. The mortar crew had seen them and were trying to stop them. The shock wave rattled the ice, and Charlie felt it travel through the skis and up through the body of the aircraft to rattle his teeth. He cursed and pushed the throttles forward, but they were already maxed out. Another round landed behind them—this one much closer—and Charlie worked the pedals to fight the shockwave as the tail of the aircraft was pushed from behind. The trees were rapidly approaching, and he was sure the next round would be on target.

With only a hundred meters left, Charlie eased back on the yoke. The plane responded by clawing its way into the sky. The soft tips of the towering pines brushed the skis as they passed over them, and Charlie waited two seconds before banking the plane left and up the valley.

The ice at the edge of the lake blew skyward behind them, and a few chunks rattled off the skin of the small plane.

As soon as he leveled off, they both trained their eyes on the mansion below. The mortar rounds had stopped, and now they saw the blinking flashes of automatic weapons fire. Tiny shapes moved across the snow, and the last of them entered the hole in the wall as they climbed. Charlie increased the turn to keep the building in sight for as long as possible.

"William," the General whispered again.

No sooner had the name left his lips, when the mansion was shrouded in a ball of orange and black flame. A series of explosions engulfed the structure, and the shock waves traveled across the snow and crushed it down until it reached the trees, stripping them of their heavy load of snow. Secondary explosions soon followed, and the north tower appeared above the cloud for a moment, only to tip and fall back into the expanding wall of smoke and snow. More explosions followed, sending stones skyward, and they rocked the tiny plane as it flew overhead.

"Do you see—"

"No, sir. He'll make contact if he did."

Charlie had cut the man off and now refused to look at him or the view below. The General swallowed his next question. He knew better. And so did the young man next to him. Without another word, he twisted back forward and examined the sky ahead. It was a beautiful night. Crisp and cold and clear. The moon appeared and seemed to light the way for them. Charlie put the plane into a slow climb, and they were soon above the mountains, heading north.

Lincoln Memorial, Washington, D. C.

"You think they're inside, by now?" she asked.

"I imagine."

The steps of the Lincoln Memorial were cold, and they huddled close as the time passed, watching the steps of the Capitol Building becoming crowded once again. The roar of the tanks and the traffic around the building had again come to a halt, and the number of flashing lights of the police cars was increased every minute. Her phone buzzed, and she showed him a picture from inside the chamber, one of several bodies hanging. It was going out to multiple sources. It lasted for a moment, and then the phones signal was cut off.

"What do you think they're doing?"

"I hope they are all getting a good look. An image in their head that won't go away. The citizens delivered a message tonight, one that cannot be ignored. We can only hope that the ones left are reading it."

Washington, D.C.

THE FORMER PRESIDENT watched out the window of the limousine as the blocks faded away behind them. The streets were clearing. Hardly a single person occupied the sidewalks now. They had all faded away. But they were out there. Watching. He could only hope that the men he had left behind in the chamber realized that. If not, they might end up with envelopes of their own.

He looked down at the one in his hands, now. It would not go to the FBI, he decided. He would keep it to remind him.

A hand found its way into his, and he turned to see his wife watching him.

"Let's go home."

THE RANDALL RESIDENCE

JACK ENTERED the house to find Debra sitting on the hard tile of the shower. The scalding water flowed over her without her acknowledgement. The gun sat on the tile next to her, and a small trail of blood still flowed from it to the drain. He reached in and shut the water off, before gathering her up in his arms and carrying her to the bedroom. He wrapped her in a comforter and pulled her close.

"Is it over?

Jack thought about the question before answering.

"It is for us."

EPILOGUE

"Never doubt that a small group of thoughtful committed citizens can change the world; indeed, it's the only thing that ever has."

—*Margaret Mead*

SYRIA-JORDAN BORDER

The camp was one color: that of the desert. It was a color that was very familiar to both of them as they made their way down the row of tents. Like the people that occupied them, their color had faded to match their surroundings and now served to identify them by how long they had been there. On each tent the faded lettering of the UN or whatever charitable organization that had provided them faded in the relentless sun, making them all as one.

The people now watched them as they passed, the desert color etched into their skin. Their expressions were those of people waiting. For news. For family. For the next obstacle to present. It didn't matter. The war had exiled them. Some now waited for word that they could leave, to travel to a new land, somewhere they could start anew. Others waited for word that they could return, to rebuild and hopefully reclaim that which had been theirs for centuries. There was no in between. The waiting now brought them together, a common burden that they shared without choice, it gave them a measure of strength, even though they wanted nothing more than for it to be over.

Dayton did his best to avoid eye contact with the refugees as he walked north, toward the border. Its high berm constructed out of the desert floor to mark the point where Syria ended and Jordan began. Men and woman stood atop it at all hours, staring north, hoping to see a loved one emerge from the desert heat. It happened just often enough to keep them there. The berm drew his attention, and he kept his head up and his gaze riveted on it, and the people made way for his towering form.

Behind him Anna did her best to keep up while greeting every face with a smile. She got a few in return but mostly looks of curiosity. The people had learned. These two were not aid workers. They were not journalist. They were not here to help. They were here for something else, and until they knew what that was even the children would stay away.

"He said the last tent in row three?" Dayton asked.

"Yes. A newer one," she replied.

Dayton reached their destination and gazed in every direction before calling out.

"Waqas ul Haq?"

The tent opened to reveal a middle-aged man wearing a stained shirt of surgical scrubs over a pair of military pants. A stethoscope hung from around his neck, and he adjusted his glasses before peering up at them.

"Yes?"

"Sir. My name is Dayton, and this woman is Anna. I was wondering if we might ask you a few questions."

"That depends. Forgive me, but I don't know you."

"We have a mutual friend."

"Who is?"

"Mr. Bunker sent us. He thought we could help one another."

"Mr. Bunker sent you? How is he?"

"He's recovering very well, and he's developed a taste for figs."

The Doctor relaxed at the remark, it was something only his friend Archie would know to say. These people were friends.

"What can I do for you?"

"I understand your wife is in the hands of Assad?"

Waqas face clouded. "Yes...that is what I've been told since I arrived here."

Dayton and Anna shared a look. She nodded, urging him on.

"My wife is there as well, Mr. Bunker said you saw her? An American. Blond."

"Yes, yes, a blond woman. That was some time ago. I work here at the camp and question everyone that comes out. A man escaped a prison transfer when the column he was traveling in was bombed. He tells me of two woman he saw while being held, one of them the blond woman. The other was possibly my wife. The description was very close. He unfortunately died of an infection before I could learn more."

"And word of your wife?"

"There has been no word, but she did not make if here. I believe the man I spoke with. I fear she is being held as well."

Anna again exchanged a look with Dayton. The unspoken message was clear.

"Mr. ul Haq, I intend to go get my wife back, will you help me?"

Waqas jaw clenched tightly, but the words were strong.

"Yes, Mr. Dayton. I will."

DELAWARE SHORE

THE BREEZE WAS NEW. The French doors had not been opened for many months and they both welcomed the sunrise and spring weather through them as they lay in bed. The beach house had become home, neither of them wishing to return to their one in the city. The furniture and other odds and ends had been gathered and stowed by a moving company without their being there before the For Sale sign had gone up. Jack didn't care. There was no way he or Debra were going to return to the house ever again, not with the stain of blood still showing in the grout of the kitchen tile. They now sat silently and watched the passing ships and beachgoers as they moved by.

"What's next?"

"For the country?" Jack asked. "I'm not sure."

"Not really what I was asking, but as long as we're on that subject."

"Lamar has called for special elections. We'll have a new government soon. I imagine they and the new Supremes will be making some changes at his suggestion."

"Such as?"

"Getting the money out of the system. I think we'll see the end of Citizen United first, then some changes to the gerrymandering laws. The banks will be broken up into several small ones, and I'm sure a new version of Glass-Steagall will be in the works. I don't really see anyone siding with the big money people after what happened."

"No, I imagine they wouldn't. I'm surprised to even see people willing to run."

"Whoever did this...they were surgeons. Every piece of information in the envelopes has so far checked out. The fallout has been huge. A lot of people are going to jail. The ones running for office seem eager to enter the new system."

"And those left behind, are they as innocent as they seem?"

"A few have resigned. If that was out of fear, or guilt, or just a desire to not be a part of it anymore, I can only guess. Each of them will have their own reasons."

"Hmm."

They watched the sun rise higher and the heat of it felt good on their faces. Enjoying the silence, they snuggled closer.

"Deacon took the director's job."

"That's nice."

She had let the answer hang on purpose and Jack now fought to stay silent. It was a losing battle.

"He wants me to come back."

"And what did you tell him?"

"Not yet. I told him I needed a break."

"From the FBI? You?"

"A break...from America."

"Oh? And where would we go?"

Jack turned his head back into the sun. It felt good on his face.

"East."

RURAL BRITISH COLUMBIA

"THERE YOU ARE, Mr. Hunting. You should have all the access you need now." The technician said as he closed the access panel.

William examined the bank of electrical boxes now lining the curb. He would have a lawn service plant a row of bushes in front of them tomorrow to hide them from curious passersby.

"Quite a bit of bandwidth for a suburban home." The tech commented as he flipped through the pages of the work order. He held it out for William to sign and he scratched his growing beard before scribbling something illegible on the document.

"I'm retired. I'm afraid it's nothing exciting. This is just for an email company I use to work for. They convinced me to operate a hub out here in the sticks, so their system has redundancy. Wouldn't want the spam to be interrupted, now, would we? I just basically keep it up and running. Takes a few minutes a day. It's a nice gig for an old software engineer to have."

"I see. Well, you have a good day."

"You too."

William watched the man climb in his truck and drive off. As soon as he was gone, he hobbled to the house and retrieved his cane. Walking without it was painful, but necessary when appearing in public. He locked the door behind him and then journeyed to the basement. The temperature dropped as he cycled through the double doors, and he made it to the console before his leg gave out completely.

He popped a few pills in his mouth before booting up the computer. A few rapid strings of text later he was into a secure communications program.

One by one, the Shepherds checked in.

END

I welcome any comments, feedback, or questions at randall.wood@scribecount.

I also welcome any input pertaining to mistakes I may have missed, not necessarily typos or grammar, as they are self-explanatory, but mistakes about procedures or content. Mistakes of this nature tend to pull the reader out of the story and make it less enjoyable. If you should find such an error, please fire off an email in my direction. The beauty of e-books and print-on-demand books is that they can always be updated to fix such things.

I also welcome any and all reviews, with one small request. With the controversy over fake reviews garnering so much attention, it gives your review greater credibility if you do so in your real name and with the verified purchase icon. Doing so helps readers call honest attention to their favorite writers and keeps the integrity of the online review process intact.

Who knows? Your review may end up on the back of the next book.

You can find links to purchase all the Jack Randall Thrillers, including links to purchase directly from me at a discount, at http://randall woodauthor.com/universal-link.

ABOUT THE AUTHOR

Randall Wood is the author of the bestselling Jack Randall series of thrillers and the Half a World Post-Apocalyptic series. He is also the founder and CEO of ScribeCount, a data aggregation company that provides sales dashboards, marketing analytics, and a variety of other services to the author community.

When he's not penning stories or crunching numbers, he and his wife divide their time between the beaches of south Florida and the mountains of western North Carolina. Whether they are hiking or swimming they are usually accompanied by Henry their giant of a Great Dane.

Randall welcomes readers to his website at www.randallwoodauthor.com and his fellow writers to ScribeCount at www.scribecount.com, where he tries hard to not refer to himself in the third person.

f

www.ingramcontent.com/pod-product-compliance
Lightning Source LLC
Chambersburg PA
CBHW031735180726
48283CB00005B/1515